MAGICAL
DISINFORMATION

AN ESPIONAGE THRILLER

LACHLAN PAGE

WJ PRESS

Published by WJ Press in 2020.

Cover designed by Ebook Launch (ebooklaunch.com)

e-ISBN (ebook): 978-0-6489669-0-6

ISBN (print): 978-0-6489669-1-3

For MSG

Magical (adjective) beautiful or delightful in a way that seems removed from everyday life.

— Oxford English Dictionary

Disinformation (noun) false information deliberately and often covertly spread (as by the planting of rumours) in order to influence public opinion or obscure the truth.

— Merriam Webster Dictionary

CONTENTS

1

ANDEAN VISIONS

IT WAS WHEN STUMBLING DOWN THE RAIN-SOAKED ANDES wearing a woollen poncho, a handwoven sombrero, and high on ayahuasca that Oliver Jardine decided to lie for love. The lying wouldn't be hard, he was a spy after all. Spying and lying formed part of his bread and butter, or as it had come to be in Colombia, his *arepa y queso*. Lying came as easy as breathing in the misty mountain air, as he drifted down a muddy track towards the warm glow of Bogotá.

If the lying flowed through his veins like a fast moving river, the motivation of his love induced fibs didn't. It froze him stiff with a guilt much like the drizzling rain filled his boots with icy rainwater, turning his feet to bricks of ice, weighing him down both mentally and physically. The dormant mist of the bleak Andean moorlands didn't help either. It hung in the air and slowly seeped into his soul bringing with it a dark cloud that hung low over his head.

It's quite likely the coal-coloured cloud of dread would have accompanied him during his entire descent, if it weren't for a hallucinogenic encounter he had witnessed under a giant ceiba tree. An event he still didn't believe had happened, as the only man able to verify it disappeared into a sea of *frailejones* plants. He would've put the whole bizarre scene down to the mind-altering plant-based drugs he had consumed earlier in the evening, but the visions continued with him after that night. They allowed him to let go of his nagging internal analytical self and believe more in the only truly natural drug he had come to trust in a post-truth digital age: love.

In Colombia, they say love is a sickness, like cholera. Although if he thought about it, that theory wasn't very romantic. A sickness that causes vomiting and rice-pudding-like diarrhoea? Let's hope no-one gets *that* sick for love. No, that wasn't the type of love he was feeling. Dangerous love? Yes, that was a much better fit. Dangerous love. That's what rattled around his brain, as he scuffled along the path, the red brick buildings of Rosales coming into sight. It was this *dangerous love* that would compel him to lie against his own country's interests, which in his case was particularly pertinent, considering he was an analyst for British Intelligence.

You see in spying for one's country, the end is always clear and focused: national preservation. Most people think that means political assassinations, undercover sting operations, and influencing foreign elections. However, more often than not, it came down to: how does one acquire a particular piece of vital information? Information that, despite what the movies will tell you, is usually not very exciting. Take his recent intelligence report for example. In it he reports on the number of submarines Colombia owns. And do they need new, British-built submarines? And if so, how many? And if a lot, what is the government tender process like? The means – in such a situation – is the process to remove the obstacles that stand in the way of acquiring such information. Thus, it involves – necessarily, of course – trickery, deception, and a good dose of motivational psychology to convince people to give you the information you need. So, to get back to his initial worries, it wasn't the means – the lying that is – that bothered him. What bothered him was he had decided to flip the whole concept on its own head. The end for him was love for a woman named Veronica Velasco. The means meant lying to her Majesty's Secret Service.

2

CALL FROM LONDON

ON THE EIGHTH FLOOR OF A FORTIFIED OFFICE BUILDING IN THE
leafy upmarket Bogotá suburb of El Nogal, a fifty-nine-year-
old man picked up a phone that was ringing incessantly on
his desk. "Dolores, if the maid has quit again, call the agency
and get another one!"

"That you Ambrose?" came the reply.

"Radcliffe? Sorry, thought you were the bloody wife!"
Ronald Ambrose ran his hand nervously through his salt and
pepper hair.

"Maid trouble, have we? Damn hard to find a good one.
When I was stationed in Sri Lanka we always had good help.
Everywhere else was bloody terrible!"

Ambrose shook his head. "Dolores always seems to rub
them up the wrong way. They think she's being rude. It seems
the Spanish are too direct for the Colombians. We never had
trouble in Jamaica, although perhaps that's because I speak
Patois and knew what they were saying behind our backs."
The head shaking had turned into a knowing nod with a
smile.

"Now old boy, I assume you've heard the rumbling about

the tight fiscal restraints that've come through from Whitehall?"

"Yes, I've read the memo."

"Good. Got to tighten the boot straps and count our pennies they've been telling us. We'll still have a sliver of our secret slice of the budget pie, which will be chiselled off in good time. However, we need to batten down the hatches and shift our resources to more pertinent…" Radcliffe stopped before continuing. "More pertinent…What was it they said? Can't bloody remember. Hang on, it'll come to me…"

"More pertinent jurisdictions to increase our synergies across our intelligence ecosystem?" Ronald Ambrose offered.

"No, that wasn't it. Although that's good. Send that through in an email, will you? I could use that. It was something to do with Shakespeare. Or at least that's how I remembered it. Ah, that's it! We need to refocus our assets to more pertinent theatres of operations."

"What does that have to do with Shakespeare?" Ambrose asked.

"The theatre part. Anyway, we need to refocus our assets. And Colombia, although it has many assets, does not rank highly on our radar at this time."

Ambrose moved forward in his chair and leant his elbows on the desk. "What are you saying, Radcliffe?"

"I'm saying there will need to be cuts to operations within Colombia."

"Budget cuts?" replied Ambrose in a serious tone moving his mouth closer to the receiver. "We're already running a pretty tight ship."

"I know, old boy. Of course, I assure you, they're completely necessary. We are in austerity measures and we don't know if we'll be part of Europe or float away out into the Atlantic by ourselves, and so we need to buckle down and work on strictly vital matters to protect the realm, as it were.

It's also a strategic matter. The Colombians will sign the peace agreement with the FARC

"FARC-U," Ambrose corrected.

"Excuse me, Ambrose?"

"Fuerzas Armadas Revolucionarias de Colombia Unida. They've added the 'unida' part to show they're united with the country in the peace dialogues."

"FARC-U? I guess when this peace business is finished, the government will need less hovercrafts then?" said Radcliffe, an air of disappointment in his voice.

"Surely there are more important matters than how many hovercrafts we can sell the Colombians?"

"Afraid not, old boy."

"What about the war on drugs? The paramilitaries? The BACRIMS? The reminiscence of the cartels? Venezuela infiltration? There are plenty of vital tasks still to be done here. There are still other guerrilla groups too. Colombia's got more acronyms than an MBA course. The ELN is still strong and growing. They say it's doubled since the FARC-U have entered the peace talks. They blew up a bloody police academy just last week."

"I thought that was the EPL?"

"EPL? English Premier League?

"No, the Ejército Popular de Liberación. Thought you knew all the groups, Ambrose."

"Not sure the EPL still exist. Our sources say it was almost certainly the ELN."

"What about M16?"

"M16 is a gun. I think you mean M19. They're disbanded now. Former Mayor of Bogotá – now an upcoming presidential candidate – was one of them."

"Calle 13?"

"Where are you pulling these names from, Radcliffe? Calle 13 is a Puerto Rican rap group."

"Heard the grandson mention it. He's reading Spanish

and French at Cambridge, did you know? The point is, the narco days are over. Haven't you seen that series on Netflix? We need to move on. When FARC-"

"FARC-U," Ambrose interrupted.

"FARC-U… sign the peace accords, they'll become a legitimate political party. They'll simply become a story of the past. Our strategies have changed to foreign direct investment and business opportunities for British companies, that's what we need. We still have a rather large order of hovercrafts from the Colombian military, not to mention the tenders going for their infrastructure projects."

"Well there's plenty of that going on. The roads through the mountains are a mess. Did you know it's more expensive to send a container–"

"That's what we need to focus on," Radcliffe interrupted. "We need to get in touch with that Brazilian company involved in the Colombian infrastructure projects. Oberricht or Odennicht, something like that anyway. Get on top of that, will you?"

"Surely stopping the narcotics trade is still a priority? Don Berna's friends are still in action. Surely we can't reallocate all our resources to investment and British business interests?"

"Ah yes, Don Berna. He's the chubby one. Very devious sort of chap. I believe he's in a taxpayer funded 'penitentiary' with the Yanks now." Radcliffe pronounced penitentiary in a faux American accent. "All that drug business is being handed over to the NCA (National Crime Agency). They'll take care of that. As long as they stop leaving bloody USBs on buses that is!"

Ambrose squeezed his hand into a fist. Bloody NCA, he thought. He clenched his hand into a fist and considered pounding the desk but stopped an inch from the surface. "So, you're saying our objective now is to provide intelligence product for British companies? I thought that was up to those private companies, Practical Solutions International, Executive Risk Focus, and the like?"

"No, course not, old boy. It's not all investment in the international sphere. Fundamental Islamist terrorism is our priority numero uno now. Not to mention the Russians and the Chinese. Who knows what the bloody hell they're up to with their nerve agents on door handles and smartphone chips listening to our conversations on 5G. You no doubt heard what happened in Salisbury? Salisbury of all places!"

"Very Cold War-esque, wasn't it?"

"Yes, it was. And this new technology these days is frightening. Just the other day I was talking to Macmillan about having a vasectomy. Next thing I knew there was a bloody ad for vasectomies on my smartphone. I don't know who's listening in – but it's not bloody us!"

"No privacy anymore, sir," said Ambrose. "Not like the good old days when it was only us or the Russians or the Yanks listening."

"Yes, bloody buggers. This terrorist business is not going away either. Getting more serious by the day. Did you know we have 1,647 terrorist suspects currently in the confines of the United Kingdom? All British citizens, of course." Radcliffe coughed and sputtered on the cup of tea he was drinking. "Bloody hell, make that 1,646, must've killed one."

"What?" said Ambrose in a surprised tone.

"Haven't you seen the new terrorist counter? Got one on my computer desktop. Bloody marvellous contraption! Displays the number of terrorists we're tracking currently on a digital counter. Goes up or down depending whether or not they've been arrested, killed or just popped up on our radar. It's like Facebook for terrorists, although none of them are my friends or post photos of their grandkids or pets."

"Is this part of the 2025 Digital Intelligence Analytics Initiative?" asked Ambrose.

"Yes. Got to show Whitehall where all their money is

going. I must say though, it's fascinating to watch. 1,648 now! Looks like two more have popped up on the radar! See, Ambrose, that's why we're focused on this Jihadi threat. It's the new frontline. I bet you don't have a guerrilla tracker? Or a cartel tracker?"

"No, you're right, we don't. Maybe we could have some funding to install one?"

"No, like I said, old boy, you need to run a tight ship. Besides, I imagine that sort of thing would be going bonkers down there. Might break the bloody internet like that big arsed woman from Los Angeles. What's her name? Kalashnikovian?"

"Yes, that's it," said Ambrose, not wanting to continue the conversation. "Will we be anticipating any layoffs?"

"Not sure, yet. Will get back to you on that. We may need to move a few assets around."

"Assets?" asked Ambrose.

"People. Might have to allocate them to more pertinent theatres of operation, as it were."

"I see."

"Right then, it's almost time for a few Pimms down at the Travellers. Day is just beginning for you I trust. My regards to Dolores. I know you might have some trouble breaking the news to your officers and analysts, but we're counting on you. Need to report through to R by the end of this."

"R?"

"Don't you read the security protocols any more, Ambrose? The current Chief is going by R."

"What happened to C?"

"They decided to scrap it and use a new system."

"Why don't they just use his name? He gives public talks now."

"Tradition, Ambrose. With everything else changing, we need to keep some things the same."

"But why R?"

"The Joint Intelligence Committee has decided to rotate the letter in alphabetical order for each new Chief we have – starting from the original C. So if Smith-Cumming was C, we're now at R."

"I see. But why have a system?"

"This is the Secret Intelligence Service, not a bloody tech start-up! It can't be all higgledy-piggledy now."

"I must admit, alphabetical order does seem a bit obvious, I'm sure our enemies could…"

"Ah, but our enemies would expect us to use something more intricate, like reverse alphabetical order for example, and so alphabetical works perfectly. Anyway, Ambrose, enough chit-chat. I must be getting on. Cheerio." And with that the receiver was slammed down.

"Understood, Radcliffe. I'll have a report sent through to R before week's end," said Ambrose, although the line had already been cut.

Ambrose stood up from his fake mahogany desk and gazed out the window over the city. The teenage sons of Bogotá's elite – future presidents and politicians – played football below on the verdant, luscious grass of *Gimnasio Moderno*'s grounds. A far cry from the muddy, scrappy pitches he was used to playing on while growing up in Lewisham. Ambrose was a career intelligence man nearing the age of retirement. Both his parents had immigrated to England in the fifties from Jamaica, and since leaving university, he'd spent the best part of his life back around the Caribbean and Latin America with his Spanish wife Dolores.

Reaching into his desk drawer, he pulled out a remote control and switched on the plasma screen on the wall opposite his desk. He flipped through the channels until he reached Canal Colombo Mundial, the 24-hour Colombian news channel. Sitting back in his chair with a slight grunt, a headline about the upcoming guerrilla demobilisation process following the peace talks caught his eye. A middle-aged man immaculately dressed in a pin stripe suit was talking to another middle-aged man in a camel-coloured suit with a navy-blue tie who was, in turn, sat next to a woman dressed in a tight-fitting fuchsia dress. Ambrose raised his hand with the control and turned the volume up. The pin-stripe suited man explained how the demobilised guerrilla fighters would receive three million pesos per month as a result of the peace process – four times Colombia's minimum wage. The other two hosts shook their heads in disappointment and tutted in Spanish. The woman spoke now, she mentioned how it was unfair to *el pueblo Colombiano* – the Colombia people – who worked hard every day to earn a decent living and now these narco-guerrilla-terrorists have decided to stop fighting and the government will provide them with a salary? Below the presenters, a fast-moving news ticker banner of incoming Tweets echoed their laments with cries of #NoaLaProceso-DePaz (#NoToThePeaceProcess) and #NoNegociamosCon-Terroristas (#WeDontNegotiationWithTerrorists). A smattering of Tweets proved positive with #AdelantePor-LaPaz (#ForwardWithPeace).

Ambrose shook his head. He knew it was a straight up lie. The demobilised guerrilla members would only receive a minimum wage and only for the initial two years until reinstated into Colombian society. To be fair, the presenter had mentioned it was merely a rumour, but the majority of people would think it's the truth.

Turning back towards his desk, his mind was cloudy, like slowly pouring milk into a piping hot cup of black tea. If R and Radcliffe wanted changes, that's what they would get. It didn't matter if the officers and analysts didn't like it. There's always someone who isn't happy. Can't please everyone, he thought, trying to justify the new changes he would have to implement as MI6's head of station in Colombia. He sighed and said aloud, "Let's hope they take it alright."

3

ON ASSIGNMENT IN THE ANDES

OLIVER JARDINE EXITED HIS APARTMENT BUILDING AND AFTER A short walk downhill, arrived at the *Carrera Septima*, one of Bogotá's main arteries. He waved his hand, hoping to attract the attention of one of the small yellow taxis that buzzed about the streets like mechanical mosquitos darting in and out of the traffic. Large crammed buses bounded down the *calles*, *carreras* and *avenidas*, revving their engines, belching smoke and honking their horns. This was the Bogotá *en hora pico* – peak hour. A rumbling sound erupted from his jacket pocket as he reached inside for his mobile phone. "Morning, Ambrose."

"Morning, Jardine, I knew you would be awake. Listen, I need you to visit Professor Villalobos this morning, he says he has something for us. Could you manage that?"

"Certainly. The usual time and place?"

"Correct. Shall I send a car?"

"No, I feel like a challenge. Matter of fact, I'm already trying my luck with a taxi."

"Very well. See you at the office afterwards. Oh, and Jardine?"

"Yes?"

"Do be careful down that side of town. As you know, La Candelaria has a reputation for violently parting people with their wallets."

A taxi screeched to halt in front of him. He went to open the door but before he could open it, the taxi driver wound down the passenger window and asked, "Para donde, mono?" *Where to, blondie?*

"La Candelaria," he replied.

"Por allá no voy, demasiado trancón," said the driver, holding his hand up with his thumb against his other four fingers like an Italian don. Jardine knew the Colombian gesture well – the streets were full. If there was one thing everyone in Bogotá could agree upon, it was that Bogotá traffic was horrendous. During peak hour, the city resembled a car park rather than a series of roads and streets.

"What do you mean you won't go there?" asked Jardine in Spanish. "Do you know how many people… Look, I'll give you 10,000 pesos extra?"

The driver looked forward at the traffic and shrugged. "Listo pues, súbete." *All right then, get in.* It was the very simple things – like taking a taxi – that seemed to involve a lot of energy in Colombia, like everything was a tussle between two opposing forces.

Jardine exchanged the usual Colombian pleasantries. He never quite knew if anyone actually cared or if it was native politeness, words floating in the air, uttered with no expectation of a considered response: ¿Cómo vas? *How are you?* ¿Como te ha ido? *How have you been?* ¿La familia, bien? *I trust your family is well?* And the typical taxi driver questions: ¿Que tal este trancón? *How about this traffic?* ¿Ya probaste aguardiente? *Have you tried sugarcane liquor?* Que tal las mujeres colombianas? *What do you think of Colombian women?*

The taxi swung left off the *Avenida Septima* zooming uphill on *Calle 53*, finally taking the mountain-hugging bypass road *Avenida Circunvalar*. Mist poured down from the verdant *cerros orientales* – the mountain range hugging the eastern side of Bogotá – and dissipated among the red brick apartment buildings of the neighbourhood of Chapinero. To his right Jardine watched the city below rush by him. It reminded him of when he arrived in Bogotá three years ago and all the things he had done since then. He had climbed the snow-capped peaks of the Andes, sampled coffee in the verdant rolling hills of the coffee zone, swam at pristine sandy beaches, been diving on the sea of seven colours, hiked through deep canyons, strolled through quaint colonial villages and trekked to a lost indigenous ruin. He'd danced salsa, bachata, merengue, choke, vallenato, and reggaetón; partied until four o'clock in the morning while still managing to turn up for work in the morning, revelling in the never-ending *joie de vivre* of the Colombian people. Jardine began to feel the prickle of the burning sun on his arm and rolled down the window to allow crisp mountain air to puncture the hot intensity. However, the last six months had been quieter, although much more important to him. He had become more thoughtful and sentimental and for once in his life, he didn't need a rational decision-making model, a SWOT analysis, or a risk assessment matrix to know why he felt this way. It had all to do with a spitfire Colombiana he had met a year earlier. She had fallen into his life and had occupied almost every waking thought and moment since.

The taxi pulled up on the edge of Parque Germania – a small plaza – and he decided to stroll through it to reach the entrance to the university. As he was placing his wallet into his inner jacket pocket and adjusting his satchel, he noticed the SUV with tinted windows trawling alongside the park, prowling as if waiting for the right moment to pounce. He picked up his pace, hoping to reach the entrance before it had circled around to the park. He glanced momentarily to the left, watching as it sped up and turn one corner of the park. The air was still crisp but the sun beating down on him brought on a sweat. He didn't think he would make it to the entrance before the SUV. He strode his legs out further, trying not to seem like he was rushing. He could see the turnstiles of the university entrance ahead as he approached the drop off point. Looking again to his left, the SUV had turned the corner and accelerated down the small street towards him. *I'm not going to make it*, he thought. A few more steps. He heard the rev of the SUV, a throaty roar like a mechanical lion. Too late. The SUV screeched to a halt in front of him. The side door slid open and a man in a dark suit jumped out, a revolver noticeable in a holster under his armpit. Jardine jolted sideways to escape, tripping. The man instinctively extended his arm catching Jardine on the elbow. *This is it*, he thought. *I'm done for*. He was ready to swing his satchel, hoping to land a blow at the neck, when the man smiled at him.

"Con cuidado, mono!" he said to Jardine, stabilising him with his other hand. *Be careful, blondie!*

"Gracias, Pablo!" said a young girl stepping out of the SUV, slinging on her backpack. Jardine guessed she was about eighteen year old. "Te aviso para que me recojas." *I'll call when I'm ready to be picked up*.

"Perdon," said Jardine to the man, straightening out his jacket. "No te habia visto." *I didn't see you*.

"No hay problema. Buen dia, caballero," came the reply. *No problem, Have a nice day, sir*.

Jardine chuckled to himself, his heart still beating a million beats per second. *Am I paranoid or what*? he said to himself. Universidad de los Andes was the most expensive university in the country. Colombia's wealthiest young minds walked alongside him, most were immaculately dressed and wearing the latest in designer fashion. *Some* were dropped off by a personal bodyguard.

After climbing an Andean mountain worth of stairs and weaving his way through the former colonial buildings of the original Spanish settlement of Bogotá – now the Law Faculty – he arrived at a small seminar-style lecture theatre. The door was open, and he could hear Professor Villalobos's voice, rambling in Spanish to his students. He stepped inside quietly and took a seat near the door. Several of the female students eyed him seductively as would often happened when seeing a fair haired, blue-eyed extranjero. Villalobos nodded and smiled towards him but continued his lecture. "And that, my dear students, is how the murderous communist regime of Castro dispatched of Batista's ex-guards and isolated Cuba's business leaders, many of whom fled to Florida and Puerto Rico. That's all for today, until next week." The professor looked down at his lectern and shuffled some papers. Jardine remained seated as students exited the lecture theatre and several female students made their way towards Professor Villalobos. It was clear from their high-pitched voices and the way they adjusted and twisted their hair in front of him that they were asking the professor to raise their latest grades. Jardine had experienced it before when he had taught on a post-grad course at a smaller Colombian university the previous year. They tugged at your heart strings, and if you were a male teacher, your pant strings. And if that failed, there was always the do-you-know-who-my-father-is routine.

Professor Villalobos was a specialist in peace, security and conflict studies at the Escuela de Gobierno Alberto Lleras Camargo at the Universidad de los Andes. Meeting with *El Profe* was relatively relaxed, there was no need for routine security protocols or surveillance evasion. It was natural for a person at the British Embassy to want to interview university professors from time to time, especially considering his cover was Third Secretary (Political). There was also another reason for the relaxed state of affairs: in the spy game there are 'desk men' and 'field men'. Jardine was unequivocally a desk man. He was an analyst, not an operative – a Jack Ryan without the balls or gun, he'd often say. He was as far from James Bond as one could get. He probably wouldn't even rate a mention as a supporting character in a Le Carré novel. No-one cares about an intelligence analyst, unless they fuck up that is.

Oliver Jardine had arrived in Bogotá three years earlier after initially being recruited while working in Central America. MI6 had decided to branch out and hire people with on-the-ground experience. Gone were the days of the old boys network and a tap on the shoulder at an Oxbridge college. They wanted operatives with a real history, language skills, travel experience, and street-smarts. Following 'the approach' from an MI6 officer in Guatemala, he had completed a six-month IONEC course at Fort Monckton — where it was decided that an analyst would suit his skill-set better — he then spent another three months training at Langley, Virginia with the cousins. Fresh out of training, the wheels of British Intelligence bureaucracy turned and in all its wisdom, spat him out to the Korean peninsula for a year as Cultural Attaché. The Seoul assignment was a strange one, especially considering his Spanish and Portuguese language skills were of little use. Although it hadn't been a pushover. He had managed to avoid nuclear Armageddon as the North sank a South Korean frigate and shelled an island on the sea border. That at least dispelled the long, bitterly cold winter, and provided him with dinner party conversation the next time North Korean nuclear threats were thrown about in the media. It wasn't until his persistence in convincing his superiors that he would be better suited to somewhere where he could 'speak the lingo' with more efficiency than his nascent Korean, that he was finally moved to the tropics. Although, Bogotá, sitting at two-thousand six-hundred metres closer to the stars would confuse the average punter, thinking the tropics was all coconuts and palm trees. The cold, rainy Andean city had more in common with London than a place to sip piña coladas or work on your tan.

Professor Villalobos eventually managed to shoo away the students and made his way over to Jardine.

"That was quite an ending, Professor. What about the murderous Batista regime itself?" asked Jardine with a cheeky smile.

"That would fall under our Caudillo week. Right before right-wing death squads and military juntas, which is followed, of course, by forced disappearances and CIA torture techniques from the School of the Americas," replied Villalobos, while taking off his glasses and cleaning them with a soft, grey cloth.

"Sounds like you've got it all covered then."

"Almost."

"What else is there?"

"Next week, we will read about violent Marxist-Leninism-Maoist guerrilla groups and the new topic of narco-guerrillas."

"That must be unique to Colombia?"

"Unfortunately, yes. Although Peru is developing some fine examples too. I'm considering including a week on the Cartels. With Medellín, Cali and the new *bandas criminales (BACRIMS)*, there should be a variety of contemporary material. The kids these days seem to love those narco-telenovelas we churn out."

"Not just here in Colombia. Anyone with a Netflix subscription is spoilt for choice in that department."

"My colleagues in the Social Sciences are telling me it's called the Netflix effect," said Professor Villalobos.

"Is it positive or negative?" asked Jardine.

"Too early to tell. Nevertheless, I'm in the middle of 'spicing up' the course. I've decided to name my weekly topics after famous movies. It helps to keep the students interested, you see. I'm brainstorming a few titles for lectures, perhaps you'd like to hear a few?"

"Humour me, Professor," said Jardine with a smirk.

"How to Lose a Caudillo in 10 Days," the professor offered.

Jardine considered it before commenting. "That seems to work."

"Seven Years a Military Junta Slave."

"That one could be risky but go on."

"Clear and Present BACRIMS, Romancing the Emerald Barons, Escobar's List... although that last one might be crossing the line?" The professor's grey bushy eyebrows raised slightly.

"How about Guerrillas in the Mist?" said Jardine, raising an eyebrow to match the professor.

"Muy bien, mi amigo. Now you're getting it," the professor chuckled to himself. "I was thinking of titling the Bay of Pigs fiasco, 'The Empire Strikes back'. I think it's very creative, don't you?"

"Very fitting, indeed. Professor, can we proceed to your office?" said Jardine in a serious tone.

"How about a coffee at the cafe instead?" Professor Villalobos motioned to a small outdoor cafe.

"Sure."

They left the lecture theatre, crossed a grass filled square and arrived at a courtyard of large terracotta tiles, white washed walls and a small fountain in centre. There was a quaint café nestled in the corner of the courtyard where they sat at a table. A view of the mountains loomed above them through the open roof. As was customary (to avoid the odd eavesdropper), the two men switched to English.

Professor Villalobos looked at Jardine with his light grey eyes. "My assistant Juanita makes great coffee, much better than Señor Valdez. But the view is nice here and, well, it's not Starbucks, at least. They have a single origin from Quindío. You won't find it at the American chain."

"I prefer coffee from Huila myself," said Jardine, while

perusing the menu. "Smaller harvest, but more care is taken in the process."

"You have good taste. I swear it is the foreigners who know Colombia better than we Colombians. I've always thought an outsider makes a better observer. After all, a fish isn't very good at describing water, is it?"

"Right you are, Professor. But there are tribes in the Amazon who can identify up to twenty different shades of green in the foliage."

"Very wise. I try to introduce these contradictions to my students, in a hope that they will realise the value of such critical thinking. My favourite is 'the pen is mightier than the sword'. But alas, in Colombia it seems 'actions speak louder than words'." Villalobos let out a deep sigh and shook his head softly.

Jardine nodded, then said, "Let's hope that the peace negotiators are right when they say it is time for the guerrillas to speak with their tongues instead of their rifles." Recognising the professor's melancholic mood, Jardine decided to change the subject momentarily. "How's the family? All well I trust?"

"As well as can be. We are trying to get my daughters into the Worthington School. Perhaps, you could put in a friendly word with the principal? He is one of you?"

"English?"

"Irish. Northern Irish, I believe. Not like those bomb makers in the south, the ones that taught our FARC how to blow things up."

"Not sure it works like that…" Jardine stopped, not wanting to correct the professor. From his experience in Colombia, there were times when it was better to nod and smile instead of challenge. Intellectual debate could sometimes be taken personally. "I'll see what I can do, Professor. I have a few contacts at Worthington."

"Thank you."

A waiter arrived, the two men ordered their coffee and then officially began their meeting.

"Have you read the latest from The Post? Blaming Colombia's increase in coca production for a hike in cocaine usage in Gringolandia," asked Jardine.

"Ha! Los imbeciles! Why do politicians that promote free-market economics fail to understand supply and demand when it comes to drugs? As long as the 'developed' world has a drug problem, the developing world will be there to supply it. It's a choice between poverty or prison for the farmers."

The professor continued ranting as Jardine nodded politely. He had asked the question, thinking it made a nice segue into the peace dialogues. After a few moments, he decided to change the subject.

"And the peace dialogues? How are the talks advancing?"

"Soto's government is committed. The FARC have come out of the jungle and down from the mountains. But, as you know, every rose has its thorn," replied the professor, as a smirk spread under his greying moustache.

"Still a few issues to iron out. Urrea still at it I imagine?" asked Jardine.

"Si, who else? But, he can only control so much. He is no longer the president. Although his protégé is an up and coming presidential candidate. In terms of the peace dialogues, I worry about the proposed deadlines from the UN. You know how things work here in Colombia. We don't always work well to deadlines. And there is also the history with La Union Patriótica lingering in the guerrillas' minds. Not to mention the ELN guerrilla talks, which will further complicate the matter."

"What's the media saying? El Tiempo? El Espectador?"

"The usual left wing, right wing talking points. Although it seems both the newspapers are in favour. The television news channels, however..."

"What about them?" Jardine interrupted, pen poised to take notes.

"It's not that they come out and directly say no to peace," the professor said as he fiddled with the wooden stirring stick in his coffee cup. "But they brush over the positive facts and then boil the pot on the negatives. They fail to cover the major changes or movements. Omission of news is almost as damaging as reporting the negatives or falsifying the facts."

"Is that what your media friends are saying?" Jardine asked.

"No, that is my personal opinion. I know all too well how *mis queridos colombianos* are not very good at filtering fact from fiction."

"That seems to be a worldwide problem these days," commented Jardine, looking down at his notepad.

"Yes, the world is in a sad state of affairs." The professor took a sip of coffee and leaned in towards Jardine, his eyes fixed in a serious stare. "However, there is something I must tell you."

Jardine nodded. "Go on."

"*El Tigre Blanco* and his Mexican cartel, *Los Betos*, are infiltrating Colombia. It seems the War on Drugs and Plan Colombia has simply shifted power to the transporters instead of the producers."

Jardine raised an eyebrow. "Are you sure?"

"Quite sure. It comes from some contacts I have on the coast. They mentioned seeing a figure dressed in white meeting with known associates of the *Oficina de Chiribito*."

The notorious Mexican cartel leader, *El Tigre Blanco*, was well known for wearing a white *traje de luces*, like an albino Mariachi. If he were in Colombia, it would mean something was afoot with the cartels.

"I see." Jardine scribbled down some cryptic notes. "This will be very useful, Professor. Who else knows about this?"

"I imagine DNI and DIJIN are aware and the CIA, of course."

"And what about…" The conversation continued as Jardine jotted down pertinent information. A cool breeze blew down the mountains as the white church of Monserrate hovered above the city. After an hour, the professor sighed and looked at his watch. "I must be off. I have some califications to do."

Jardine noticed the professor had used califications, a Spanglish word for marking assignments or tests, but didn't comment. "Very well, Professor. Thank you for your time."

The two men shook hands and Jardine watched as the professor walked back to his office. Having finished the meeting, Jardine continued to note down a few remaining points. With the professor gone he noticed that it was eerily quiet for a university campus. He looked around him, trying to work out why when he saw a sea of glowing faces around him. Students, some sitting on the grass, some at tables and others waiting in line to buy their coffee, were nose deep in their phones. It was as if there was a worldwide conspiracy where palm sized rectangles of enchanted Plexiglas had been handed out and the humanoid apes had fallen under its spell, unable and unwilling to free their eyes. As a spy – well, an analyst actually – and not wanting to stand out, Jardine followed suit and he pulled out his phone.

He scrolled to V for Veronica.

4

LIFE IN BOGOTÁ

THAT EVENING, JARDINE ARRIVED AT VERONICA'S APARTMENT. She was sat at the kitchen table surrounded by mountains of grey covered books of *código civil colombiana.*

"Hola amor," she said, standing up and moving forward to hug him. "I missed you. I've been working on this case all day. My boss said that when it's finished, we can talk about a potential promotion. How was your day?"

"The usual, interviews and reports followed by reports about the interviews." Jardine placed his satchel on a chair and then walked to a cupboard pulling out a bottle of wine. "That's great news about the promotion! I told you you could do it. *Eres una chica muy pila,*" he said in a playful way. You are a very smart girl.

Veronica Velasco smiled and felt an injection of electricity run through her body as she looked on fondly at her partner. Ever since she could remember, Veronica Velasco had been curious about the world. Having grown up in the days before Google, her father – due to her incessant questioning of everything and everyone around her – decided to buy her the entire encyclopaedia Britannica. The books were crammed into her bedroom filling up every inch of space, under the bed, under her pillow, behind the door and even stacked around the tank of her pet fish who – if it weren't for his short-term memory – would have no doubt become quite knowledgeable about all things to do with the letter M. The lack of space didn't seem to bother her, as she set about reading methodically from A to Z in an attempt to quench her thirst for knowledge. This quest for knowledge had continued all her life until the current day, which, paired with her fiery demeanour – an aspect she had developed through her teenage years – had ultimately led her to a career as a lawyer. Because the law, as she would say, contained *un poquito de todo el mundo. A little bit of all the world.*

It was this attitude, passion and knowledge that led to her getting the position of Senior Associate at the boutique law firm Garcia y Velasquez, situated in the centre of Bogotá. Her bookish ways expanded beyond the courtroom into the class-room as she also taught law in código civil at her former university, La Universidad Nacional. Educating fresh minds from the same background as her own really gave her purpose. Those who would, in turn, help others like them-selves, made all the long hours worthwhile. Despite her cere-bral success in work, her love life success was often left wanting. It appeared as if the section on love in her ency-clopaedias was sadly lacking in real world examples. And the real world lessons she had learnt did not match the additional books she had read on the subject. However, this all changed when a young man of unknown origin mysteriously appeared in her life. After a month of dating, when it was established they were in a relationship, she would confide in him that he was her *príncipe azul.* Her blue prince. A term which confused the man, until it was established that a blue prince was in fact, not blue, but Prince Charming. Alas the clichéd, lovey dovey talk didn't end there. What followed between them was a variety of terms of endearment mani-fested in a range of bilingual pet names which were – fortunately for those around them – used sparingly and with thoughtfulness and wit. These sweet words continued until the end of their six-month honeymoon period. They had celebrated with a small weekend trip away, a trip where she found herself still hopelessly in love with him, consolidating her thoughts of building a solid and stable future with her blue prince on a foundation as strong as the walls of the white-washed houses of the small colonial town on a lake over the eastern hills of Bogotá.

"Glass of wine, my love?" Jardine held up the bottle with a smile.

"Yes!" She closed her laptop, stood up and moved towards Jardine, receiving a glass of Argentine Malbec.

"You didn't tell me about your day?" Jardine asked, taking a sip of wine.

Veronica nodded and took a large gulp of her wine. That morning, she had arrived at the university and had taught her class with her usual flair and passion. Her petite yet voluptuous figure glided effortlessly in front of the whiteboard. The fluorescent lights caught her eyes, causing them to fluctuate between light brown and smoky caramel. Her silky straight hair swayed and swished over her face as she turned to speak with her class, her perfect white teeth shone between her dark red lips. Her students would comment on her balance of sophistication and humility, a fact her friends would second. The type of woman who could enjoy a fine dinner party with important guests, but then throw back rum and aguardiente in a cantina, holding her own. Her pale-eyed blue prince would comment that everything she had accomplished was due to her own intellect and persuasive personality, a rare thing in Colombia where nepotism was as ubiquitous as cheese in hot chocolate. A local delicacy.

A little before nine am she had left her class and had travelled to her office in downtown Bogotá, arriving to the security checkpoint of the building. "Hola," she said with a flirtatious smile, whilst striding along effortlessly in high-heels and the latest designer handbag from Brazil over her shoulder.

"*Y por qué tan feliz, señorita?*" the security guard at the law firm asked her. *Why so happy, miss?*

"Do I need a reason to be happy, Alfredo?" she replied, winking.

"Not at all. It's just the last few months I have noticed you have an extra bounce in your step. Maria told me you have a new man in your life. Un gringuito."

"Maria, really? Those coffee ladies never stop with the gossip, do they?"

Alfredo let out a chuckle. "They are their own network of intelligence, as we used to say in my military days. They know all the secrets that go on around here."

Veronica frowned and then smiled. "I think I'll need to have a little chat with Maria."

Veronica continued through the metal detectors and security checkpoints, which exist at the entrance of all Colombian office buildings, rode the elevator to the fifteenth floor, walking down the corridor, entered her office and sat down at her desk while opening her laptop.

Jardine took a sip of wine. "A pretty standard Monday then."

Veronica nodded.

"Although it sounds like you can't keep a secret from anyone in Colombia!" said Jardine. "Well, I think it's my turn for dinner. Would you prefer gnocchi or fettuccine?"

"Whatever you decide, cariño."

5

NEW THEATRES OF OPERATION

THE BRITISH EMBASSY IN BOGOTÁ SITS ON A LEAFY STREET IN THE neighbourhood of El Nogal. During the day, there are two shotgun-nursing security personnel who patiently stand guard outside, sipping sweet black coffee and shooting the breeze with those that enter and exit the building.

Stepping out of a taxi, Jardine handed the driver the fare in crumpled peso notes and swivelled to greet the two security guards. A man with black hair and a trim moustache both cropped short approached him, a Beretta M9 visible under his jacket. "*Usted tiene autorización para estar aquí?*" the man asked in a terse voice. Are you authorised to be here?

Jardine smiled, reached out his arms and hugged the man. "It's been a while, Don Carlos."

They stepped back to face each other. Don Carlos reached forward and placed a hand on Jardine's shoulder. "Too long," he said in Spanish. "I've been away with the Ambassador in Los Llanos."

"Los Llanos? What's going on there?"

"Nothing important. The Ambassador was on a trip to promote British-made farm machinery."

"Sounds like a high priority," said Jardine dryly, as the two men walked towards the building's entrance.

Don Carlos was an easy going, jovial man with the appearance of a Hispanic Sean Connery (in his later years). Despite his happy demeanour, Jardine knew his life had been far from what most would consider happiness, growing up in the department of Antioquia. Some of his family had been killed by guerrillas and so he joined the military at eighteen. He had spent the better part of a decade in the jungles around La Macarena as part of an elite group of Colombian commandos that undertook reconnaissance missions in guerrilla territory, identifying potential guerrilla camps for aerial bombardment. This group would later become the *Compañia Jungla Antinarcóticos,* the Counter-Narcotics Jungle Company, alias: JUNGLA. After leaving the Military, Don Carlos had worked as a bodyguard for the Minister of Agriculture before finding work as a private security contractor, which led to his current position as Head of Security for the British Embassy. The two men had met in Jardine's first week in Colombia. Jardine thought Don Carlos' expertise might be useful for his intelligence reports. Gradually, their professional relationship had blossomed into a friendship where Jardine would regularly spend Sunday enjoying lunch with Don Carlos' family, who had unofficially adopted him as their *hijo inglés*.

Having said goodbye to Don Carlos, Jardine entered the building, passing his satchel through the metal detector while exchanging the daily exhibitions of banter and pleasantries with the two security guards in the entrance hall. Then he took the lift to level eight. After passing through a security airlock, he ambled down a corridor towards his office, and sat down at his desk.

The office seemed remarkably quiet for a Tuesday morning. Then, looking at his desk, he noticed a small post-it note stuck to his monitor.

Don't forget the weekly briefing changed to Tuesday this week! Jane

Shit! The weekly briefing.

The Bogotá MI6 Station had recently invested in an encrypted internal messaging system known as HushApp. Despite the utility of such a service, there were members who still preferred the old-fashioned method of pen and paper for important messages. "You never know when technology will be breached," many older officers would say.

He exited his office and strode towards the conference room, slipping into a chair close to the door. Inside, a projector beamed the important issues of the meeting: the on-going peace process, the status of ELN — Colombia's other active guerrilla group, and the upcoming presidential elections, which were panning out to be as polarising as whether or not a smallish island nation should leave a large continental trading block.

The meeting wrapped up and Jardine stood up, turned and reached for the door handle to exit when he felt a tap on his shoulder.

"Ah, Jardine, a word if I may?" said Ambrose, trying to sound cheery.

"Of course." They both returned to Ambrose's office, Jardine sitting in a leather armchair opposite the desk.

"Fancy a cuppa?" asked Ambrose, switching on a small electric kettle on the top of a filing cabinet.

"No, thanks, already had a tinto this morning." Tinto was strong back coffee, Colombian style. "How was El Country Club?" Jardine asked.

"You know me, enjoyed the nineteenth hole more than the first eighteen!" said Ambrose with a light-hearted chuckle. "Picked up some interesting information from Senator Restrepo, though. Might lead somewhere in learning more about the Oficina de Chiribito. It's funny, most politicians in this country — even the president — say publicly that these BACRIMS don't exist. But a few glasses of scotch and it turns out they know all about them! Greene was right, alcohol is better than a lie detector."

The kettle had boiled, and Ambrose poured some water into a teacup with the union jack on the side. "How about you? Off gallivanting with that new chica of yours?" asked Ambrose, raising the cup but not drinking.

"Was up in Guatavita for the weekend, quiet spot. Try the rabbit if you ever go."

"Ah yes, not often you find rabbit these days. Not like in my day where..." Ambrose continued for a few more minutes about his youth in London and how they would hunt rabbits on the heath and then cook them in a stew.

"Not sure if you've read my latest report," Jardine asked. "Not sure I got the analysis right."

"Haven't had a chance, I'm afraid. I rarely have time to go through the CX reports these days," Ambrose acted disinterested. Jardine always had the feeling he was irritated at something, like he read the report and it wasn't up to scratch but didn't want to mention it. "I'm sure it's fine. Don't doubt yourself, we always like to give you analysts a wide berth," Ambrose added in a cheerier tone.

A wide berth in plausible deniability on their behalf as well, Jardine thought. "Right, well, I met yesterday with Professor Villalobos. He's confident former president Urrea's influence will be minimal and the Peace Dialogues will go ahead as planned. Although the deadlines could be pushed back, depending..."

"Actually, Jardine," Ambrose interrupted. "That's why I called you in here. We've had similar intelligence product from our other sources. Seems everything's tip top, and well, things look like they'll get quiet in the future..."

"Agreed," said Jardine sharply. "With the FARC out of the drugs game, we'll have whoever fills their vacuum to contend with. You said yourself the BACRIMS were rising in influence. And no doubt some dissident FARC members will take up offers from them. The professor mentioned—"

"Yes, you're quite right," Ambrose interrupted again. "It seems some ex-FARC already have joined the Oficina de Chiribito and more will in the future—"

Jardine interrupted now, a hint of desperation in his voice. "The Professor mentioned that El Tigre Blanco and Los Betos are moving into Colombia, it's important we follow it up—"

Ambrose held up his hand. "Yes, yes, I heard that from our American cousins over the week. Is that all he had? You do know that any collaboration between cartels will fall under the jurisdiction of NCA, not us? We're strictly political, as you know."

"What does that mean?" asked Jardine, although he knew exactly what it meant.

"It seems that we are being asked to move to more pertinent theatres of operation. Those are the words of the top brass, of course, not mine. Looks like there will be some budget cuts around here and potentially some moving of assets. Syria and Yemen are heating up and the Russians and the Chinese are becoming more and more active. Need to go where the action is," said Ambrose, shaking his head with eyebrows raised slightly, giving him the look of a worried elderly person lamenting the world these days.

He wasn't sure if it was his heart or mind reacting, but Jardine began to feel an acidity swell in his stomach. His mind became like a television with bad reception, a fuzzy mess of black and white. His throat began to itch like small particles of crisps were tickling his oesophagus. "What are you saying, Ambrose?" he asked, although again, he knew exactly what he was saying.

Ambrose reached into his side drawer, pulled out a bottle of dark rum, held it out and raised his eyebrows towards Jardine.

Jardine replied, "No thanks. Like to keep a clear head these days."

Ambrose shrugged and tipped the bottle horizontally into his cup. As the burnt orange liquid trickled into the teacup, he began. "They'll let us know exactly what will happen soon enough, but thought I'd warn you, all the same. The crux of the matter is our main priority around the world is to stop international terrorism. The FARC have now been taken off the international terrorism list and so Colombia is no longer a threat. Our next priority is to combat instability which might weaken British interests — the peace talks have stabilised and now Colombia is open for business. As you know, budgets are tight, and Whitehall is pulling in the reigns all over the shop. There's even talk of a merger. Imagine that! Five, six and GCHQ all one big happy family. We sure as hell wouldn't all fit in the bloody ring, that's for sure!"

Jardine didn't reply, his mind raced with possibilities.

Ambrose continued, his eyebrows raised with concern. "We should know something later in the week. It really is over my head, I'm afraid. The powers that be have spoken and the new head is saying that fundamental Islamist terrorism is here to stay — ISIS, Al-Qaeda, Hezbollah and all their bloody friends. They seem to be popping up left, right and centre at the moment — Philippines, Indonesia, Afghanistan, Kenya, who knows where they might rear their heads next! Could be Venezuela for all we know!"

"The world was simpler when it was one ideology versus another, wasn't it?" said Jardine. Although Jardine had never lived in that era, he knew elder members of the Service said it all the time. "I mean, you knew where you stood. Not that I'd know anyway. Wasn't my era."

"Aye, t'was," replied Ambrose, putting on a Scottish accent. "You knew what you were fighting for and you knew what to read and believe. And don't even get me started on the bloody social media. It used to be you could trust what you read in the public sphere. Now it's all tabloids and pseudo Russian news sites. It's only us old hands that have seen how this Russian propaganda machine works. Shall I go through the six steps of disinformation?"

"Think I've heard it from you before. Just last Friday, in fact."

Ambrose nodded and then chuckled softly. "That's right, I had forgotten. Anyway, I'm coming up to retirement age. Once the Peace Accords are signed, I might look at packing it in. Dolores and I are still undecided between Montego Bay and Malaga."

"You'd fit right in in Malaga," said Jardine. "You'd be the only Englishman that actually speaks Spanish down there."

"I can imagine it now. A small olive plantation, some orange trees, living off tapas and cheap red wine. I'm sure I could find some contracting work to do. Keep me busy if I'm bored."

"That might be what we all need to do if they think about sending us to these new theatres of operation," said Jardine.

"It's not certain yet, Jardine. I'll know by the end of the week."

Ambrose felt the need to lie and downplay the budget cuts as if it would somehow soften the blow, although deep down he knew it wouldn't help at all. He added, "Soon we'll be shifting focus to British business interests. By the way, don't suppose you have any information about how many hover-crafts the Colombians might need?"

"Three months ago, my report from General Esguerra showed the need for at least five. Although he told the Ambassador the same thing."

"I see. Anyway, speaking of the Ambassador, I've got a

meeting with him now. "Ambrose stood up and pulled on his jacket from a rack next to his desk. "What do you think?" he asked, his arms splayed wide.

"Arturo Calle?" asked Jardine.

"No. It's a custom job from Miguel Carvajal. Bullet proof suit jacket. We've been issued them by the Foreign Office."

"I didn't get one…" said Jardine, his voice trailing off sulkily.

"Ah yes, well only for the top brass. Guess I qualify as that now." Ambrose looked sideways in confusion, like a small truck of realisation had just hit him. "Never thought I say that about myself. Top brass. Has an air of sophistication, doesn't it?"

"I guess it does. What material is that?" Jardine stepped forward and rubbed the lapel between his thumb and index finger.

"They say it's some sort of tightly woven blend. Top secret, of course. Can't give away trade secrets said the man, Miguel."

Jardine stepped back closer to the door. "Better get back to it. Report's due this week. Will be in touch, Ambrose. Give my regards to the Ambassador."

Jardine shuffled back to his office and slumped in his seat. His first thought was Veronica. What would she make of all this? His chest began to thump. Best not to tell her for the moment, he thought. Not yet. Not until he knew for sure what was at play. Instead, the analyst in him wanted to gather data and information about these so-called 'new theatres of operation.' Luckily, in his line of work, he knew people. He decided to pull out his phone and send a WhatsApp message to a journalist friend, Orlando Garzón.

El Villano as usual on Friday? Need to pick your brain about something.

— SENT

Placing his phone on his desk and mustering as much motivation as he could, he opened an encrypted file on his laptop and began to type up his weekly intelligence report.

6

CX REPORT

INTELLIGENCE REPORT

SECRET INTELLIGENCE EYES ONLY

LOCATION: BOGOTA, COLOMBIA

ANALYST: O.W.J./#397664

COLOMBIA WEEKLY BRIEF:

1. Eleven killed in Bogotá - non-political.

Analysis: Eleven people killed in Bogotá this week, albeit ten of the victims occurred during and after the Colombia World Cup qualifier match against Uruguay. This is a regular occurrence during such matches. One death attributed to gang violence. Thus, the deaths are not classed as political in nature.

2. Five social activists killed in Huila, Cauca, Nariño and Putumayo.

Analysis: Five social activists were assassinated. One in Huila, two in Cauca, and one each in Tumaco (Nariño) and Mococa (Putumayo). Media reports show they are cartel related. However, several local sources and the Progressive Democratic Party contradict this information and suggest there is paramilitary involvement. Members of the right-wing Democratic Power Party suggest it was the guerrillas. Nevertheless, confirming the exact cause has proved difficult due to the unwillingness of the public to come forward with any knowledge. Our sources suggest a strong likelihood the victims were social activists. Suggest further investigation to ascertain the impact.

3. Peace dialogues have potential to be delayed several weeks.

Analysis: Recent intelligence from the peace talks in Havana suggest a delay due to the public holidays of Saint Peter and Saint Paul, the Assumption of Mary, Columbus Day, Colombian Independence Day, the Battle of Boyacá, National Plantain Day, and the week-long festival of the potato.

4. Presidential candidate with the right leaning Partido Poder Democratico (Democratic Power Party) falsely accused of showing support for paramilitaries at popular vallenato concert.

Analysis: Presidential candidate with the right leaning Partido Poder Democratico (Democratic Power Party — a party established by the former hard-line president Urrea) was accused by the candidate from the Progressive democratic party of yelling '*Viva los paramilitares*!' while onstage with a popular vallenato singer. This was accompanied by a video on Twitter as proof. However, it was later established that the video had been doctored using a technique known as a 'deep fake.'

5. Presidential candidate with the left leaning Partido de Progresistas Democratico (Progressive Democratic Party) erroneously attributed to having an alliance with President Madera of Venezuela.

Analysis: Conversely, the candidate of the Democratic Power Party accused the left-wing candidate of the Progressive Democratic Party of having a secret alliance with Presidente Madera of Venezuela to convert Colombia into a communist-socialist utopia like Cuba. This was later disproven as there was no real evidence to the former statement. In addition, Starbucks has opened its first store in Colombia, providing further proof it is not moving towards a communist regime.

6. A supposed photo of the current President Soto, during his university years, meeting with Fidel Castro was shared online by the former president Urrea.

Analysis: A photo circulated in Colombia media purported to show the current President Soto meeting with Fidel Castro in his university years. In fact, it has been established that this was in fact a more recent photos of an official state visit which had been doctored by a Russian based mobile phone application designed to make the subject appear younger than they really are. This App has received worrying feedback from the US State Department.

7. It has been confirmed that the Mexican Cartel leader, El Tigre Blanco, is in Colombia and establishing links. Please Refer to NCA for more details.

Analysis: Regarding El Tigre Blanco, please refer to the latest NCA report.

CONCLUSIONS:
Colombia's death rate continues to rank among the highest in the world, although it has improved considerably in recent years. It should also be taken into account that Colombia is, in fact – according to the latest Gallup Poll – the happiest country in the world.

The country remains polarised still, which is manifested in the two election frontrunners: an ex-guerrilla from a now disbanded revolutionary group, and the protégé of a former hard-line, right-wing president. This has also had an impact on the controversial peace process with the FARC guerrillas. The country, like much of the world, is suffering from a social media rumour mill, which is as abundant and robust as the coffee plantations Colombia is famous for, but also as corrosive as the acid-fuelled process to manufacture cocaine.

The ongoing peace talks — currently being held in Havana, Cuba — are due to wrap up in the coming weeks, once the somewhat excessive bank holidays are finished.

END REPORT

7

A WEEK IN BOGOTÁ

WITH A NERVOUS WAIT UNTIL LONDON'S FINAL DECISION ON Bogotá Station's future, the whole office was on edge. The small team of intelligence officers and analyst were equally split between two camps. On the one side there were the we'll-all-be-bloody-relocated hysteria camp, and on the other, the they-always-do-this-to-put-us-in-our-place-and-remind-us-we're-dispensable camp. Despite the feelings of angst, the week passed much as it had every other week for Jardine, as he tried to coax up as much motivation as he could to continue with his work. Head down and show London what it is to rustle up intelligence on selling hovercrafts, finding oil rights for BP, and perhaps even develop a new market for marmite in Colombia. Whatever it took to stay in Colombia and be with Veronica, he thought.

Each morning he checked the news like he did every week, keeping abreast of major world developments and the good, bad and ugly of the Colombian media ecosystem. The 24/7 news cycle meant there was always something new, something bigger, bolder and more shocking than the next. On Wednesday while surfing the internet, there was one headline in particular on the BBC that caught his eye:

'Ex-DAESH members from UK to have citizenship revoked'

An interesting development, he thought. By threatening to revoke their citizenship, it would give the Service a bargaining chip with which to coax the ex-fighters to become informers. Perhaps, that'll be my new job? Debriefing DAESH informers. Continuing, he read that the world was still rife with political polarisation from Argentina to Zambia. Governments in Latin America were starting to elect populist leaders, there was another terrorist attack in France, which was used by both sides on the political spectrum to prove a point instead of being considerate to the victims. He scrolled further, reading about a string of volcano eruptions in Indonesia, a corruption scandal in China, and the English were actually winning in the cricket. Whenever reading the news and watching the comments on social media, he couldn't help but think that most of the world's problems today were due to people living in echo chambers where the idea of debate had been lost. All that seemed to matter was a one minute sound bite on the talking point of the day with little in-depth analysis.

Whilst reading the local news, Jardine came across a particular headline that seemed to sum up the news in Colombia that week:

'Después de los acuerdos de paz, Venezuela planea empezar, en Colombia, una revolución de castro-chavismo'

'Venezuela planning Casto-Chavista style revolution in Colombia following the Peace Accords'

The article sighted unidentified sources within the Colombian intelligence apparatus with the information. *The old trick of using an 'unidentified source' as a key supplier of information*, thought Jardine. One of the oldest tricks in the book. It was in this moment that a small chime alerted Jardine to an incoming meeting request. He clicked the small box to see that Ambrose wanted to speak with him at eleven thirty on Friday morning. *I hope this is good news*, he thought as he finalised his reports for the week.

Several times during the week he left the office to meet his sources. His cover as Third Secretary (Political) at the Embassy meant he didn't need an elaborate cover story most of the time. Occasionally, he would use English language teacher as a cover, as it enabled him to explain one-on-one meetings. Colombia was opening up to international business and many Colombians, even those within Government, were required to speak the language of Shakespeare more than ever. A language teacher avoided questions from the security guards, who may or may not be working for any number of illegal groups in the capital. When he thought about it, a teacher, or a private tutor, was an excellent cover for a spy. It worked in almost every situation. "What were you doing at that Russian oligarch's home?" *His son needs a bit of help with his English, you see.* "Why were you having a coffee with that Cuban dissident in Miami?" *He's just moved to the USA, needs help with his business English vocabulary.* "You met with the Head of the Colombian Armed Forces, getting some intelligence product, were we?" *Nothing of the sort, helping him with his phrasal verbs.*

On Wednesday afternoon Jardine met with General Esguerra Martinez, the General in charge of purchasing for the Colombian Armed Forces. The General never failed to wear his khaki green uniform complete with medals, combat boots and worn military cap. Their discussion entailed what the military were doing while the peace dialogues were wrapping up, and whether or not they were interested in purchasing any more hovercrafts.

"Do the British use hovercrafts?" asked General Esguerra Martinez at the meeting.

"Not really," Jardine replied.

"Then why do you make them?"

"We're good at it, I suppose?"

"In Colombia, we enjoy and partake in all our exports. Coffee, emeralds, gold, the women…"

Jardine tapped his nose. "What about…?"

"No!" said the General with an uncharacteristic shout, before calming himself. "That is an exception." Jardine had forgotten never to mention cocaine to Colombians.

Normally, General Esguerra wasn't interested in talking military tactics, the peace process or hovercrafts. He mostly wanted to speak about his experience working in Dubai as a private military contractor for a sheik, and how his family had enjoyed their life there. "The sheik paid much better than *la patria*, unfortunately," the General lamented. "And the work was much less dangerous than here. Dubai has many fantastic restaurants, especially Lebanese restaurants. I've grown a liking to it. My grandmother was Lebanese, did you know? Although the Lebanese food in Colombia is usually adapted to our tastes. Do you think Colombian food is bland?" The General had the habit of asking many questions without stopping for an answer before moving onto a further comment and another question, a characteristic he shared with Veronica. "Because that's what all my American counterparts say. Not enough taste and flavour they say. I tell them American food has too many condiments, we have a word for it: 'condimentado'. It means too much flavour, ruins the true taste of the food. I used to cook for the Yankees when I studied at West Point Academy. Did you know there is even a Syrian restaurant in Teusaquillo now? I've been there a few times. The owner is a real Syrian, although he is becoming more and more Colombian. I am teaching him Colombian slang. Do you know any Colombian *modismos*? I can teach you some. There's…"

Jardine would usually let the General talk. He knew he

enjoyed it and it was rare for Colombians to open the conversation with business without a lengthy chat about everyday topics first.

After the General had stopped talking and whilst sipping his tinto, Jardine asked a question. "And what of ELN, General? What are their movements these days?"

The General placed his coffee cup gently on the table and took a bite of an arepa. He began speaking with remnants of the arepa between his teeth and small pieces dangled gently in his neatly trimmed beard. "We know that some FARC dissidents have joined the renegade groups of the ELN and are setting up a new base outside of Valledupar. That region has a lot of cattle farms in the valley between the Sierra Nevada and the Serranía del Perijá. We know they are trying to establish a base somewhere in that area, but we don't know which side of the valley. Although it is likely the Perijá side, hiding in Venezuela with protection from the Madera regime." The General made a Gallic shrug as he finished his sentence.

"Is this group likely to join the new peace talks that are rumoured between the Government and the ELN in Ecuador?"

"We don't know for sure. To be honest, we just want to aerial bomb them and see where they run. That is our usual tactic. Then we know where their base is located."

"I see, General. It sounds like you've got your work cut out for you."

Jardine made a mental note that he would need to modify that part for his report. Something along the lines of: 'The General foresees further aerial attacks on the ELN/FARC dissident group's new base in the mountains surrounding the Valley of Upar.' He would often need to adapt the speech of his reports to London's taste. One couldn't be as frank as the General had just been. He wouldn't get away with putting: 'To be honest, we just want to bomb the *hijos de puta* and see where they run!' in a report. Even if that were a legitimate and desirable objective, it was too personal and too close to death for London, nowhere near vague enough and it most definitely didn't leave room for plausible deniability down the track. It needed to be expressed in a more concise yet delicate manner, an aspect every good intelligence report should contain. Succinct and to-the-point, yet vague enough to be wrapped, gerrymandered and denied if need be.

Following the morning meeting with General Esguerra, Jardine met with Señor Quintero, a Senior Executive in the Financial Superintendent, the regulatory body that covers money laundering. It eventuated that Señor Quintero did not have a whole lot to contribute, apart from running commentary as to why Santa Fé was Colombia's best football team. What he did produce were statistics on projected GDP growth, which had no bearing on whether or not hovercrafts would be purchased.

On Thursday morning, Jardine met with Señor Zuluaga, one of Colombia's largest coffee barons and a general importer/exporter of all sorts of goods — legal and illegal. The man was an archetypal Colombian coffee farmer, or *arriero*, as the early explorers of the coffee region were known. He regularly wore a light blue shirt tucked into twill trousers with a large poncho-like cloth draped over his right shoulder. His light grey eyes, alert under his woven Panama hat, stared right at Jardine as he spoke. Drug smuggling, and smuggling in general, was big business in Colombia, and Zuluaga knew the Colombian landscape better than anyone. He could chat for hours in his office in Santa Barbara, explaining every intricacy of the country's geography on a giant relief map, which held pride of place beside his desk above two sacks of Colombian coffee. He knew all the smuggling routes and tricks of the trade the *contrabandistas* used to ship everything from cocaine to whisky, to plasma screens to inflatable Chinese-made blow up toys. His family were wealthy landowners and his father had been killed by the FARC. This meant *hijos de puta* usually preceded *guerrilleros* in their talks. It also meant that much of his intelligence product was provided for free, which pleased Jardine's budget conscious superiors. Not to mention the bags of premium coffee Jardine would bring back from their rendezvous.

Thursday evening, he met, for the first time, with a Social Activist from Sucre in a billiards hall in downtown Bogotá. The recent spate of assassinations conducted by unknown right-wing groups as a result of the FARC's truce with the government had left a power vacuum, which was currently being filled by a number of former paramilitary and criminal organisations. Without the guerrillas for protection, social leaders had been targeted. Jardine felt guilty meeting with the activist, knowing that it was unlikely to continue in the future if he was transferred or made redundant. Unless, of course, the activist required a number of well-built hovercrafts, had a large taste for a yeasty British spread, or perhaps owned a parcel of land containing black gold.

8

PACK YOUR BAGS

On Friday morning at eleven thirty, Jardine knocked on Ambrose's door, then entered and sat opposite him.

"Morning Jardine, I suspect you've had a busy week. I imagine you met with Esguerra Martinez, Quintero and Zuluaga?"

"Correct. Nothing too important to report. Most of it went in the weekly report to London."

"Right, I see." Ambrose avoided eye contact as he stood up and moved behind his desk looking out the window. "And what about the others? Any updates on Señor Leonardo Gabriel Murillo Rico, the National Director for Anti-Corruption."

"Not too well, I'm afraid. He was arrested, sir," replied Jardine.

"Arrested? What for? Surely his collaboration with us wasn't discovered?"

"No, it wasn't that. He was arrested for conspiring to launder money for the purpose of foreign bribery."

"Good heavens! And what of your meetings with the Commissioner for the police's anti-kidnapping task force, GAULA isn't it called?"

"He's gone missing."

"Missing?"

"It seems he's been kidnapped, sir."

Ambrose still avoided eye contact and seemed to be bringing up news that he already knew. Jardine could tell he was stalling before telling him the news about the austerity measures. "Kidnapped? Bloody hell! Well surely there must be something from your contact at the National Truth Commission? I mean he must be making some progress with all the atrocities committed during the civil conflict?"

"He's been a little tied up at the moment."

"Tied up? He hasn't been kidnapped too, has he?"

"No, he was fired."

"Fired? Whatever for?" asked Ambrose incredulously.

"Lying. About his university degrees, apparently. He's not a Doctor Rodriguez, just a Señor Rodriguez."

"Well, it all seems quite normal for Colombia really. Now, I shouldn't delay any further." Ambrose turned from looking out the window to face him. "I've spoken with Radcliffe, who in turn has been speaking with R, who has been bent over by the Foreign Secretary, the Prime Minister and most of White-hall, and…" Ambrose reached forward for a cup of tea, leaving the words hanging in the air.

"And…?" asked Jardine.

"And it seems you're wanted in Yemen."

"Yemen?"

"The Houthi rebels are well and truly down from the mountains and marching on Sana'a. It appears we'll need 'Our Man in Yemen' to make contact and find out what their position is."

Jardine gulped. Vero is not going to like this.

"*Si dios quiere*," Ambrose continued. "All will be well, and you'll slip in nicely to the new environment."

It had never occurred to Jardine that this phrase, "If god wants," in Spanish, used ubiquitously in Colombia, was on par with the Arabic *inshallah*. God willing. Or perhaps, it was just because he'd found out he would be transferred to Yemen.

Ambrose sipped his tea then continued. "Of course, all the arrangements will be made for you. You have the usual relocation allowance, a short sojourn in London. You'll need to learn Arabic pronto, of course...." Ambrose's voice trailed off.

Half an hour later, Jardine returned to his office and slumped in his chair. He switched on his laptop, logged into Twitter and aimlessly scrolled, not caring or interested in anything in particular. An announcement proclaimed that in a few weeks, it would be the last day of the Colombian conflict. The hashtag #UltimasSemanasDeLaGuerra was trending. He should have felt elated and happy for Colombia, but all he could feel was an empty hole in his stomach and a scratching throat that was starting to develop into a lump. Scrolling further he came across the more negative hashtags aimed at the President Soto. #NoMasSoto (#NoMoreSoto), #Soto-Traidor (#SotoTraitor), and #SotoMentiroso (#SotoLiar). Incredible that people could be against peace, he thought.

His mind shifted to Veronica. Would she want to go with him? What would he do if she said no? As an analyst he was used to weighing up two sides of a situation. From what he could surmise, it was a tussle between duty for country and love for a woman. But which held more weight? He felt an obligation to his country and his profession. Yemen would be more dangerous than Colombia, but where there's danger, there's more respect and promotion. There's no doubt it would be good for his career. But would he choose that over losing Veronica? No, not a chance. He couldn't walk away from her.

With merely the thought of her caramel coloured eyes, her calm demeanour and her soft affectionate caresses, he felt in a world of peace. What was it about love that affected the brain? The analyst in him didn't want to believe it was real.

He had always been taught that there were only four motivations for spying: money, ideology, compromise and ego. This seemed to work in life as well. Although, he thought maybe he could suggest that they add *love* to the course at Fort Monckton. Because to him, it seemed like love was the most powerful emotion of all. It felt like it was rewiring his brain, for the better.

He glanced out his office window at Bogotá's eastern mountains. Maybe she would come with him? Sure, she's due for promotion, but there must be opportunities for her skills set in Yemen. We're in love. Maybe she would enjoy the hotter weather? Maybe we could start a family there? It would be a hell of an adventure. We'd live in a villa and she could do yoga and join the local Colombian expat club. Can't be that hard to pass the bar in Yemen. Although she doesn't speak the language or know anything about sharia law. I wonder if they have yoga in Yemen?

The thoughts raced through his mind. He needed more information — intelligence product — before he could mention it to Veronica. He needed to speak to Garzón, he's been to Yemen. He would guide him in the right direction. A short beep from his mobile phone snapped Jardine out of his trance. A WhatsApp message appeared on the screen:

El Villano tonight. Any time after 5pm

— GARZÓN

Perfect. He could talk to Garzón at El Villano – a popular local bar — and then dinner with Veronica. Speaking of which, what time was it, 7pm or 8pm? He picked up his phone and called Vero.

"Hello?" she answered.

"Hola, mi cielito. ¿Que haces?" *Hello my little sky. What are you doing?* Came the response from Jardine.

"My little yellow birdie. I'm going over the case from this week. How are you? What are you doing? I wish we were still in Guatavita, snuggling by an open fire with hot chocolate."

As always, her response would include three different questions or comments in which Jardine didn't know to which he should respond. "I've just had a meeting with my boss," he thought on his feet about what to say next. "Needed some information for a report I'm writing. I'd much rather be with you, hot chocolate and an open fire though." Along with combined questions, Jardine had become accustomed to answering multiple questions in a sentence.

"Aww. That's so sweet of you. I wish we could be together right now. I have so much work to do. *No te imaginas*. But I can feel my promotion is so close. My boss just told me, if this case is successful, I'll be made Directora! It's what I've waited for my whole life."

"Fantastic!" He tried to imbue as much confidence and warmth in his voice as could muster. "You can tell me all about it over dinner tonight. What time was it?"

"Eight pm mi amor. Te amo mucho. See you at dinner!"

Veronica's sweet tones and positivity had managed to coax out a stream of optimism in him. It seemed love could cloud the analytical abilities of even a professional intelligence analyst.

Jardine brought his focus back to his monitor. She was very happy and upbeat, he thought. A quick chat with Garzón and then break the news that we're moving to Yemen at dinner. I'm sure she'll forget all about her promotion with the prospect of adventure and international travel. Why wouldn't she?

9

FRIDAY NIGHT DRINKS

JARDINE ARRIVED IN A TAXI STOPPING RIGHT OUTSIDE EL Villano. "Cuidado, por acá hay mucho ladron," said the taxi driver, looking in the rear view mirror at Jardine whilst scratching his cheek, a Colombian sign for 'be careful: thieves!' "Especially with your monkey appearance," he added, cackling away to himself. Each Spanish-speaking country in Latin America has their word to describe people of a lighter complexion. In Colombia it was *mono*. Monkey.

Climbing the narrow wooden stairs, a slow Cuban song played a hypnotic rhythm of bongo drums and piano with the occasion outburst of brass horns. Reaching the top, Jardine turned into a dimly lit room filled with plush leather sofas and dimly lit booths among short palm bushes. On one side was the bar with a line of stools. Whoever sat there would have their back to the open doorway, not his preferred seating arrangement. But much more sociable if alone. However, in El Villano, there was always someone he knew.

A voice drifted through the air in heavily accented Spanish. "My good friend *ron* is a little sour and by that, I mean he likes lime. The perfect couple. Actually, it's rather a good name for a cocktail don't you think, Jose? A sour ron! Rum, lime juice and lots of ice." The familiar voice drifted through the air, its timbre unmistakable to Jardine's ears.

"Suena bien, you're onto a winner there. A sour ron for me, Jose," said Jardine. Jose, the bar tender signalled a thumbs-up and swivelled around to prepare the drink.

"Jardine, old boy!" A man in his 60s, wearing a tropical linen suit with white runners spun around on his stool. "Was wondering when someone I knew might get here." He stumbled off the stool and moved forward to shake Jardine's hand. His eyes were slightly red, and his light grey hair resembled a certain bike-riding British Prime Minister. "Knocked off early today, you see. Can't miss happy hour at El Villano. What's new with you?"

"Nothing too much to report, Alfie. Reports, reports and more reports. All on the peace dialogues, of course. Although it's quietening down now."

"Yes, seems the conflict will be over in few weeks. Ha! We know that won't be the case, don't we? How's that woman of yours? Keeping you out of trouble?"

"At least out of the bars. How about you?"

Alfie scratched his head. "Oh, I'm alright. Been a busy week, working, as it were."

"Working? Do you mean amber liquid lunches, vino-filled dinners, and post-dinners rums and port? Imagine a liquid rainbow of yellow, red and dark brown, that's your fluid intake for the day," said Jardine squeezing his shoulder.

Alfie smiled. "It's networking, you know, schmoozing with clients, getting them to bill more hours of English classes, or sales training, marketing, intercultural babble, or whatever." Alfie White had arrived in Colombia in 1980s as an English Language Assistant with the British Council and never left. He was now the owner of Oxford English Solutions. The premier, according to him, English language provider in the city.

The two men continued chatting as several other

customers filed through the doors for happy hour. A little before six pm, another familiar voice drifted over their shoulders.

"What a bunch of absolute douche-bags! What up, fellas?" If voices were unmistakable to Jardine, there was no doubt this voice belonged to: Mike Brady. "Off the red eye from Cartagena this morning and ready to start the weekend with a bang!"

A tall, dark-haired American with a square chin and defined cheek bones entered the room wearing a dark navy suit around a crisp white open neck shirt. On his feet he wore chocolate brown brogues which made a hearty clonk as he walked in, oozing his usual charm and confidence. Except this time, something was off. His usual effortless strides were stifled by the movement of his hand to his crotch making slight adjustments and chancing an itch while his hand hovered in the region.

"Have fun in Cartagena did we Mike?" asked Alfie.

"Let's say I took some advice from the leader of the free world's secret service agents on where to grab a drink…"

"I can imagine what that entailed. Did you find true love? Love in a time of cholera, perhaps?" offered Jardine.

"Far from it. It was more like lust in a night of chlamydia. The itching hasn't stopped…" He moved his hand again down to his crotch and itched furiously. "Doesn't matter though. I'm ready for tonight. What are we drinking, mother-fuckers?"

"Are you sure you don't need medical attention?" asked Alfie looking towards Mike's nether regions.

"I'm fine. Rum? I'm buying a bottle. Jose…" Mike Brady walked over to Jose, patted him on the back and they looked at the bottles of rum on the shelf behind the bar together. The number of expats in Colombia was low compared to the other Latin American destinations of Rio, Buenos Aires, Santiago or Lima. Stereotypes are powerful beasts and unfortunately

Colombia was one of the most stereotyped countries in the world. Internationally known for its bone-cracking violence, squeaky powdery cocaine, Don Pablo Emilio Escobar Gaviria, the Miss Universe crown fiascos, and a failed-state crawling with blood-thirsty cartels battling it out in the street. That's what the international media portrayed anyway: sex, drugs and…well, sometimes salsa and Shakira. As such, Colombia was not your standard international destination. Years of violence inflicted by Marxist-Leninist guerrilla 'freedom' fighters, paramilitary 'self-defence' units, the 'entrepreneurial' cartels, and an increasingly well-equipped and trained military had given *la tierra querida* — the promised land as Colombian's affectionately called it — a bad name in the international sphere. Not the kind of place your ordinary citizen would go for some rest and relaxation or a career change. It was because of this that Colombia seemed to attract an eclectic cast of eccentric, adventurous and unique individuals, read: misfits. Because in reality they were a rag tag bunch of digital mercenaries, embassy mandarins, travelling teachers and anyone who felt more attractive to both sexes in Bogotá than Boston, Bristol, Brisbane or Berlin.

By seven-thirty, the bar had filled up and Jardine, Alfie and Mike had managed to commandeer a sofa and a small parcel of real estate near the bar. Alfie sat next to Mike as he recounted his week in Cartagena, while Alfie told him about his latest way to make a few pesos on the side — receiving cash wire transfers for rich Venezuelans exiled from the Madera regime. Over time others joined. Zac, an Aussie stoner, Tomas, a German engineer, Etienne, a French telenovela actor, and finally Jonathan Lloyd, a tall and slender Englishman with short dark hair, a prominent nose and thin lips that seemed to quiver when he spoke. Jonathan was a veteran teacher on the international circuit. Eight years in Hong Kong, two in Beirut, three in Jakarta before spending the past four in Bogotá.

Jardine looked nervously at his watch. As he lifted his head and looked towards the entrance, a man with shoulder length brown hair and a goatee entered and worked his way through the throngs of people now occupying the area in front of the bar. Orlando Garzón was a typical *rolo* — resident of Bogotá — which meant he often wore a scarf and tortoise shell rimmed glasses. A bookish middle-aged man, he'd lived through the darker days of Colombia, the advances of the guerrillas, the massacres, the Miss World pageants, and more recently, had contributed several 'feel good' articles on Colombia's transition from dangerous no-go zone to intriguing international destination du jour. He'd spent part of his childhood in the US, but had returned to Colombia and felt more Juan Valdez than Uncle Sam.

It was Garzón Jardine had wanted to see most of all tonight. He knew he'd recently travelled to Syria and Yemen and would know what it was really like. He quietly hoped for a positive outlook, so he could break the news to Veronica over dinner with a more 'upbeat' vibe.

"Well if it isn't the motley-est crew of ruffians this side of Panama," announced Garzón, as he back-slapped and high-fived his way around the group. The men returned the greeting and partook in a round of drinks.

As the men enjoyed their libations, Jardine ushered Garzón aside. "Mind having a quick chat?" he asked. "Heading out for dinner with Vero but wanted to run something by you."

"Sure. I'm all ears."

The two men stepped away from the group to a quiet corner of the bar.

"There are some changes afoot at the Embassy. When the Peace Talks are done, I'll be transferred to Yemen."

"Yemen? I guess that's where all the action is happening?" said Garzón, shaking his head. "People in our business always end up in the rough and tumble places. As soon as

there's some good news or a breakthrough in something positive, our work dries up. Seems no-one's interested in good
news."

"What was your experience there?" Jardine asked. "I
remember you telling us about it, but it didn't seem as relevant then."

"If it bleeds, it leads. Isn't that what they say?" Garzón
chuckled, still thinking about what he had said earlier.
"Everyone's focussed on these 'foreign' members of ISIS."

"ISIS are in Yemen?"

"Everyone's in Yemen. But you can divide them, roughly,
into two camps: those receiving cash from the Saudis, and
those from the Ayatollah."

"That was our ten second analysis as well. Not that I'm an
expert yet. I guess I'll need to be."

Garzón nodded. "This morning I read an article, from a
friend of mine at the BBC, about foreign fighters in Syria, Iraq
and now Yemen."

"I think I read the same article," said Jardine.

Garzón's eyes lit up. "That's the second in a week! Last
week they stopped three guys from London with a cash-filled
suitcase trying to get to Turkey. It seems they'd been financing
around the UK. Reminds me of the days when money was
flowing from the triple frontera region. Arab immigrants
made millions from illegal contraband and counterfeit goods
and funded Al-Qaeda and Hezbollah. Although the US
attempted to put a stop to it. I imagine it's still going on
though, hard to stop anything like that on this continent."

"Al-Qaeda operating in Latin America?"

"Yes, and Hezbollah. But that was years ago now,"
answered Garzón, taking a sip from his beer.

A loud obnoxious accent yelled across the room at them.
"Yo guys, listen up! I've got a story for you, douchebags." It
was Brady. He very much lived up to the unfavourable American stereotype of being loud and obnoxious. Jardine and

Garzón joined the group once again. "One of my lady friends in Cartagena told it to me," Brady said.

"You mean one of your whores?" said Jonathan, followed by a tutting sound.

"Ha! You can talk. I've seen you at La Piscina!" Brady replied.

"Fuck you! You fucking twat!" Jonathan screwed up his nose and walked off in a huff to the bathroom.

The group of men looked at each other startled.

"Girlfriend just broke up with him," said Alfie. "Seems she was only using him for fancy dinners, trips to Europe and the occasional Instagram post. That's all my woman gets out of me as well." Alfie shook his head.

"He'll get over it. Not like we're in a fish-less ocean here! We're balls-deep in a school of marlin and we're the goddamn bait!" said Brady, high-fiving a few random people passing by. "Anyway, as I was saying, a little birdy señorita from Cartagena told me…" Brady began to recount what he had heard in Cartagena. A woman Brady had spent the weekend with was a *prepago,* a unique, escort-like arrangement in Colombia where a woman is pre-paid to spend an evening with a man. Dinner, dancing, drinks and *maybe* 'dessert'. She told Brady how a certain American government agency – the DEA – became involved with a group of gorgeous Colombian women working in a club they frequented. Not a big issue in and of itself. However, the story got interesting when a mysterious sheik from an unknown Middle Eastern country began to use the services of these señoritas too and began to glean the odd piece of vital intelligence information.

"Like a honey trap?" asked Alfie.

"That's right! A honey trap – attractive and sticky," replied Brady.

"I think we would call it an arequipe trap in Colombia," offered Garzón, to a roar of laughter from the group.

Arequipe was a soft caramel similar to the Italian dolce de leche.

Brady continued to recount how at first, there was no real valuable intelligence. That was until the US president himself was due to attend a week-long summit of the Americas in the city of Cartagena, and the Sheik – with the prepago's help – employed the same tactic on the President's Secret Service Agents in the lead-up security protocols.

"So, there you have it, fellas! And you guys thought I was only taking part in the pleasures of life!" said Brady, his arms outstretched.

"American stupidity knows no bounds," said Jonathan, having returned from the bathroom.

"Eh, marica, we're all Americans in these parts," said Garzón. "Por favor! Why do people always think that America stops with the Yankees?"

Jonathan looked at his shoes and shuffled his feet. "Sorry, Orlando. Fuck, I miss her…" he muttered under his breath. He leaned on the bar. "Double ron, José. Some of the good stuff, añejo 8 años."

"So, who's this sheik then?" asked Jardine. "Any leads on that, Mr. Crab crotch?"

"Well, let's say, gentlemen, the conversation didn't go that far. My curiosity was piqued and well, then something else peaked, if you get my drift," Brady exaggerated a wink at them.

Friendly jibes and witty remarks filled the air as the laughter and banter continued until a voice broke the atmosphere.

"Hello? Ah, mind if I join?" asked an American accent coming from a tall man with neatly parted hair.

"Fark yeah! Pull up a pew, mate," offered Zac, an Aussie who had backpacked his way down from Mexico and had decided to stick around in Colombia. The man stepped forward. He wore a pale blue shirt with hiking boots. "I'm glad I found this place. I was a little lost and starting to worry." The man pushed his glasses up his nose and chuckled nervously. "In New York, I'd simply pull out my iPhone and Google it, but my company warned me against taking my phone out in the street down here."

"Ah, no need to worry too much about that, old mate. Look at the size of you! You tower above most around here," said Alfie.

"Well that's just the thing, I stick out like a sore thumb! Anyway, you chaps seem to know the ropes around here." The word 'chaps' sounded strange through the vocal chords of an American. "Are you guys British? I guess you all live here in Bogotá. I studied at Durham on a study abroad during my senior year. Lovely place, England."

"What brings you to Bogotá?" asked Garzón.

"In town with the VizFeed to do a story on demobilising guerrillas, and anything else I can find an angle on."

"You should watch yourself. A journalist from the Times was threatened by the military, had to get out of dodge quick smart," said Brady.

"That's what I'm worried about…" the man trailed off.

"Well, Garzón's your man. Fellow scribbler and he'll put you in touch with almost anyone in the country," offered Alfie, his speech starting to loosen into his trademark slur.

"Garzón?"

"A la orden," said Garzón, outstretching his hand. *At your service.*

Jardine looked at his watch. "Dinner with Veronica, guys. See you later."

"Come on, have one more. You know she'll be half an hour late," said Brady reaching for a bottle of rum.

"Maybe next time, fellas. Watch yourself, Brady. Don't go spreading around your new condition. The last thing we need is you spreading around your lustful chlamydia."

The group continued drinking into the night, as Jardine

stepped out into the cool Andean night air and hailed a taxi. Sitting in the backseat Jardine realised he hadn't got any useful information about Yemen from Garzón. *Looks like I'll have to make something up,* he thought, as the taxi weaved its way through the dark streets of Bogotá.

10
___

VERO IN YEMEN?

HEADING NORTH IN A TAXI, JARDINE ARRIVED AT A SUSHI restaurant in the neighbourhood of Rosales for dinner with Veronica. The sushi train moved around displaying small-coloured plates of sliced marine life. He knew it wasn't a good idea to order fish in an inland Andean city, but what was one more risk now that he would be stationed in Yemen?

Jardine entered the restaurant and saw Veronica sat at the sushi train. She smiled, stood up and wrapped her arms around his neck and kissed him on the lips, then burrowed her nose into chest affectionately.

"I missed you!" she said softly.

"I missed you, too," he replied.

Sitting down, Veronica looked at his face. "Mi amor, you seem nervous," she said in Spanish, a deep and genuine affection in her voice. Colombian women were masters at reading one's body language and could always sense when something was wrong.

"Me? Nervous? Well, perhaps a little. It's just work. You know, lots of information flying in these days, changes happening. Nothing to worry about though," he replied in English, he always felt less emotional in English. Spanish changed the way he thought and made him feel like a different person, more sentimental. He needed less of that if he was going to tell her what had happened, what would happen. They both ordered large glasses of a Chilean Carménère and glanced dreamily into each other's eyes as a skilled chef coarsely chopped a small octopus in front of them.

Veronica recounted her day of research on a crypto currency scandal she was working on. "There are so many lies these days, these *estafadores…*"

"Scammers, grifters, con artists," Jardine offered.

Veronica swilled her wine in hand. "Yes, scam artists, they convinced people to invest in a crypto currency fund. Then, they created websites which seemed to be independent from their business confirming their information. It gave legitimacy to their business. It also gave the impression you couldn't lose if you invested."

"Incredible. So what's the next step?"

"We are building a case, but it could take years." She looked into Jardine's eyes and smiled.

He smiled back and then took a sip of wine. "Vero, you're right. I am nervous. There's something I need to tell you." He reached across the table and grasped her hands in his.

She looked at him and smiled. Her large eyes shone like smooth, moistened pebbles caressed by a gentle river. "Yes, mi amor?"

"You know I've been here a few years now."

"Of course."

"And I have been covering the peace talks with the guerrillas."

"Yes, they've dragged on for quite a while, haven't they?"

"Yes. They have." Jardine looked down at the table and squeezed Veronica's hands slightly.

"But it will be great when they are finalised. My country can finally revert to peace. Although we still have the ELN and the criminal gangs and 1.5 million Venezuelan refugees…" she continued.

"And the FARC dissident groups, and evidence of infiltration by the now powerful Mexican cartels… But I'm getting off track here. There are going to be changes at the Embassy."

"Change is good. Change brings opportunity," she offered. That was another of Veronica's attributes, the cup was always half-full, there was always a rainbow after rain, and there was always a new day to make the impossible, possible.

"I mean, the peace talks are ending, and well, I'm… I'm being transferred." He turned his head upwards to look her in the eyes.

The sparkle in the glistening pebbles dried up and her pupils dilated to form large black spheres. She leaned back slowly, and her brow moved downwards causing ripples of skin across her forehead. It seemed as if her wavy crespo hair was emitting sparks and began to expand and radiate outwards. Her hands moved down to her hips as if to gain leverage for what was to come.

"Como así? *What do you mean*?" she asked in a terse tone.

"It's my job. I'm being transferred, there's little reporting to do here now. The talks are—"

"What do you mean?" she interrupted. "What about us? Where are you going? When? How? What about me? You're going to leave me?" The questions flew out in rapid fire Spanish, like red hot embers from a chainsaw cutting through steel.

"Well, you would come with me, of course. I mean, we would go together?" his voice raised at the end of the sentence with uncertainty.

"What about my career? My family? My friends? I can't just leave! I have a small puppy, for Christ sake." Shit, I'd forgotten about the dog, thought Jardine.

"It could work. The main thing is we'll be together," he

tried.

"Dónde? Where are they sending you?"

"At the moment, there's talk of Yemen or Syria. I can't remember which. Actually, I think it's definitely Yemen. The culture is meant to be fascinating…"

"YOU WANT ME TO GO TO A WAR ZONE? *Estás loco*?" Small droplets were starting to form in the corners of her eyes, although they did little to put out the sparks still flying from her mouth.

She stood up with her hands on her hips and a cloth napkin in one hand.

"Por qué siempre me pasa a mí esa mierda!" she said, as she slammed the napkin down on the bench of the sushi train.

A table situated behind them looked on and made disapproving sounds while shaking their heads.

"It'll be okay, we'll work it out," said Jardine standing up and outstretching his arms towards her. He wanted to say calm down, but then remembered that 'calm down' is the last thing you should say to someone who needs to calm down. Nevertheless, the words slipped out. "Look. Calm down, please."

"Calm down? Aha." She seemed to consider this while drinking from her glass. But then, after she had swallowed a large gulp, she returned to her high-pitched screams. "You want us to move to a war zone and be happy!?"

"It'll just be for a few years, tops. I can earn good money there. They'll pay extra danger money and then we can do whatever we want. Maybe buy a small boutique guesthouse somewhere nice? We've talked about that before. We could really set up a new life for ourselves…"

"Bah! You and your idiotic plans!" And with that she left not in her usual hopping grace, but with a determined salsa stomp, slamming the door so that everything in the restaurant rattled like a small tremor had engulfed the building.

Jardine stood up as the small coloured plates continued

their circular trajectory around the sushi train. He placed his wine glass on the table. She'll come around, he thought. Although, he was anything but sure.

After bursting out of the restaurant, Veronica hailed a taxi, slamming the door as she got in.

"Suave con la puerta, por favor!" shrieked the driver. *Gentle with the door, please.*

She thought about unleashing a torrent of expletives but instead burst into tears, sobbing into her hands in the back seat.

"Perdón, no quería ser tan brusco. Estás bien señorita? asked the driver. *Sorry, I didn't mean to be so rough on you. Are you okay, young lady?*

"Si, problemas del corazón, nada más." *Yes, nothing more than problems of the heart.*

"Ah," replied the driver nodding. "Todo saldrá bien, tu verás." *Everything will work out fine, you'll see.*

Arriving home she poured a large glass of wine and sat on her balcony looking over the twinkling lights of Bogotá. She took a sip and sighed. It felt like everything was falling into place. Studies, work, working her way up the career ladder, the man of her dreams and poof! It all comes crashing down because HE wants to move. She took another sip of wine. It wasn't really his decision, was it? Maybe she was too harsh on him? It's not his fault they want to transfer him. *It's just that I'm making so much progress in my career and I can't just give it all up and move to the other side of the world. I mean, I love him dearly, but there must be another way for us to be together. There must be.* Veronica Velasco stared off into the night. She wanted to believe that everything would be alright, but this was real life, not a fairy-tale. And real life didn't always have a happy ending.

11

GARZÓN: THE PHILOSOPHER

JARDINE DRAINED THE REST OF THE RED WINE – A FULL, LARGE glass – and paid the bill, apologising to the manager.

"Perdón por el show." *Sorry, for making a scene.*

"No se preocupe, caballero." *Don't worry, sir.* "Ya estamos acostumbrados aquí." *We're used to them here.*

Calling Garzón – who mentioned he was at a small tienda bar in La Candelaria – Jardine got into a taxi and directed the driver to take him to Bar Doña Ceci. He asked the driver to leave him at the Centro Colombo Americano, preferring to walk through Parque de los Periodistas. Stepping out of the taxi his legs felt like noodles, swaying slightly as he walked. He moved through the square, eyeing a statue of Simon Bolivar ahead to help steady his walk when he heard the low buzz of a motorcycle approaching. The area was quiet and dark, a red transmileno bus passed by on his left. The wind blew a solitary empty diet coke can along the cobblestones in front of him, letting off a metallic rattle which echoed off the surrounding buildings. The buzzing grew louder as it too bounced off the surrounding walls like a small mosquito approaching his ear. He turned just as a motorcycle with two men pulled up alongside him. The man on back with an outstretch arm holding a handgun. "Dame tu billatera y celu!" the man shouted. *Give me your wallet and mobile phone!*

Jardine stared at them a moment, swaying from side to side. Then he calmly reached into his pockets and handed over his wallet and a cheap mobile phone. "Fucking take them, you fucking malparidos de mierda!" he spat in Spanglish.

The man with the gun tilted his head to the side like a curious kitten, obviously amused at the verbal abuse from their victim. With the objects in their hands, the two men sped off through the square and down a dark side street.

Jardine entered the bar and saw Garzón sat at a quiet table in the back with eyes glued to a plasma screen. He slumped down in the seat opposite. "Your shout, just got fucking robbed. Although, they only got my *flecha*," said Jardine grinning, holding his smart phone up in his hand. In Colombia, it was common to carry a cheap decoy phone – a *flecha* — in case of robbery.

"Robbed?" Garzón took sip of beer and chuckled. "Bloody gringos, can't take you anywhere." He motioned for the waiter to bring them two drinks.

On the screen, the announcer described the recent round of negotiations between the Colombian Government and the FARC: "Consensus has been reached on a number of issues between the FARC and the government, including agrarian reform, public education and land redistribution. But the Colombian people, on the other hand, are still divided," the announcer reported. "Recent polls have shown the country is following a similar path to the 2016 US election and Brexit as society becomes more and more polarised. Following the upcoming signing of the peace accords in Cartagena between President Juan Miguel Soto and FARC guerrilla leader Ramon Lopez, alias: Simonchenski, a plebiscite is scheduled for October 2. The peace deal will be sealed by *el pueblo colombiano*, the President had announced. However," the

announcer continued, "discrepancies still remain as to the fate
of ex-combatants and their role in society. How will they
make a living?" the announcer asked rhetorically to his audience. An image was displayed on the screen of a recent Facebook meme spreading the information that the ex-guerrillas
would receive free housing and a monthly stipend four times
the minimum wage. The news was clearly false, but the
announcer framed it as if the fairness of this was up for
debate.

"Hijuep…?" said Garzón. *Son of…* "They're playing to
people's emotions, not the facts. If there's one thing that
makes people angry it is unearned benefits. Very cleverly
done too. Because it's true, the guerrillas will receive around
620,000 pesos, a little below minimum wage, per month. Plus,
a one-off payment of two million pesos. They've embellished
the numbers substantially and because they've wrapped it in
a kernel of truth, *el pueblo colombiano* won't even notice it's a
lie."

"A kernel of truth?" asked Jardine. "Sounds like something the Russians would do. Very sneaky. Well, the lie's out
there now."

"They say a lie can travel halfway around the world while
the truth is still putting on its boots."

"One of yours?" asked Jardine.

"I think it was Hemingway. Everyone seems to quote him.
Or maybe it was Twain, or Churchill, or maybe Stalin?" said
Garzón. "How was dinner? Didn't go well I'm guessing..."

"Fucking terrible." Jardine was slumped in his seat. "She
went mental and I think we broke up. And now I'll be single
in Yemen. Don't imagine the singles scene is too hot over
there. Plus, I loved her, Garzón! Really thought she was the
one."

Garzón raised his drink. "Maybe she still is?"

"Not if she doesn't come to Yemen. It will be *finito, acabado,
terminado*."

"Welcome to my world, always moving. Living out of a suitcase. Forever single. Sometimes I would try desperately to pitch new ideas to my editors to see if I could stay somewhere a little longer."

"And?" asked Jardine, sitting up in his seat.

"Worked sometimes, but you end up lying about the importance of the articles. You know, make the issue you're writing about sound like something big is happening. But in the end, it leads you down the wrong path."

"You'd make it up to save your job?" Jardine asked, raising his eyebrows.

Garzón took a sip of beer and considered the question. "No, not make it up. But find a new angle, a new way to show the information. Gave me some extra time in some places. I'm not like that VizFeed guy!"

"Oh yeah, him. What did he have to say for himself?" asked Jardine.

"Works for VizFeed. Some new news website. Seemed very, very dodgy. Not sure how credible their content is. Reminded me of when an Italian newspaper published an article claiming Hezbollah were planning a missile launch site in Cuba."

"Sounds very 'Our Man in Havana', doesn't it?"

"Or maybe it was a training camp?" Garzón stroked his goatee, trying to remember. "Anyway, they claimed Hezbollah were up to no good in Cuba. Then a Republican senator in the US picked up on it and spoke about it publicly. Then the news outlets picked up on the speech and it almost became the truth."

"What stopped it?"

"You guys."

"The Foreign Office?"

"Ha! Come on. You don't think I know who you work for?"

Jardine gave a knowing smile. "So we saved the day?"

"The analysts discredited it as overblown and with unreliable sources," said Garzón, taking a sip of beer.

"Ah yes, the old blame-it-on-the-source trick," teased Jardine.

"If only they'd been that diligent with that 'sexed up' dossier about Iraq," Garzón joked.

"I'm not sure anything's changed," said Jardine smirking. "We have a strong history of spy-turned-fiction writers too. Seems to be in the blood. "

Garzón smiled. "If there's one thing that's true, everybody loves fiction. Especially for your kind. You deal in human intelligence. Humans are not cold, rational, calculating creatures. We deal in coloured, exaggerated, word-of-mouth all the time. Then we repeat it and repeat it until it becomes legend, a myth. Stories only exist because we invented them, just like we invented God, money and taxes. They're not necessary to survive per se but try living without them!" said Garzón.

Jardine nodded. He considered what Garzón had just said and then turned to face him. "I guess we all lie everyday if we're honest about it."

"Maybe you need some of that?" Garzón motioned to a group of students necking aguardiente straight from the bottle and others throwing it back from small plastic shot glasses.

Ah, to be a student again, Jardine thought. Maybe he could go back to that lifestyle? *I'm still young enough to party hard*, he thought.

"Hold that thought," said Jardine deciding to visit the bathroom. To reach it, he had to descend a spiral staircase to a dimly lit lower level where the music was quieter. Beyond the stairs, he walked down a corridor and passed several rooms set up like a Moroccan harem. At the end of the corridor was the men's bathroom, a small alcove with a urinal covered by a curtain. Entering and pulling the curtain behind him, he managed to overhear a group of students in serious discussion coming from one of the open rooms off the main corridor. The hushed tones made it sound important, like a piece of juicy gossip one just cannot stop from eavesdropping. Instinctively, Jardine listened. It was just audible enough for him to make out the words "todavía activa en la sierra nevada de santa marta – lado valledupar". *Still active in the Valledupar side of the Sierra Nevada."*

After finishing his business, he remained behind the curtain for another minute, enough time to realistically still be doing his business and not arouse suspicion. Yanking the chain to flush, he came out from behind the curtain and saw the group seated a few metres from where he had been standing. He needed to pass them to return upstairs, but knew he wanted to hear more. He shuffled his feet a few steps to not give the appearance of sneaking around, and then he noticed some antique photos of Bogotá on the walls along the corridor. With the pretence of looking at the pictures, he stopped and swayed from side-to-side, giving the illusion that he was just another drunk foreigner, interested in the history of Bogotá. The afternoon of beer drinking helped in this department. He inched closer and closer to the group, but accidentally kicked a chair leg causing it to tumble over. The group swivelled and gazed at him.

"Oye, que haces?" one of them yelled.

He replied in slurred English and broken Spanish. "Oh, well, ah, hola? Sorry, no Español," he said in his best gringo accented Spanish. He raised his finger in the air and smiled as if a lightbulb had just gone off in his head. "Ah, turista, bonitos fotos, no?" He placed his hand on his chest and then motioned to the photos on the wall.

The leader of the group swatted his hand in a not-worth-it gesture, muttering: "gringo borracho" before continuing his dialogue. *Drunk gringo.* "Así que los grupos disidentes de las FARC han aliado con ELN para formar un grupo nuevo y están…" *So the dissdent FARC groups have allied themselves with the ELN to form a new group and they are…*

This Jardine recognised was what El Espectador had run with on the front page that very morning. Several dissident FARC groups had allied themselves with the ELN guerrilla group, although the article mentioned this was happening in the south of Colombia, towards Tumaco. The leader, Daniel, of the Allied Pacific Front had been killed in action with the Colombian military. However, the leader of another dissident from FARC group, Juancho, was now in control of parts of Tumaco, the department of Nariño. He couldn't remember reading anything about active ELN or dissident FARC groups near Valledupar. He knew ELN were still active in some parts of Serranía de Perijá on the other side of the Upar Valley, that's what General Esguerra had told him. But, he thought the Sierra Nevada had been cleared of all guerrillas and para-militaries years ago.

Stumbling upstairs and still playing the act of drunk gringo – which wasn't hard given his state – Jardine arrived back at his table and pulled out his phone and rechecked the El Espectador article. There was no mention of the north or the Sierra Nevada de Santa Marta. Strange, he thought. Maybe this can be a new line of investigation. Therefore, I *am* still needed here. He opened the HushApp and typed a brief message to Ambrose:

New intelligence. Appears important — requires further investigation of approx. 6 months.

— SENT

The message quickly acquired two ticks but hadn't turned blue. *This is my ticket to stay here,* he thought. A new story. An investigation of potential new FARC guerrilla groups joining forces with the ELN. He began to feel himself again, upbeat and ready to advise on his new intelligence to prolong his stay and investigate a renegade group of ex-FARC combatants, hiding in the Sierra Nevada de Santa Marta. He leant back in his chair and smiled.

"You look happy about something," said Garzón.

"It's amazing the stories you hear in the bathroom in Colombia." His phone vibrated, a response from Ambrose.

Good work. Send whatever you've got to NCA and the cousins, they'll take over from now on.

— AMBROSE

Immediately, Jardine's heart sank. The sides of his mouth drooped.

Garzón looked over at him. "Bad news?"

Jardine nodded.

Garzón leant forward and put his arm around Jardine's shoulders. "Tell you what, tomorrow I'll take you up to the mountains. I've got something I think you might like."

12

SEEING CLEARLY

JARDINE WOKE FEELING A THROBBING PAIN IN HIS HEAD, LIKE A taut rubber band tightening and loosening every five seconds around his temples. There was a fog behind his eyes giving the impression of watching a shaky 3D movie. Despite the hazy feelings, he didn't feel the usual alcohol-induced depression nor the insatiable yearning for an unachievable hangover remedy which didn't exist.

Rising from bed, Jardine rambled through his apartment to the kitchen to make himself a coffee and an arepa with cheese. As he waited for the machine to warm up, he slid the cornmeal tortilla into a hot pan, almost knocking over an open bottle of dark rum on the counter. *I vaguely remember buying that last night*, he thought. A rich aroma filled the apartment with a warm, roasted smell, like burning pine needles in a small fireplace. Next to him in a small frying pan, the crispy yellow arepa sizzled softly with bubbling melting cheese on top. He slid it out of the pan and onto a wooden chopping board before picking it up and biting into it with a soft crunch. He poured the coffee into a large cup placed on his kitchen bench, and then, eyeing the rum bottle, tipped a generous slosh into the dark coffee. As he sipped the coffee and rum concoction, he held it in his mouth, as if it had some medicinal quality and the longer he kept it there, the more healing it would bring. After all, there wasn't an abuela in all Colombia that didn't swear by fermented sugar cane as an anecdote for a myriad of life's problems. Only it wasn't healing that he needed, but rather, a problem to be solved.

"You're starting early," came a deep voice from behind him.

Jardine jumped and turned around. He hadn't noticed the man on the sofa. "What the fuck!?"

"Sorry, thought you remembered I was sleeping on your sofa," came the reply from Garzón, lying on the sofa with his hands resting behind his head. "Down that coffee, we've got a big day ahead of us."

The two men, now in Garzón's 4WD, cruised north on the Avenida Séptima. The sun shone brightly and one half of the avenue was closed to traffic as hordes of runners, cyclists, skateboarders, walkers and the occasional roller-blading clown zipped up and down the closed off street. An initiative known as the *ciclovia*. Large swathes of road were closed to vehicles and opened for the citizens of Bogotá to enjoy. Reaching the Calle 84 they transferred onto the Avenida Circunvalar and then onto La Calera road, twisting and ascending higher into the mountains. Bogotá, sitting at 2,600 metres above sea level, meant it was surprisingly cold in the early morning and evenings. San Luis, where they were heading, sat at an altitude of 3,100 metres. It was a far cry from the clichéd Hollywood movies which portrayed the capital as a sweltering, tropical war zone full of *sicarios* and will-inhibiting drugs. Although, it was no paradise either.

"The shaman said it's good to loosen up a little before the ceremony."

"Shaman? I thought we were hiking up there."

"Don't you remember what I told you last night?

Jardine considered this for a moment and then throwing

caution to the wind, nodded and commented, "I thought those Shamans usually prescribed coca cola?"

"Shit! Maybe they do…" Garzón shrugged. "Too late now."

"You haven't done this sort of thing before?" asked Jardine.

"I have. But, I can't remember the colour of the can the Shaman was holding last time."

Jardine looked puzzled, but then nodded.

The bus continued its ascent passing *asadero* barbecue restaurants and wooden craft furniture shops with panoramic views of the city. On a Sunday, it would be full of families chowing down on chorizo and traditional meats from Los Llanos, but on Saturday it was relatively quiet and calm. The air was notably cooler as they arrived at a small settlement known as San Luis, an area partly organised as a small town and partly a *barrio de invasion*; an invasion neighbourhood where houses and shacks had been constructed wherever and with whatever materials the residents determined.

As they walked up through the winding streets, a small group of children ran up to Garzón and high-fived him. Stopping at a small corner store, they stocked up on packets of crisps and a large bottle of coca cola.

"Now that I think of it, we will need coca cola for the Shaman. Helps him think, I guess. Also, livens the shindig up a bit and makes it more bloody entertaining!"

Jardine took out his phone and typed 'Ayahuasca ceremony' into his mobile phone. "Garzón, it says here we're supposed to fast before an ayahuasca ceremony too. No food, drugs or alcohol," said Jardine lifting his head from his phone.

Garzón considered this for a while and then said, "Para nada! No te creas todo lo que leas en internet." *Not at all. Don't believe everything you read online.*

Jardine nodded, unconvinced, but was prepared to go

with the flow. "Don't suppose you know how we'll get back?" Jardine asked.

"My 4WD," Garzón motioned with his lips towards his vehicle.

"You'll be able to drive after a shamanic ceremony?"

"I'll be fine. I drove home okay last night didn't I? Besides, if we're desperate, I know a track down the mountain. Doesn't take long going down."

"How long?"

"Two hours?" said Garzón, shaking his head from side to side.

"Is it safe?"

"During daylight, yes, very safe. Besides, who'd want to rob two *borrachos* like us?"

Arriving at a grassy clearing with patches of boggy mud, they turned left onto a dirt track and continued for a few blocks before coming to a stylish mud brick house with smoke pouring out a rustic chimney.

"Looks a bit out of place compared to the other concrete block shacks," commented Jardine.

"Plenty of dollar-carrying gringos looking for liquid enlightenment to fill the middle-class void of conformity."

They approached the house. Garzón knocked twice before turning to face Jardine with a cheeky smirk. "This is it. Beware of unearned wisdom."

"Freud?"

"Jung. Just don't lose your shit, alright? It'll be bad for my karma."

After a few moments, the door opened, and an elderly lady dressed in a soft grey *ruana* – a woollen poncho – answered the door.

"Señor Garzón! Mijo, pase por favor," she said. *Mr. Garzón, my boy, come in please.*

They entered the house and were led through to a back-yard encircled by a wooden-slat fence. A round mud brick hut with a cone-shaped thatched roof stood in the centre. Smoke slowly sifted out of a metal tube wedged into the thatched roof. The two men entered and waited a few moments for their eyes to adjust to the darkness. Situated in the middle of the hut was a small fire emitting smoke up through the metal tube. On the fire sat a small caldron-like pot. Around the outer edges of the fire were an array of coloured cushions spread out with plastic buckets behind them. Directly opposite Jardine and Garzón on the other side of the entrance, was a small man with a greying beard, dressed in a white and blue striped shirt and jeans, with a colourful woollen knit jumper slung over him. His eyes were a dark grey with hues of green and brown and his smile revealed a perfect set of white teeth, false no doubt, thought Jardine. This guy, Jardine imagined, could pass as Keith Richards' grandfather.

"Bienvenidos!" he said warmly. "We must begin at once if we are to be ready as the sun sets. This is, of course, when your subconscious comes alive. This is when the jaguar awakens to hunt, when the wise owl begins his night of watching and waiting, and when life in the jungle begins to buzz and hum with the activity of its living organisms, all living and breathing as one. Please come in and sit."

"Gracias," they both chanted in unison.

"This guy sounds like the real deal. Much more professional than I was expecting," Jardine whispered to Garzón.

"He's the real deal, alright."

"Sounds like he knows the jungle well. Must have grown up there."

"He's from Sogamoso actually. Probably never set foot in a jungle. But, he knows his stuff."

The men sat down on two cushions next to each other as a few other people entered the hut and were seated. Outside the wind picked up and a gust blew in through the open door, and with it a flurry of petite yellow butterflies entered the hut. They filled the room with a moving mist of fluttering gold amongst the smoky haze. Jardine looked up with amazement as the small creatures fluttered around him. As the group took in the beautiful scene, they heard a scream, "Malparidas mariposas!" shouted the shaman. *Bloody butterflies*!

Next, the group heard the metallic hiss of an aerosol can as the shaman doused the small yellow creatures with a can of insect repellent. The stench of the noxious chemicals mixed with the smoke made it hard to breathe. Several people began to cough and splutter as the butterflies slowly tumbled to the ground, like small autumn leaves. "Eso se puede usar," said the Shaman cheerfully. *I can use these.*

The shaman darted around the hut, scooping up the minuscule yellow winged bodies and when he had enough to fill his hand, he added them to the bubbling pot in the centre. "In China, the yellow butterfly is a sign of wealth, but here it is a sign of…" his voice trailed off and the Shaman stared downwards shaking his head with a frown, like a priest giving a sermon and losing his place. Jardine tilted his head towards Garzón and covered his mouth. "Off to a good start. If the roots don't get us high at least we can inhale a can of insecticide."

Garzón sniggered. "Don't worry. Like I said, he's the real deal. He knows what he's doing. After the torrential rains and floods of 2011, various councils in Bogotá hired him to stop it."

"Stop the rain?" asked Jardine.

"Si."

"And how did he do that?"

"How should I know? He's a maldito Shaman. Who knows how he does it?"

"Magic!" The shaman raised a hand in the air, his eyes the size of marbles. "Magic! That's what they mean. It's proof that magic exists and that the extraordinary can happen. Although I can't remember why, it's also a sign to all of you." He pointed now with his bony right index finger and motioned around the circle. "For change to take place, something inside you must die. Death is never nice, but it's necessary for life. New life. Anyway, we must get underway."

The shaman stepped towards the pot and stirred it, chanting in a rhythmic throaty bellow. It wasn't Spanish. Jardine assumed it was a Bora or Witoto, or another language from the Amazon. After an hour of chanting with the group sat there, eyes closed and instructed to focus on their breathing, an assistant entered and poured the murky contents of the pot into small coconut halves, which were distributed around the circle. Jardine received the bowl and looked down at it. A slight breeze entered the tent and crawled down his neck. *Just like in the refrigerator in the shop*, he thought. But, that was before he'd even spoken to Garzón…

"It is time!" the Shaman said.

The shaman motioned with his hand for everyone to drink, while he pushed play on an old iPod. The chant continued now via a small speaker hung above as everyone in the circle gripped their coconut cups and stared down into the murky contents. Jardine examined the liquid and tried to imagine it was a darker coloured cup of milo. He lifted the coconut half to his lips and downed it in one gulp. He felt the gritty liquid flow through his teeth and a numbing bitterness streak across his tongue. The numbness continued down his throat as along with a slight burning sensation, which tickled his oesophagus. After a few moments, the shaman began to talk softly as more cups of the murky dark liquid were distributed. The group downed another cup full of the liquid. By now, the entire tent was dark, and it was hard to make out where everyone was sitting.

"You must trust the spirit vine," said the shaman. "It has its own intentions. Do not fight where it takes you but be ready for what will come."

The music continued in the low rhythmic chant.

After half an hour, Jardine turned to where he thought Garzón was sitting. "Do you feel anything?"

"Not yet. It will come," he replied.

Another fifteen minutes passed, Jardine was still focused on his breathing with his eyes closed, the chanting still droning in the background. For all the analytical scepticism he harboured, he wanted something to happen. He wanted to feel the effects and see where it led him. Maybe it would hold the solution to his troubles? He opened his eyes and saw only darkness around him. Still nothing, he thought. He sighed as a small wave of disappointment began to wash over him. Maybe this was a waste of a day? Maybe he should have started to get up-to-date on events in the Middle East, worked out how to convince Veronica to come go with him. It wouldn't be so bad for her, would it?

He closed his eyes again and lay back further onto the cushions. He began to notice brisk movements flickering out the corners of his eyes, like dancing shadows. He looked up to the top of the hut as the smoke escaped through the metal tube. Around the tube he began to see light green geometric shapes forming, twisting, turning and spinning away before reappearing again around the chimney-tube. The music seemed to be louder now, and it filled his ears as if he wore noise-cancelling headphones with the volume turned up. The music built up and up and up, until he began to fall into what felt like a deep dark hole that had opened up under the cushions. It felt as if the world were falling away. Falling and falling into endless blackness, but somehow, it felt claustrophobic, like there was an external life force crushing him slowly as he fell. The geometric shapes spun around him now, but after a few moments, they disappeared. *This is not at all what I imagined*, he thought as he tried to find the will to push against the hopeless crushing sensation he felt. Past, distant memories came flooding through the darkness, not as clear pictures or visions but vague thoughts and ideas that clouded his mind and confused him. He could remember all of the negative experiences of his life. When he was teased as a child, all of the embarrassing moments he had had in his life, the mistakes he'd made, the insecurity he sometimes felt, it all came rushing in, engulfing him at once.

What the fuck is this? he thought, as he slowly slipped into a darkening despair.

13

DESCENDING AWAKENING

JARDINE AWOKE WITH A SUDDEN JOLT, GASPING FOR AIR. IT WAS still pitch black in the tent and so he switched on the torch from his mobile phone. He looked around the hut, there was no-one left inside. Standing with shaky legs, he hobbled to the doorway and stepped outside. The chilly Andean air blew softly across his body and sent a shiver down his spine. It was now dark, and the temperature had dropped considerably. "Where the fuck is everyone?" he said aloud. He stepped back inside the hut and picked up a ruana lying on some cushions and took a woven sombrero vueltiao hanging on the wall. He slipped the ruana over his body and slid the sombrero on his head. *At least this will keep me warm and the rain off my head,* he thought.

He stepped out once again into the crisp night air. "Garzón?" he shouted. "Shaman? Hay alguien allí?" *Anybody there?* But the darkness of the night swallowed up the sound like a galaxy into a black hole. He managed to exit the backyard and made it to the street passing in front of the mud brick house. Below, he could make out a blur of orange and fuzzy yellow lights – Bogotá – probably not far to walk as the crow flies. *I've hiked these mountains a few times before*, he thought. *What did Garzón say it was? One hour to the bottom?*

He stepped forward with a few shaky strides. "Hello? Anybody here?" he tried again. Nobody answered. He began to feel the earth spinning and felt an acidic aniseed flavour burning up the back of his throat. The vertigo caused him to fall on his hands and knees as he hauled up a bile-tasting brown liquid, causing him to dry retch until it seemed like only air came out. With the contents of his stomach on the dirt road, he wobbled to his feet and wiped his mouth with the ruana. The night remained silent, no-one to be seen or heard. *Where the fuck is everyone?* he thought again, looking down at the hazy orange lights of Bogotá.

He rambled away from the mud brick house, swaying like a palm tree during monsoonal rains, and walked through a small green field surrounded by small concrete houses. Eventually he found a path leading downwards, seemingly towards the bright lights of Bogotá. He trudged down the path, twisting and turning until it became a muddy track. A light rain began to trickle down. He continued like this for thirty minutes before stopping to catch his breath, bent over with his hands on his knees. Having regained his normal breathing and straightening his back while glancing around at his surroundings, he recognised the terrain – a paramo – the misty and marshy moorlands which straddled the snow-capped peaks and the alpine forests found in the high-altitude tropics of South America. These areas acted like sponges, holding vast quantities of water and were almost constantly shrouded in mist and drizzling rain. Around him were hundreds of frailejones plants, a tall, slender, cactus-like plant of large, soft and spongy leaves atop twisted brown trunks. They encircled him like worshippers in a cathedral, standing to attention and swaying slightly in the breeze. It gave off the eerie feeling he was not alone but accompanied by a small army of plants. The rain stopped. A slow mist moved across the night sky as the moon shone through the clouds, casting a fuzzy lunar blue across the landscape. Jardine looked up at the moon as it spun slightly and morphed into a crescent shape, then into an oval, and then grew arms and formed a star before splitting in half releasing a shower of green-outlined hexagon patterns that fell from the sky, like geometric hail stones. *This stuff hasn't worn off*, he thought.

He continued further downwards along the path until he reached a small clearing. The mist began to clear now revealing the full moon again. The clearing formed a small circle and was surrounded by more frailejones cacti plants, as if the plant-like entities had followed him and had now trapped him in a ring. In the middle of the clearing sat a giant ceiba tree with wide buttress roots splayed out like pythons. Its canopy spread out above like an intricate system of arteries and veins blocking the shine of the full moon. Approaching the ceiba, Jardine glimpsed a man wearing a long white tunic with white pants and black wellington boots. On his head sat a gnome-like white hat and the man held what looked to be a book of some sort. As Jardine inched closer, the man didn't look up. Jardine could see it wasn't a book the man was holding, but a report – a report strikingly similar to the intelligence reports he dished out each and every week. The kind of report that comes with a clear plastic cover and is regularly handed around a table at serious meetings, glanced over and then never seen again. Jardine inched closer still and was now within five metres of the man. However, still the man did not look up. He seemed to be engrossed in the report, flicking through the pages and nodding with approval, a slight smile on his face. The man's long black hair softly lapped at his shoulders and a hand-weaved woollen mochila bag with a zig zag pattern hung at his side.

Inching closer again, he could see the report appeared exactly as he had expected: clean and clinical with headers and footers, sensible tables and pie charts, headings in bold and sub-headings underlined. Everything meticulously planned and organised according to the Secret Intelligence Service style guide and report specifications. The man continued studying the report, occasionally frowning or moving his hands to his chin in a pensive motion as if considering an important point in the report. Jardine took a few more steps forward until he was within a metre of the man. Then the man glanced up, smiled and reached forward to hand the report to Jardine. It was at this stage that Jardine realised he was not scared of a random man sitting under a ceiba tree in a misty paramo at night. Uncharacteristically, he also didn't feel alarmed at a stranger reading classified material. Jardine reached forward to grab the report, but as he did, the man stopped and moved backwards, closer to the tree, and put up his hand to signify stop. Jardine lowered his brow and tilted his head slightly in confusion. The man smiled a toothy grin and held the report up in the air above his head with both hands.

As he raised his hands, a bright green vine snake with a pointed head and cherry-red eyes slid down the trunk of the ceiba and dangled from a branch above the man. It appeared to glow a fluorescent, neon-green as it slithered down the man's left arm, around and behind his head, then back up the right arm onto the spiral binding of the folder. As its bright green skin touched the report, the pages transformed into a rainbow of glow-in-the-dark colours, like dipping a rope in multi-coloured paint and then sliding and slapping it over a white-wash wall. The snake continued wrapping its body tightly around the report as its pages became saturated in the bright, neon colours. The more the snake wrapped around the report, the brighter and more vivid the colours became. Without warning, the snake began to squeeze the report. Tighter and tighter with enormous intensity, layer after layer of bright verdant scales pulsating and flexing while the colours got brighter and brighter, illuminating everything under the extended canopy of the ceiba tree until, eventually — BOOM! The snake and the classified intelligence report exploded into a thousand small yellow butterflies, which fluttered up into the air. Jardine stood gazing in awe, his mouth wide open as the butterflies filled the air around him like small buttery flashes flapping around his head. He looked at the man, who was also watching the butterflies with a smile, his eyes glistening with enchanted wonder. The butterflies continued to flutter around the two men before rising into the foliage above the tree, like fire-flies casting a glow over the clearing, revealing the watchful frailejones cactus encircling them. Bringing his eyes back down, the man dressed in white smiled, gave a satisfied nod and winked at Jardine.

Then, the man slowly walked around behind the ceiba tree before scampering off, pushing his way through the frailejones and disappearing into the night. Jardine stood there under the ceiba tree not quite knowing what to do next. He looked up at the moon again, hoping the geometric shapes would return to prove that he was still feeling the effects of the ayahuasca. The analyst in him wanted answers and he felt a burning desire for meaning. He thought about running after the man, but something kept him from following him. His stomach began to gurgle unpleasantly, and he felt the sudden urge to lay down. As he did, he gazed upwards at the butterflies as they now drifted downwards softly towards his face. He felt several of the dainty yellow creatures flutter on his face, right between the eyes. Gently at first, and then grew in intensity, so much so that the soggy creatures created a wet sensation on his brow. He shook his head lightly trying to make them go away, but they continued — a flurry of soft moist thuds. Shaking his head more violently, a shot of bright light shone into his eyes, temporarily blinding him, as he looked upwards to see small droplets of water beaming down from a branch of the ceiba tree, landing with a methodical drip between his eyes. Gradually, Jardine sat up to see that the sun was rising. *That* was the light that had blinded him. And they weren't small yellow butterflies, but droplets of water falling from the tree. He scanned around the clearing, looking for signs of the man, a snake or a techno-coloured report of classified British Intelligence. But none was to be found.

Looking to the east, the sky was beginning to fill with streaks of burnt orange and rose as the sun continued its ascent. He could see the tops of red brick buildings past a group of trees below. Bogotá seemed closer than before. Standing up on wobbling legs, blood seemed to rush through his body with great intensity, a sudden surge of adrenaline pulsating throughout. He couldn't yet describe it in his head, but he knew what he had to do to stay in Colombia. It wasn't an analytical, data-driven decision, but a sort of intuition. He knew how he could stay close to Veronica and not be transferred to Yemen. The gloomy uncertainty of the past week felt as if it were being expelled, and the world was opening to new possibilities.

He trudged forward, drifting slowly down the muddy track towards the red brick buildings and soft warm glow of Bogotá.

14

TO LIE FOR LOVE

Sofia Hernandez de la Torre had always dreamed of studying in the United Kingdom, just like her tweed-jacketed Anglophile father, Don Jaime. Don Jaime Enrique Hernandez had consumed all the great British authors: Dickens, Orwell, T.S. Elliot, and Greene. He had read all the works by Roald Dahl, C.S. Lewis, and Tolkien to his daughter at bedtime when she was young and had posted Churchill quotes sporadically around his house in dark walnut frames. The door to his study sported a sign reading 'Keep calm and carry on,' a phrase he would regularly parrot to Sofia, in English, as she left the house each morning. He would wax lyrical about the United Kingdom being the most sophisti-cated, advanced and decent country on the planet, even if the people did seem somewhat cold and reserved at times. At least once a year he would travel to London and wander around Hyde Park, remembering his days as a graduate student of politics at University College London. Ever since young Sofia was old enough to salsa dance, which in Colombia is not long after exiting the womb, he had enrolled her in the Anglo-Colombiano bilingual school in the leafy northern suburbs of Cedritos. More recently, he had her attend extra evening classes at the British Council to improve her accent and accustom her to British English, the way the Queen spoke it, in preparation for university in the United Kingdom.

However, on this fine morning, nothing had prepared Don Jaime Enrique Hernandez for the sight of a British man, in a grubby rain-soaked ruana and tattered sombrero vueltiao, wrestling through the trees lining his backyard nestled in the foothills of Bogotá's eastern mountains. The man eventually broke through into the yard and walked past Don Jaime and his daughter while they were having breakfast on their outdoor terrace. In most cities around the world, this would cause quite a stir. In Colombia, however, and especially in the upmarket neighbourhood of Rosales, it was considered a high-security breach with the added threat of potential kidnapping. In fact, had it not been for the man's obvious gringo appearance, Don Jaime Hernandez may have pulled out the ancient revolver he kept in his office desk and aimed it at the intruder.

"Muy buenos días," said Jardine, tipping his hat slightly and smiling confidently as he strode past the father and daughter enjoying their breakfast. He stopped in front of a high brick wall separating the terrace from the street and stroked his chin while sizing up the height of the wall. After a few seconds, he jumped, caught the top and hoisted himself up and over, disappearing over the other side. Don Jaime Enrique Hernandez, his mouth still wide open, rested his fork on the table in front of him and looked at his daughter. "Creo que este señor trabaja en la embajada británica." *I think that man works at the British Embassy.* "I've seen him leaving the building as I arrive for my English classes with the British Council."

"Ah si?" replied Sofia Hernandez de le Torre, trying not to seem impressed and excited by the intrusion.

Don Jaime looked down blankly at his changua soup.

"Maybe it's best we send you to an American University instead…"

***

Walking down through the leafy, well-heeled neighbourhood of Rosales, past expensive dogs being walked and navy-jacketed security guards on every corner, Jardine only had one wish: to be with Veronica and stay in Colombia. Yes, he was a spy, or an intelligence analyst at least, but he'd happily throw all his ambition out the window just to be with her.

He wasn't sure if it was the DMT of the Ayahuasca still rattling around inside his mind, but he felt a sense of creative energy and freedom flowing back through his veins — a sensation he hadn't felt since he was a child, dreaming of becoming a successful cartoon artist, or as a teenager when he dreamt of becoming a rock star — fantastical ideas which propel one to follow their passions. Because any logical person would take a more practical approach, like accounting or teaching. It somehow seemed clear to him what was holding him back from being assertive and taking control of the situation. It was the inner critic in him. It was his ego that was holding him to account and not letting his mind wander. With that critic gone, he realised there was an inner artistic rebel that yearned and dared to be different, something that drove an intense curiosity, a curiosity which had once troubled him but now propelled him forward. The clarity punctured his mind and inseminated his plan moving forward. He had a solution to his problem. He would embrace creative chaos, but apply rational reasoning. His mind buzzed with ideas like thin tentacles of grey matter unfolding and creating a web, tingling under his scalp. It felt as if there was a flowing river of neutrons gushing through his cerebral estuaries.

Reaching the Avenida Septima, as the heavy traffic flew past him, the ideas continued to swirl, and he began to mentally map out his plan, which entered his brain in a gushing internal monologue, much like the smoggy air entering his lungs from the exhaust-fume belching buses chugging by. *I used to sort fact from fiction, now I'll just combine the two and become a story-teller.* It's not like it would be anything new in the world of espionage. Spy stories are up there with fishing tales, ghost stories and urban legends. It's normal to mix the real with the imaginary. It's almost expected to some degree. *And I am in the land of magical realism, after all.* His thoughts flew in a stream of consciousness: *First off, I'll need to decipher my audience.* His old instructors' mantras came floating back to him: 'When one writes a report; one must think of one's intended audience'. *My audience is a middle-aged man approaching retirement and an organisation that wants to concentrate on new theatres of operation, whatever the fuck that means. Oh, and fundamental Islamist terrorism.* It seemed easy enough. *I'll simply report that Latin America is the new theatre of operation with a threat of fundamental Islamist terrorism. That ought to do it. But I'll need to add something big. Something with bite. Something believable, but fantastical enough to warrant attention and make my superiors think, 'No-one would be crazy enough to fabricate this! Our man must be on to something!' I'll need a lie so big that its very scale will leave a residue of truth and credibility.* His mind raced with the possibilities. And then, as if the rational was breaking through the creative barrier, a small pang of guilt swept across him. A guilt that was swiftly and efficiently answered by his creative self.

What if someone does a 'fact check'?

Wait, there's no fact-checking website for intelligence work. I'm the bloody fact-checker!

What if they question my sources?

This is top secret, highly-classified intelligence product and therefore the sources must remain anonymous. Not only that, the sources must be protected with codenames. That should cover most of the questions coming from Ambrose and London.

But what about my own internal moral questions? Was it wrong to lie?

I'm only doing what every intelligence officer already knows: professional and state-sanctioned deception. *If governments have course for legitimate violence, why can't I, as a Government employee, have course to legitimate lying? Besides, it's not like I can be prosecuted. There's an Official Secrets Act, but there's no Official Lying Act.*

Furthermore, he considered, there's nothing sinister involved. There was no extortion or blackmail or assassination or torture. There was no ulterior motivation. No hidden resentment that controls my actions, no secret angst harboured only to be unleashed unconsciously on the world. It was nothing more than my pure unadulterated passion for someone I love, being manifested in a creative, slightly deceptive manner. They would be merely white lies, nothing more. Isn't that why white lies exist? To protect the ones we love? You wouldn't tell a child that Santa Claus doesn't exist, so you lie. That ugly sweater your grandmother gave you? Are you going to tell her that it's ugly as fuck and you'll only wear it to ironic bad-Christmas-sweater parties? Of course not. It would be no different to politics. Politics is all lies. Even the so-called experts or the pollsters and pundits couldn't work out *la verdad* from *las mentiras*. Not only that, the most powerful country in the world couldn't sort out the truth from the lies in their elections. One candidate had an unstructured problem with truth and the other a structured approach to untruths. The whole world is full of lies, nowadays. Truth has been democratised, which means no-one appreciates it. All you had to do was open your social media account to see fake news, post-truths, clickbait, and 'factual' lies. They hadn't been that bad, had they? It had only meant an attention-seeking, temper-tantrum-throwing leader of the free world was elected. Only caused a large supranational regional bloc, based on years of economic integration, to slowly decay and disband. Merely divided the world between open, global-minded citizens with a closed, protectionist, xenophobic mindset. But apart from that, what else had it done?

A few white lies about new theatres of operation and fundamental Islamist terrorist organisations operating in the backwaters of South America won't end the world. *All it will do is keep me in Colombia for a prolonged period of time to be with Veronica. And anyway, I'll be lying for the noble cause of love. The noblest cause of all the causes that were ever caused.*

The monologue subsided. Jardine felt happy with himself and held out his hand to hail a taxi. A taxi pulled up next to him. Entering the taxi, his mind allowed one more internal foray before engaging with the driver. The transformation from intelligence report writer to Garcia Marquez-esque story weaver is just beginning. All in good time, he thought. I will become the spy that lied for love. Well, actually, the intelligence analyst that lied for love. But before I do that, I need to fucking sleep.

15

EL TORO

JARDINE EXITED THE TAXI AND ENTERED THE LEAFY TREE-LINED Parque Santander. The sun shone brightly as wrinkled men in fedoras sat on wooden stools shining the shoes of suited men with slicked back hair reading El Tiempo and El Espectador. Jardine strolled through the park before passing in front of the National Tax Office building, arriving at Avenida Jimenez. He waited patiently as a red Transmileno bus slid by before crossing the Avenida, arriving at Plazoleta Del Rosario. The square was filled with university students sitting in circles near a fountain, and men in ill-fitting suits standing in small clumps, chatting and mingling around the square. Street vendors and pigeons fought for space on the pavement as every few minutes streams of passengers disembarked from the Transmileno station, causing a flurry of movement along Avenida Jimenez and onto the Plaza.

On the southern side of the Plazoleta Del Rosario sat Café Pasaje. Jardine entered and allowed his eyes to adjust as cigarette smoke streamed through the air, like wispy spider webs. The room was dimly lit with wood panelling sporting antique advertisements for Coca Cola and Club Colombia beer. Wooden booths sat on one side, while an enormous

Colombia flag covered part of the ceiling, hovering over red-vinyl chairs circling round metal tables in the centre. Jardine approached a man sitting at the back in one of the wooden booths, a newspaper hoisted up covering his face. The antique setting gave it an air of a 1950s noir detective film.

"Profesor, sabes que no es seguro encontrarnos afuera de la universidad," said Jardine.

"I know, I know, is dangerous meet outside the university, but I love it," said Professor Villalobos with a shrug. "You know El Gabo used to live around here and frequented this cafe. And Cafe Molino, it no longer exists. I believe it's where he first saw a deer."

"A deer?" asked Jardine.

"Ah, don't worry," replied the professor, swatting his hand as if to say not important.

Jardine took a seat and ordered a strong black coffee, a tinto. He smiled at Professor Villalobos. "You should have cut eye holes in the newspaper. It would have been easier for you to spot me."

The professor chuckled. "You have been watching too many detective movies, my friend."

"You got my message?' asked Jardine.

"Yes, yes, I received it."

"So? Tell me. What do you make of it?"

"To be honest, I didn't really understand what you were asking… Something about the Sierra Nevada, Maicao and Arabs? I don't see any connection."

"The Arab connection in Maicao. What do you know about it?"

"Well, in the late 20th Century—"

"I haven't much time, Professor," Jardine interrupted. "So, I'll be brief. I've been hearing about Tafur Kabachi in Venezuela, the Foreign Minister. Seems to be in loads of trouble with the Yanks. But anyway, it got me thinking about Maicao."

"Maicao is good if you need a cheap TV, but San Andresito is closer, my friend," said the Professor with a smirk.

"Yes, I know. But what if there is still an Arab connection there? And perhaps, they still have a connection to Hezbollah in Lebanon, or Al Qaeda, or maybe even Islamic State? Is it possible?"

The professor lifted his coffee cup. "Well yes, this is Locolombia, *todo* es posible, my friend. Although I haven't heard anything like that for long time." He placed the coffee cup back on the table. "I don't think you will find much, to be perfectly honest," he said with an earnest look on his face, before sipping his coffee again.

Now Jardine lifted his coffee cup. "Do you have any connections there? Anyone who could show me round if I were to visit?"

"I'll see what I can find. Although I must say, honestly, I don't think it's worth your time. Islamist terrorism in Colombia? Maybe in Argentina or Brazil or even Paraguay in the tri-border area. But not here. However, I do have an acquaintance and, well, he is always on about such conspiracies. He's always blaming the USA for the worlds' ills."

"What this professor's name?" Jardine asked.

"Professor Ramos, Vladimiro Ramos, the name gives it away, doesn't it? I mean that he's a left-winger," said Professor Villalobos with a smirk.

Jardine stood up abruptly and turned to leave the cafe. "Professor, thanks for your information. Estamos hablando."

"But your tintico?!" The professor shook his head and took a sip of his coffee, returning to his newspaper as Jardine fled.

Stepping out into the Plaza, Jardine retraced his steps across Avenida Jimenez, crossing through Parque Santander until he arrived at the Carrera Septima, outside of a store selling emerald jewellery. He saw the muscular hind legs of what appeared to a large four-legged animal dash behind a building a block away. He shook his head as if to shake some sense back into him. *Maybe the Ayahuasca is still coursing through my veins?* he thought. He lined up his sources for the story in his mind. *I can introduce the idea of Professor Rojas as a sub-agent through Professor Villalobos. What would float London's boat more? A Hezbollah faction with QUDs-backed operatives, or a radical fundamental Islamist Al-Qaeda cell operating and fundraising out of Maicao? Or perhaps a newly established ISIS group? Surely ISIS was the new terrorism theatre of operation? Sunnis or Shiites, which held more sway in London?* He pondered the plot line. *General Esguerra had mentioned a Syrian restaurant in Teusaquillo. That could be useful. It also kept the options open over which group to mention. Maybe it's best to keep the options open for the time being, before I narrow it down. What about other potential sources? Don Carlos was once an operative in northern Colombia... Surely, he had come across something of value in the past?*

Jardine had decided to base his theory around the town of Maicao, a place notorious for smuggling contraband and had a sizeable Muslim population. Garzón had planted the seed with the embellished story from several years ago in an Italian newspaper. Now it was just a matter of watering it and watching it grow.

Maicao was also close to the Sierra Nevada de Santa Marta where, based on the students he had overheard, he planned to base his fictional terrorist training camp. His narrative was slowly gaining ground, but it was still only an amateur fly-by-night airport thriller rumbling around in his head, full of clichés and flat conversations between paper-thin characters as hollow as a ceiba tree full of greedy termites.

As his mind filtered through the possibilities, an unusual quiet came over the busy downtown centre. The streets had a feeling of the calm before a storm that is common before a motorcade comes barrelling down the street.

Jardine gazed to his left down Carrera Septima to the intersection with Avenida Jimenez. The usually busy road was devoid of cars. Groups of people still flooded out from the Transmileno station and the emerald merchants on the corner still chatted animatedly together. But it was as if all sound had stopped. He half expected green geometric shapes to come spinning out of somewhere as he continued to glance towards the intersection. He couldn't say exactly why he felt it, but he knew something was coming... he assumed it would be an important politician in a series of black SUVs escorted by police on motorcycles. Still glaring towards the small clusters of emerald dealers milling on the corner of Septima and Jimenez, he witnessed a surreal sight.

A large black bull appeared from behind a building and casually strolled down the Septima. It passed the emerald merchants, bringing a Transmileno bus to a screeching halt, and continued its journey towards Jardine, coming up alongside where he stood and turning its snout towards him. He could feel the warmth of its breath huffing through its enflamed nostrils as he outstretched his hand. It felt like his hand was under a sporadic electric hand dryer. Moving his hand slowly up to its head, he patted it and ran his fingers through the tuft of jet-black hair between its ears. The bull huffed some more and knelt down in front of him, cooing like a baby kitten. Instinctively, as if a rodeo-bull rider, Jardine carefully climbed up onto the bull's muscular back, grabbing it by the horns to balance himself. With a slight affectionate caress from his boots on each side of the enormous beast, the bull grunted and began to trot north along the Carrera Septima to return him to the Embassy.

16

THE SETUP

INTELLIGENCE REPORT

FOR SECRET INTELLIGENCE SERVICE EYES ONLY

LOCATION: BOGOTA, COLOMBIA

ANALYST: O.W.J./#397664

SOURCES: Flaming Flamingo; Real Macaw; Toucan Loco

REPORT TITLE: THE NEW FRONTLINE IN TERRORISM — A POTENTIAL threat of fundamental Islamist terrorist cells operating and training in northern Colombia.

EXECUTIVE SUMMARY: From an examination of new intelligence product from established sources, and recently acquired sub-sources, it can be concluded that there is a medium-to-high chance of potential fundamental Islamist terrorist cells operating and training in northern Colombia.

Please note: due to the highly secretive nature of such intelligence, codenames have been used.

This assessment had been concluded by:

A. Reports from sub-sources (#397664-003/01) of Agent (#3597664-003), alias: Flaming Flamingo that a fundamental Islamist cell has emerged and is active in the mountains of northern Colombia with connection to the contraband market town of Maicao. This intelligence is based on recent revelations from a Professor privy to such group's inner workings.

B. Anecdotal evidence provided by Agent (#397664-001) alias: Real Macaw, a former commando and security contractor with the Embassy, from his considerable military experience in that region that: "Al-Qaeda and a host of other Islamist groups have a history of operating out of Maicao with access to adequate funding and support from local merchants."

C. Report from Agent (#397664-006), alias: Toucan Loco — a Colombian General — that a Syrian national, operating a restaurant in the neighbourhood of Teusaquillo, is in fact a front for potential Bogotá operations of alleged fundamental Islamist terrorist network. It has been reported, and confirmed, that the incredibly good hummus is in fact a known recipe from an infamous Islamist fighter by the name of 'El Cocinero'.

• • •

ADDITIONAL POINTS: In addition to the above direct intelligence product, the current instability of the region should also be noted:

1. The current situation in the Bolivarian Republic of Venezuela with known connections to several Middle Eastern terrorist organisations, and the financing of various illegal drug trafficking groups — such as the Cartel of the Crescent Moon — across the Venezuelan/Colombian border should also be considered.
2. In addition, it has been alleged by the Central Intelligence Agency and the US Drug Enforcement Agency that the current Venezuelan Foreign Minister, who is of Lebanese/Syrian heritage and has personal links to Hezbollah, has a past family connection to the Ba'ath Party in Iraq.
3. Reference to a previous article in the Italian daily Corriere della Sera, which claims that a Hezbollah cell was operating in Latin America (Cuba and other countries) with regards to attacks on foreign owned infrastructure in the region.

FINAL SUMMARY: Due to the above mentioned intelligence product, it is requested that further resources are required to undertake more in-depth and in-region analysis of the situation to ascertain the extent and veracity of these claims.

This request includes:

A. A reconnaissance trip to northern Colombia to provide additional HUMINT intelligence.

. . .

B. A request that Analyst #397664 is to remain in Colombia indefinitely to undertake further investigation and analysis.

C. A further request that Analyst #397664 is given temporary field officer status to conduct HUMINT intelligence in northern Colombia.

END REPORT

Jardine leant back to read his report. It wasn't perfect, but he suspected it would be enough to arouse interest in London. In Bogotá, however, it was a different matter. His reports were routinely read by the British Ambassador. He imagined he would be sceptical. Ambassadors were usually only diplomatic with officials from the country they were posted in but scathing to their fellow compatriots. Although the Foreign Office would never know the true identity of his sources, and at least they couldn't comment or alter the report in any way. In terms of the response from London, he doubted it would make the special red book delivered to 10 Downing Street each morning. Not yet anyway. The American *cousins* would no doubt be interested, but they wouldn't be brought in until something substantial was to come of it. The tone was political, so that should keep out the NCA and DEA and any other acronym heavy drug related organisations. And so, the only person Jardine could think of that stood in his way was Ambrose, Head of Colombia Station. He said himself that he didn't have time to read the reports. Let's hope his mind is still firmly on retirement and not looking to be critical with 'sexed-up' intelligence reports.

17

THE PITCH

HE STOOD AT AMBROSE'S DOOR AND REHEARSED HIS SPEECH. "Although I am *primarily* an analyst, I believe I would also be a good controller of agents. My position as analyst is not all that different from an agent's. I conduct interviews with sources, which is not a far cry from running an asset. I am familiar with the cycle of intelligence: collection, analysis, dissemination, and action. It is only the action part in which I have had limited experience."

"What are you mumbling out there, Jardine?" Ambrose asked.

Startled, Jardine mumbled a reply and proceeded into Ambrose's office, handing him the report. Ambrose received the report in his left hand as his right reached for his glasses and once perched on the bridge of his nose, he began to read. The report was brief, maybe a page at most, and after a minute, Ambrose took off his glasses and stared at Jardine seriously. "You are sure about this, Jardine?" he said, raising his eyebrows as he finished the last part of the sentence.

"Is an analyst ever sure, Ronald?" Jardine tried Ambrose's first name to give a sense of familiarity. "I only know what my sources have told me. All verified of course. Even did a social media trimetric analysis: Facebook, Instagram and Twitter. There are some rumblings on these topics online as well," said Jardine, trying to inject some certainty and authority into his voice.

"Oh really? I haven't come across anything."

"I'll include it in the next report," replied Jardine.

"Very well."

Jardine nodded politely. Shit, how am I going to pull that off? Inventing a falsified intelligence report was easy enough when you're the author, but an article in the media?

Ambrose continued. "So the gist of what you're saying is that this sub-source of yours, he has said that Hezbollah…"

"Not Hezbollah necessarily. It could be Al-Qaeda, ISIS, or even a radical Palestinian faction. Don't want to let a centuries old religious schism narrow the possibilities." Jardine chuckled and then stopped abruptly.

"Right. So, there may be a connection with…" Ambrose looked down at the report to find the right words, "…fundamental Islamist terrorist cells active in northern Colombia. How certain are you that this chap is telling the truth?"

"Which one?"

Ambrose lowered his eyes to the report once more. "The sub-source of flaming flamingo."

"He confirmed he had heard there are groups active there, he's a close acquaintance of flaming flamingo."

Jardine felt blood rush to his head. This was the first time he'd lied so openly to Ambrose. He'd also never said flamingo aloud before, perhaps he should have chosen different code names …

"Flaming flamingo?" Ambrose accentuated the 'f' as it rolled off his tongue.

Jardine nodded.

Ambrose put on his glasses and looked down at the report again. "Why haven't I heard of this sub-source of flaming flamingo before?" Ambrose looked up from the report, his head tilted downwards, eyes looking at Jardine over his glasses. "And what have I told you about using a modal verb in reports? Modal verbs are for tabloid journalism and click-bait, no 'mays', 'mights' and 'could quite possibilities...!'

Jardine nodded. "Understood, sir." This time Jardine went for the more formal 'Sir' as if he were being scolded by a headmaster. There was no official protocol between the two. When it was serious it would be 'Sir' and for more light-hearted moments, 'Ronald'. "Flaming flamingo has known him for quite a while, trusts him. I believe they studied together at La Nacional. He put me in contact because it's something additional that he was worried about. Seems sub-source 397664-003/01 is a bit of a lefty at heart and has become disillusioned of the violence in the world of late. Of course, it's simply his word at this stage, that's why I want to verify it for myself. You know, get some meatier intelligence on our plates!" Jardine finished in a jolly tone.

Ambrose looked at the report again. "And why have you been so quick to trust this friend of flaming flamingo?" Ambrose looked back up at Jardine. "You know it usually takes a few months to verify new sources."

"Well, that's the thing, sir. He's an ex-M19 guerrilla and a fully-fledged professor of political science at La Nacional. I would've mentioned him earlier, but it's all been very hush-hush, got to keep a lid on these things for as long as you can, never know who's listening. Especially with the peace process going on. He doesn't quite know where he stands in that regard. He's very secretive, doesn't trust the Colombian government at all, especially after all the wiretaps with DAS a few years back. Personally, I believe he's speculating. He's costeño, you know how crazy it is up there on the coast, magical realism and all that."

Ambrose looked sideways for a minute as if contem-plating to say something important. "Had a costeño girlfriend once. Crazy girl. Used to drink aguardiente like a marathon runner drinking Gatorade in the Sahara. Couldn't keep up with her in the end. Lost touch eventually, until a year ago. She contacted me on Facebook. Nearly had a bloody heart attack, what if the missus had seen it?!"

"I didn't know you were stationed to Colombia in your youth, sir."

"Not Colombia. Caracas. Met her there. Turns out she's living here now."

It seemed Ambrose had changed his tune.

"We're living in a new age, Ambrose. Things happen at break-neck pace these days. Not always time to check, otherwise you'll end up last."

The feeling of rushing blood had subsided now. It was amazing how quickly he had adapted to lying. He was almost convincing himself that there might be some truth to his report.

"Remember that smuggler we were tracking for a while? What was his name?" asked Ambrose. "You remember, the one that was doing business with all the guys we were interested in: the narcos, the paras, the guerrillas, the BACRIMS. If I remember correctly, he was even providing plasma TVs to corrupt local officials. Ha! Crazy stuff."

"El Lobo?" Jardine offered.

"El Lobo! That's what they called him. Can you imagine that happening back home? The press would have a field day! Not sure it's magical realism, more like a case of truth's stranger than fiction," chuckled Ambrose.

Jardine didn't know how to respond but decided to laugh along. It appeared that something Jardine had said stirred a nostalgia in Ambrose and it had changed his mood. Jardine's heart began to beat faster. He decided to take advantage of the situation as a mantra came floating into his mind, he didn't know from where: *If you want to convince someone, make it seem like it's their idea.*

Ambrose's chuckling began to subside, and his voice took

on a tone of wanting to wrap the conversation up. "Of course, one always needs a range of HUMINT to verify, Jardine."

"You're one hundred per cent correct, sir. Couldn't agree more. Additional HUMINT is always beneficial. Another great idea of yours."

"Yes, also, as you know, we're being asked to start living in the multimedia digital age. Which means you need to supply some video evidence. Preferably in short bursts, like a Tik Tok video. Attention spans are waning you know."

Shit, Jardine thought. That's something he hadn't considered. It was all right to write lies on paper but providing video evidence was another thing. Nevertheless, he replied with his new-found confidence. "Of course."

Ambrose was about to speak again but raised his eyebrows and held his index finger in the air, as if a sudden thought had popped into his head. "I hadn't told you this, because it had never occurred to me until now. A while back, before your time here, we were tracking a man who went by the name Benbow. He met with Al Qaeda affiliates in Miami before flying to Bogotá. We lost track of him after he entered Ciudad Bolivar, but then he resurfaced in Cartagena several months later. It seemed he had links to anyone and everyone who wanted to buy radioactive material out of Eastern Europe. He left eventually, and nothing was heard from him again. So, naturally, resources were angled elsewhere."

"You think he still might be active?" asked Jardine.

"No. The last I heard he had defected to Russia and was living out his life at a former Soviet resort in Yalta. But, it goes to show you. There just might be more at play in Colombia than drug trafficking cartels, blood-thirsty paramilitary defence units, violent Marxist guerrillas, and ruthless urban criminal gangs." Ambrose picked up his tea cup but didn't take a drink. "Of course, Jardine, all of this will need to be based on facts. It's all become very analytical these days. In my day, well, we ran on gut feeling and hunches, and it worked fine to some extent, but these days we need to cover out behinds," said Ambrose, before taking a long gulp of tea.

"Of course, sir."

"Unbiased facts, no opinions, no judgment. We leave that to the politicians."

"Absolutely."

"Free of outside interference. You know the Colombians will tell you the nice, clean fluffy tale rather than the truth," said Ambrose, his eyebrows raised with an earnest look on his face.

"Indeed, and what about inside interference?"

"That too. Keep office politics out of it. Although the Foreign Office and Whitehall will also want to look at your reports. But they can't add or edit, just advise. Is that inside interference?"

"I suppose it is," commented Jardine.

"Hard to avoid though."

"Quite. Impossible, in fact."

"Inside interference is fine," said Ambrose.

"Okay, done deal," replied Jardine.

The phone rang and Ambrose answered. His answers were short, it seemed as if he was deciding on the toppings of his *arepa rellena* for lunch. After a minute he hung up the phone. "Right, now then. Where were we? Yes. That's right, your intelligence trip to the coast. You will be responsible for recruiting additional sources and writing the intelligence reports and I'll filter them and pass them on to London. Talk to Jane and go over what you might need and then get back to me with a timeline and budget. Things are tight, but we have some funds available for terrorism-related activity. As R said, 'We must disrupt terrorism at its source.' Meet them at their end of the wicket, as it were. That's exactly what we're doing. Bloody good work, Jardine!"

A flood of relief swept over Jardine.

Ambrose went on. "I'll authorise a month extension. Any

more than that and we'll need approval from London. You'll need something concrete to convince them of that. They're strong headed and will want a pint of your blood with any work you do."

"My reports will be like a brand-new Forsyth novel. They won't be able to put it down," said Jardine without a tinge of irony in his voice.

"Ah, and before you go, Jardine. Why tropical birds?"

"Tropical birds?

"Your code-names. We usually like to use birds of prey, such as eagle, falcon, hawk, etc."

"We are in Colombia after all. So, I thought a little avian tropic touch might do the trick."

"Very well." Ambrose nodded like he had just come up with an ingenious new plan.

"Thank you, sir," said Jardine as he exited the office.

18

AMBROSE TO RADCLIFFE

AMBROSE PICKED UP THE RECEIVER AND DIALLED THE DIRECT LINE to Radcliffe. After two rings Radcliffe answered.

"Morning Ambrose! Of course, it's not morning here. Just about to nip down to the club for kippers on toast."

"They still serve kippers on toast?"

"No. Well, it's not on the menu anymore, that's for sure. Some new bloody fusion thing these days. They still make kippers for us old dogs, though. They've taken to making the dishes sound a hell of a lot fancier than they are. Anyway, have you mentioned the budget cuts to your team? How are they taking them? I know it will cause some distress, but one must do their duty for Queen and country. And as you know, this new Islamist business is not looking too tickety-boo in Syria, and the spill over into Iraq and Lebanon. Yemen not too good either. The worse thing is we don't know who to bloody support! The Venn diagrams coming out of analytics look more like a game of Chinese checkers than something to guide us."

Ambrose stood up and moved over towards the window. "It certainly is a complicated situation, sir." He let out a coughing sound, as if to change the subject. "There's something we've stumbled across here, Radcliffe. It may be of interest."

"What? A threat more important than ISIS?"

"It's related, sir. May have wider implications than just Latin America."

"Well?"

"I'm sending you a brief outline now. It's still in the early stages, but it could be something significant. It seems there could be a Hezbollah, Al-Qaeda or ISIS cell working here in Colombia. On the coast, possibly with support from Venezuela."

"Ha! Right in the yank's backyard! That does sound substantial. Imagine the look on their face when we uncover a terrorist cell three hours from Miami. Let's follow this up, Ambrose. I was just reading the other day about the Suriname president's son inviting Hezbollah to set up shop in the country. Seems they're trying to spread all over the continent."

"Yes, that was my analysis as well," said Ambrose, wanting to appear like he had already thought of the same thing.

"Well then, pending my reading of the outline, I'll send through a modest bursary, although we won't be able to send any more personnel."

"That's fine, sir. We have a man working on it as we speak. Actually, he's the one who came across the information."

"One of ours, is he?"

"Yes, analyst. Been with us a few years and knows the lingo. First posting was to South Korea."

"Right. Good work, old boy. As you know, R is saying that we must disrupt terrorism at its source, meet them on their side of the wicket, as it were."

"That's exactly what I said," chimed Ambrose.

"Great minds think alike, Ambrose. Will be good to out-do the cousins in their neck of woods. We still owe them for Fuchs and Nunn May."

"Wasn't that in a Greene novel?"

"Which one?" asked Radcliffe.

"Never mind."

"Jolly good then. It will be good to get back in the good books with the Yanks after all this time. I look forward to the outline. Keep up the good work and keep me informed."

Ambrose hung up and smiled to himself. Jardine will be happy with this, he thought. Just hope the little bugger's right about it all. And with that he sent through a confirmation email to Jardine, just as his assistant walked in with an arepa overloaded with shredded pork and coleslaw.

19

TRIP PLANNING

JARDINE SAT IN FRONT OF HIS LAPTOP, LOOKING OUT ACROSS THE skyline of Bogotá and the red brick buildings of El Nogal. He felt a curious mix of excitement blended with doubt and a dash of regret. What he'd written in his report was at best a fantastical overstatement and at worst a gross embellishment. And now came the nervous wait to see if it would even be believed by London. He played the BBC World Service on his laptop as he leant back in his chair, looking at the large relief map of Colombia on the wall. A present from his source, Señor Zuluaga. The three prongs of the Andes rose up from the map like paper mâché slugs. The world seemed so much smaller in map form, he thought, as a BBC announcer did the rounds of the top international news stories. The names of the towns and cities on the map seemed exotic and mysterious, the reality of slogging through the traffic-choked streets, the crime and chaos of it all was not visible. The announcer spoke about the Colombian peace dialogues, announcing they were progressing as planned. A special signing ceremony would be held in Cartagena in the coming weeks as a symbolic gesture of the end of the conflict, and to promote peace and prosperity in Colombia. That might be my last event in the country if this doesn't turn out, he thought. His eyes trailed up to the northern-most point of the South American continent: La Guajira. Lowering his eyes slightly, he passed over Maicao. That will be my first port of call. His eyes trailed west to a particularly protruding lump on the Caribbean coast, apart from the three strands of the Andes: The Sierra Nevada de Santa Marta. That's where he'd heard the university students talking about dissident-FARC and ELN groups re-emerging. No-one, not even the Colombians, knew about that. That will be my next destination. A remote outpost in the Sierra Nevada de Santa Marta, who would suspect that? A good place to establish an Islamist terrorist cell training camp. I'll need to enter from the Valledupar side. The side rarely visited by tourists. He trailed his eyes from there further west to Cartagena. With an extra month now confirmed, I'll be able to attend the peace treaty signing in Cartagena on the twenty-sixth of September, after visiting Maicao and the Sierra Nevada. Jardine sat still looking at the map, lost in thought when he heard the bright chime of a new email. It read:

Further investigation approved for one month. Further funds available from London if pertinent. Good luck! :)

— Ambrose

And just like that, Jardine was now officially an operative, guaranteed at least an extra month in the country. He started to plan what he would need: cash, to pay potential sources and a vehicle of some sort. There was potential to get a hand from the military, perhaps General Esguerra had some contacts? Crucially, he would need to develop a watertight cover story. Third Secretary (Political) served him in Bogotá visiting Government offices, but it would be harder to explain that on the side of a mountain in the jungle. It would be difficult for Jardine to be a Mr. Grey too. For one, he was six-foot tall with light brown hair and blue eyes. He stood out like dog's balls in most of Colombia. On the coast, however, he was able to at least blend in with the crowd of backpacking foreigners. Yes, that's it! Everyone would know he was a gringo, but at least they would lump him together with all the other harmless travelling weed-smoking gringos. Instead of a Mr. Grey, he would be more of a Grey dude. But most gringo travellers visited the Sierra Nevada on the Santa Marta side to visit the Lost City, so he would need to develop a bloody good reason for visiting the Valledupar side. He'd need to adapt his clothes as well. In Bogotá, he would normally wear a suit to his sources. It gave the appearance of being more refined and it fit in well with the other businessmen in the Andean capital. For the coast he would need to tone down his appearance, blend in more with the environment. The project began to overwhelm him slightly. He felt a small seed-sized lump begin to expand in his throat and a hot rush of blood from his forehead down to his neck as his stomach began to toss and turn like a small squall on an acidic sea. Realising he needed some help with the planning, he decided to check in with Jane, the Embassy Office Manager, to see what other paperwork was required. He collected all the required budgeting and planning documents and, standing from his desk, exited his office and walked down the corridor to Jane's office.

"Hiya, Jane. How are things? Jose well, I trust?"

"Hiya, all right here. Jose's the same as always — crazy, but I still love him all the same. Just read Ambrose's email. Now, you'll need…"

Jardine thrust a loaded folder in her face.

"Wow! That was quick. You must be chomping at the bit to get up there?"

"Desperate measures requires…" For a moment, Jardine couldn't think of what to say next. Then as if a charge of electricity had overtaken his brain, he responded: "...requires measured action."

"That from a Bond film?" asked Jane with a smirk on her face. She opened the folder and ruffled through the papers. "Everything here seems to be in order. Have you contacted DNI?"

DNI was La Dirección Nacional de Inteligencia. Colombia's newly formed intelligence agency.

"DNI? Why? Oh, that's right, got to register our movements with them. Got it."

"Exactly. We are still on friendly terms with the Colombians, so you'll also need to team up with a DNI Officer."

"Err, what? I thought I would be... flying solo."

"Afraid not. We've done many operations with the Colombians in the past few years and they have some very good officers. Besides, you're an analyst, you're no Bond."

"Do you mean Bond, the Secret Agent? Or Bond the Ornithologist?"

"There's a birdwatching Bond? I only know the Secret Agent..." said Jane, confused.

"Right, well, never mind," Jardine interrupted. "I hadn't considered that. It's just that—"

"Don't worry. We'll sort it out for you." Jane stood up and moved across the room to a filing cabinet, pulling out a pale manila folder. "Look, he's a good agent, trained with the best — that means us — and knows the coast. He operates out of Santa Marta." Jane motioned for Jardine to sit in one of the two leather armchairs facing each other opposite her desk as she began to read from the report: "Jorge Francisco Leon Jaramillo, aka, Paco Leon..."

Jane continued introducing the DNI agent, Paco Leon, a former elite commando from the Compañía Jungla Antinarcóticos (Counter-Narcotics Jungle Company) known as JUNGLA. A group originally trained by the British SAS, and subsequently the US Army Special Forces. Afterwards, Leon was seconded into Colombia's intelligence services in operations becoming a member of an MI6 training program as a trusted, vetted unit — a group of Colombian intelligence agents that were polygraphed, interviewed and trained to infiltrate the drug cartels to gleam valuable intelligence. An expert in patrols, ambush, counter-ambush and surveillance. The group was also trained in how to make the perfect cup of tea, a valuable skill when entertaining members of the British security establishment. This training, however, paled in comparison to Paco's former training. Coming from a small farm in the foothills of Serranía de Perijá, Paco had been 'recruited', taken against his will to serve with a small group of guerrillas at fourteen. The excuse for taking him was to 'fight for a more equal Colombia.' However, Paco soon found that the group mainly dealt in extortion and drug trafficking. Escaping at the age eighteen, he knew he wouldn't be able to return home to his family and so instead fled to Bogotá, where he enrolled in the Navy and studied nightly to finish his high school requirements. After five years, he left temporarily to study Economics and Political Science at Universidad Nacional before returning and being moved into the JUNGLAS. Since then, he had been selected to study at the Western Hemisphere Institute for Security Cooperation at Fort Benning, Georgia.

"So, as you can see, you'll be well taken care of, Jardine. He's mellowed since his JUNGLA action days. You'll find he will keep a low profile and be discreet in his judgements."

"Does he know why I'm on the coast?"

"He knows enough not to ask questions. He'll help in whatever capacity needed.

However, we must keep this tight-lipped. So, it will help if you have a cover to tell others you encounter. In fact, I've already taken the liberty of assigning you a cover." She handed Jardine a satchel which contained a long-range camera, a small recording device and some type of log book.

Jardine rifled through the bag. "Let me guess, investigative journalist?"

"Ha! Are you kidding? You'd be more likely to be killed being a journalist than a spy in Colombia."

Jardine thought for a moment and then it came to him. "Professional birdwatcher?"

"Like James Bond?" asked Jane, a feigned look of surprise on her face.

Jardine smiled. "You're a quick learner."

"I'll see what I can find and rustle up some documentation for you," said Jane.

"Excellent. Well, I'll finalise everything, contact this Leon bloke and I'll be off." Jardine stood up and moved towards the door.

"Good luck! Enjoy the cazuela de mariscos on the coast!"

Jardine exited the office and strode down the corridor. *I'm like a double agent to myself*, he thought. *Lying for my cover as an intelligence officer and lying to my employer as myself*. It was then that he realised, for the first time in his life, the only person he wasn't lying to, was himself.

20

LAS ÚLTIMAS PALABRAS DE VERONICA

HAVING COMPLETED ALL THE REQUIRED DOCUMENTATION FOR HIS trip and having contacted Paco Leon — the DNI Agent he would meet — Jardine returned home that evening exhausted, and collapsed on the sofa. His mind raced with a million thoughts, mainly about what other intelligence he could invent to keep the story going. As he thought about his story, his mind drifted towards Veronica. The authorization had come for a month's extension, but he couldn't let it slide to her just yet. He had to be sure that he could stay and be with her. Nonetheless, he couldn't leave for the coast without speaking to her one last time. Even if she wouldn't listen to him, he had to try. He worked up the energy to stand, walk outside and hail a cab, arriving at her apartment just before nine pm. He spoke to the security guard through the intercom at the door of her building.

"Hola, para hablar con Verónica Velasco. Apto 601, por favor."

"Sí señor, un momentico," replied the guard.

Jardine looked inside and saw the guard switch to another phone and dial a number. He could faintly hear the guard speaking with someone, before switching back to the intercom phone to speak to Jardine.

"¿Eh, señor Jardine? Dice ella que no quiere hablar con usted."

"What? Why? Did she say why she doesn't want to speak with me?"

"No, ella..." Jardine took a few steps away from the door and looked up at the building while pulling out his mobile phone and dialling Veronica's number. After a few moments, she answered, "Que quieres?!" *What do you want?* Jardine jerked the phone away from his ear. Her voice was so loud a dog barked from across the street.

"Veronica, I'm sorry all of this has happened. I'm going to fix it. I'm going away for a little while. But, I promise you, it will all be okay."

She answered with the *humpf* of a small child and he imagined her crossing her arms and pouting. He felt the acid rise in his stomach. He wanted to explain everything, pour out his plan like dominoes on a card table, but he couldn't. He had to maintain secrecy, at least for now.

"You don't love me!' she said, now at a more audible tone. "You just want to party before they send you to Iraq or Iran or Afghanistan, or whatever *país de mierda* they're sending you to."

Jardine took a deep breath and rolled his eyes.

"You're rolling your eyes, aren't you?" she said.

Jardine mouthed an obscenity. "No, not at all... Honey, I'm going to fix things. You'll see. I love you."

"Huh", again the childish sound came out of her mouth.

"I'm working on something that will keep me here a little while longer. I can't tell you what it is. But, I'm flying to the..." he almost mentioned where he was flying to. It's no wonder, the honey trap is so effective, he thought. Women can get anything out of a man, all they have to do is wait for him to slip up. "I'm flying out tomorrow. I'll call you when I can, but I'll be in some remote areas. Everything will be okay. You'll see."

"You're flying out tomorrow?"

"Yes."

"Where to exactly?" her tone was calmer now.

"I can't tell you. Look, can I come up and we can chat?"

A few seconds passed. "Si, come up," she replied.

Jardine entered the building and took the lift the sixth floor. Entering the apartment, he noticed paper everywhere and several wine bottles scattered around the room. Veronica moved towards him and looked up at him with her moist brown eyes. She looked angry, but then her eyebrows rose and she burst into tears, hugging him tightly and sobbing into his chest.

"Vero, I'm sorry. Everything will be okay, I promise."

"No, I'm sorry. I overreacted. I was scared and I love you and I don't want to lose you. I just can't, I can't...'I can't go to Yemen with you."

"I know. I'm not going to Yemen any more. At least not for the time being. I've got an extra month here now and I think I'll be able to stay indefinitely. Until we can work out something for the both of us."

"All I can think of is a future with you. I don't want or need anyone else." She had stopped sobbing now and again looked up into his eyes.

"You're all I want, too. Everything will work out, mi amor. Tu veras." *You'll see*.

21

SANTA MARTA

THE FLIGHT ATTENDANT ANNOUNCED THEIR DESCENT INTO SANTA
Marta as Jardine crunched on the final remnants of a bag of
peanuts and glanced out the window. Clouds blanketed the
ground like a bumper year of cotton with the snow-capped
peaks of the Sierra Nevada piercing it. The lush volcanic-rich
foothills of the Sierra Nevada de Santa Marta cascaded down
into the Caribbean Sea, providing fertile agricultural land.
This had led to enterprising locals planting marijuana during
the seventies and eighties, putting Santa Marta on the famous
hippy trail, which in turn had led to *el boom marimbero*,
making the Santa Marta Colombian gold strain of the green
herb legendary among weed connoisseurs. Not to mention, it
made many families from the northern Guajira region rich.
During the nineties, the guerrillas moved in and then the
paramilitaries, and thus, the whole Sierra became off limits.
That is, until the late two-thousands when the hippy trail
returned as the gringo trail, as backpackers began to amass in
the small fishing town of Taganga, a fifteen-minute drive
from Santa Marta. It was on this gringo trail that Jardine had
travelled, from Mexico, after leaving university, a time and
place — in Guatemala — where he was approached and

encouraged to apply to work in the clandestine world of espionage. So apart from his mission, Jardine was also intrigued to witness how the area had morphed into the behemoth backpacker town he had heard his colleagues mention.

The plane landed with a screech and a thud and the passengers erupted into applause, as was custom in Colombia. Jardine sat still, quietly mulling over the assignment ahead. The passengers grappled like small children for their hand luggage as the air hostesses did their best to explain that the fasten seatbelt sign was not switched off. The thought of being near the beach gave him the sudden urge to throw his whole mission in, eat some fried fish, neck some rum and cold beer and begin a new life on the coast. But, wrestling with his mind, he managed to concentrate on the job at hand; he had added purpose this time. He was determined to find the connections, recruit sources, extract the required information and prolong his stay in Colombia by writing the best intelligence story to end all stories. That was his mission.

The air was damp and sticky as he approached the taxi rank, like a wet towel wrapped around one's body — it couldn't have been anymore different from Bogotá at two thousand six hundred metres up in the Andes. The skin was darker, the Spanish faster — and devoid of the letter S — and the streets were alive with people treating it as their living room. Despite the heat, many of the men wore jeans with striped polo tops and huge square-rimmed sunglasses. In Colombia, like in many South American countries, stereotypes tended to follow the altitude: the higher up a mountain one goes, the more colder and reserved, the closer to sea level, the more outgoing, friendly and loud. Santa Marta and its residents, the *Samarios*, were most definitely at sea level.

Jardine took a taxi from the rank to his hotel near the main seaside promenade in the old town of Santa Marta. The taxi driver interrogated him in the friendly curious way that Colombians often do. Did he like Colombian food? Had he tried aguardiente? And did he think Colombian girls were the most beautiful in the world? To be polite, he replied yes to all of the above. Arriving at his hotel, Casa de Isabella, he left his luggage and headed out to meet the DNI Agent. The Dirección Nacional de Inteligencia (DNI) was Colombia's sparkling new intelligence agency. It had been scrubbed clean with a diamond tipped brush, following a string of fiascos as the former agency DAS. British Intelligence were known for their expertise in clandestine listening technology; DAS were known for wire-tapping every man and his donkey in the country without warrants.

After leaving his luggage at the hotel, Jardine headed out to meet Paco Leon at Hotel Don Pepe, a former colonial mansion one block back from the beach on Calle 16. As he walked the three blocks to his meeting, the sun was setting slowly, yet the air was still thick and humid. The sizzle and smell of fried fish wafted through the air as families pulled out their rocking chairs to sit on the pavement and chew the fat. The sound of a tinny accordion and the rhythmic thud of bongo drums from a vallenato trio bellowed up from the beach as Jardine arrived at the entrance to the hotel. A man dressed in white linen opened the grille-gated door and he entered, taking a seat in a wicker chair placed at a round marble-top table in the courtyard. Behind him was a swimming pool surrounded by palms and lush ferns with earthen-ware pots. Normally he would prefer to sit facing the serene view, but he was on assignment and an operative now and wanted to make sure he could see who was entering the hotel. He ordered an Aguila beer and took a deep breath. He had been so busy organising his trip that he hadn't had time to consider how he would explain to Paco what he was looking for. Or how, or if, he would be able to pull the wool over the agent's eyes as well as his employer's. The grille gate creaked and Jardine, still seated, peered around a square column to see a tall man enter. His hair was closely cropped on the sides but slightly longer on top. He wore cream-coloured linen pants with a light pastel-orange linen shirt. On his feet were the Guajira version of rope-soled espadrilles, which had a band at the heel. The man continued to Jardine's table, his hand outstretched. "Me han dicho que buscas un guía turistico?" *I've heard you are looking for a tourist guide?*

"Solo si el servicio es bueno, bonito y barato," replied Jardine, standing. *Only if the service is cheap and cheerful.*

A repertoire they had decided on over the phone from Bogotá.

"A pleasure, Paco. I just arrived from Bogotá, or *la nevera* as I believe it's known here." *The refrigerator.*

Paco smiled and chuckled. Like many Colombians from the coast, he was taller than his Andean compatriots. "That's right, the fridge. We Costeños aren't used to the cold mountains. It's always easy to spot a *cachaco* here in Santa Marta, they're the ones wearing a scarf on the beach."

The two men laughed together, ordering two ice-cold beers as they sat on wicker chairs. When the drinks arrived Jardine raised his bottle in an amiable toast. "A la nevera!" *To the fridge.*

"To la nevera, compadre," Paco replied, raising his beer bottle.

"Cigarette?" asked Jardine, his hand outstretched with a soft packet. Paco hesitated. "It's not going to shoot a poison dart at you!" Jardine added dryly, with a serious look.

"Ah, my British friend. Always cracking jokes without changing their expressions. You are very much like Los Rolos in Bogotá, so *formalitos*, never smiling in your tweed jackets and ties. But, you are always listening and analysing, I know that." Paco took a cigarette from the packet, leant back and lit it with a match he pulled from his breast pocket.

"Let's not start with the stereotypes just yet, Paco."

Paco ignored the comment. "Yes, always listening." A curious expression spread across his face and he smiled with a slight frown — it meant you never knew whether what would come next was a joke or a small moment of fury. "Experts in eavesdropping, the British. I heard what you did with David 'El Loco' Bautista. Good job. Although, you know what?"

"Humour me, Paco," said Jardine.

"I think we Colombians are more seductive. In the case of Bautista, I think our Colombian women were the real stars. I haven't met a man yet that could resist a Colombian honey trap."

"Ah yes, Bautista was a tricky one. We had to use some of our best technology to record those conversations."

"From Q branch?"

"Doesn't exist I'm afraid."

"Oh…" Paco looked disappointed.

"But it was you guys that really made the headway. We were merely support," added Jardine.

"Yes, it was a fine example of our joint collaboration in the war against drugs."

Jardine lit a cigarette, took a drag and exhaled. He didn't usually smoke but had been told that it helped to have a packet on hand when on assignment to offer. "You know, I only really smoke when I'm nervous," he said holding the cigarette out in front of him and examining it.

"You are nervous now?" Paco asked.

"I suppose I am. It's just, I really don't know what the bloody hell I'm doing here."

Jardine felt a slow burn begin in his stomach, a feeling of uneasiness. It was the first time since his ayahuasca experience that he had felt a slight pang of anxiety. He felt like a fish out of water. His previous work trips involved being driven from office to office, conducting interviews and then typing up the report. However, this time was different. He knew he'd have to get his hands dirty. The only problem was, he didn't exactly know how to dirty his hands. How far should he go with his story?

Paco spoke. "No te preocupes. I can assist in any way possible. What are you thinking for tomorrow?"

"I was thinking tomorrow we head for Taganga. I wanted to survey the scene, check it out for leads. You know I visited there ten years ago. I imagine it's changed."

"Si señor, Taganga used to be a small town of pescadores and then in the seventies and eighties, it was mostly hippies. *Gente divertida y tranquila." Fun and relaxed people.* Paco looked directly at Jardine with eyes motionless and lips straight. "But now, it's a den of a cocaina y putas, a town that never sleeps and is partying 24/7. Ever since Los Israelitas took over it's gone from Guate-mala to Guate-peor." *From Guate-bad to Guate-worse.*

Jardine nodded solemnly. "How worse can it get?"

Paco smiled. "This is Colombia, *mijo.* It can always get worse."

LUNCH & LAGOS

THE PHONE SOUNDED IN JARDINE'S HOTEL ROOM AND HE PICKED
it up on the second ring. "Muy bueno' día' señor, hay un
señor León aquí," said a voice on the line.

"Muy bien, ya bajo," replied Jardine.

Jardine and Paco had finished the night early after talking
some more about their work while dining at Hotel Don Pepe
before Paco had walked Jardine back to his hotel. Now, as
Jardine walked down the stairs to the Hotel lobby, he saw
Paco sat on a chair flicking through the daily paper.

"Good morning, ready to begin our birdwatching tour?"
asked Paco, following Jardine's instructions from the night
before. Their cover story would be that of a local tour guide
and a keen British birdwatcher. Jardine took the camera out
and slung it over his shoulder. This overt display of a valuable object was usually a no-no in Colombia, but it fit better
with his cover story.

Paco led Jardine to his battered khaki-green jeep, and they
drove north to the outskirts of Santa Marta. As they left the
city the road was winding, hugging the barren hillside as
cacti and small shrubs lined the road. Rounding the final
bend, the former quaint fishing village turned backpacker

party paradise came into view — Taganga. Barren brown hills, which would be green during the wet season, led down to lush green trees amid low rise buildings near the beach. Small fishing boats bobbed in the bay like corks in a bucket. Continuing downhill into town, they parked under a shady mango tree and walked a block along a sandy pedestrian street to the beach. As they walked, Jardine peered down the street and swivelled his head, nonchalantly, in a radar-like sweep. Always need to know what the devil everyone's up to, he could hear his old MI6 instructors saying. *I'm an operative now, need to keep my wits about me.* He picked out barefoot Australian surfers, noticeable by their multi-coloured shorts and trucker caps — overhearing one of them utter the phrase, "Yeah, nah mate," confirmed it. A cacophony of "che" and "boludo" wafted through the air from a posse of guitar-playing, jewellery-making dreadlocked men and women sat on the side of the street — Argentines, he thought. A group of lanky Dutchmen passed them walking away from the beach, carrying scuba tanks and oversized flippers. This observation he deduced solely on one of their football jerseys — the Dutch team, Ajax.

The two men found a small thatched shack on the beach, sat down in rickety wooden chairs and ordered cold beer — a mango juice for Paco — and crispy fried fish served alongside fried plantains and coconut rice. They discussed how the peace deals would affect the coastal regions of Colombia, while admiring the laidback stream of people passing by. After lunch, Jardine strolled out to the edge of the beach and looked out. The cool Caribbean water lapped against his feet as the sun blazed down on his neck and face. He turned and looked back towards the beach and the small beachside promenade. A stream of foreigners strolled along the foreshore, outnumbering the locals three to one. He wasn't used to so many foreigners. They tended not to stand out in the big bad metropolis of Bogotá, there were simply too many people.

Here, he could blend in as a tourist, a world away from the grey drizzling Andean plains of Bogotá.

He glanced back at the beach and saw a small convenience store with pre-packaged mobile phones for sale out the front. Seeing the phones, an idea popped into his head. The first scene of my story, he thought. He motioned towards Paco with his thumb and pinkie extended and held up to his ear. Phone call. Paco nodded and continued talking, arms waving as he spoke like he was performing an intricate karate move. Jogging over to the store, Jardine bought two of the pre-packaged mobile phones, paying in cash. Taking them out of their packets, he turned them on and displayed each phone's number on the screen. Next, he walked two hundred metres to a *minutos* lady - the ubiquitous, usually elderly women, street vendors who rent out mobile phones by the minute.

"Para llamar a…" Jardine asked. Before he could finish the lady shoved several phones in his face without looking up. He dialled the numbers of the two phones he had bought and then answered them but didn't speak. After a minute, he hung up. He thanked the lady, handed her a two thousand peso bank note and strolled back to where Paco was sitting. Before arriving, he opened the service's encrypted messaging service on his own mobile phone and sent through the phone numbers of the pre-packaged phone he had bought to GCHQ.

Conduct tracking on the following numbers +57 3215758349 and +57 3145749975 — Ref. #397664

— Sent

After typing the two numbers of the decoy phones into the message, he then dumped them in a small rubbish bin next to a mango juice stand. The woman at the stand smiled and offered Jardine mango biche — salted mango strips with lime juice. He shook his head and continued. The false-flag phone tracking would give the beginning of his story an air of authenticity. I've been here barely twenty-four hours and already actively pursuing leads, hot on the trail of an international ring of fundamental Islamist terrorists, he thought. At least that's how they would see it.

He looked up towards Paco and saw the waitress now waving her hands in the air, mimicking someone sprinting and then falling as if being chased and knocked down. Jardine strolled back to the table as the waitress left carrying dirty plates back to the kitchen. Paco leaned forward in his chair and took a swig of beer. "Parece que había un asesinato aquí hace una semana."

"Who killed who?" Jardine asked.

"Seems a man committed some *violations* and the Paramilitaries killed him." Jardine assumed Paco was using the literal Spanish translation of *violation*: rape. Paco continued. "The girl worked for a man with connections. Justice can be sorely lacking or salsa-spin fast in Colombia. It all depends on who you know or who you've pissed off."

What Paco said was true. Nepotism was as ubiquitous as the smell of coffee in the morning in Colombia. In his case, nepotism would work in his favour, Jardine thought. "What type of connections?" asked Jardine.

"Paramilitary or whatever they've turned into now," replied Paco. He leant forward in his chair and wrote in his notebook. "I must report this right away to Bogotá."

"Can't it wait, Paco?" Jardine asked.

"No, I must report it now. This is a serious offence and we must encounter the perpetrators."

"Surely that's the police's job?"

"Las policías aquí no harían un culo!" he hissed. *The police here won't do anything.*

It was in this moment that Jardine realised that Paco was very insistent in asking questions and doing things by the book. Just my luck, he thought. Jardine wished that the normal Latino stereotype of lazy, late, and corrupt was true. But it seemed he had been teamed up with the most efficient, effective and by-the-book agent Colombia could offer, going above and beyond his call of duty. Paco walked away and made a brief phone call. While he was away, Jardine raised his hand with his index and middle finger in the air and mouthed, "Dos cervezas, por favor," to the waitress.

Paco returned and raised an eyebrow at Jardine.

"For my cover story. It's always a give-away when the undercover agent doesn't drink."

A moment later, two more beers arrived and a cup of coffee that Paco had previously ordered.

Paco spoke to the waitress. "Mira, Vanessa te presento mi amigo. Bond, James Bond. He's a birdwatcher, a Caribbean bird expert, in fact."

"Mucho gusto, soy Vanessa Ospina," the woman smiled to reveal ivory white teeth contrasting against her skin.

"Igualmente, Vanessa. What a lovely spot you work in, shame about the customers." Jardine winked at her and motioned with his mouth towards Paco with a smile. The old Jardine wouldn't have been so comfortable in such a situation, but the new-found confidence and ease with words was something that he put down to the rewiring of his brain following the ayahuasca.

"Yes, I know, but what can I do?" she said in Spanish looking at Paco with a loving smirk, before turning and walking away.

"So those two beers are just for you?" Paco asked, motioning to the two bottles.

"Do you want one?" said Jardine sliding the beer forward on the table.

"Oh no, no señor." Paco slid the bottle back towards Jardine. "I only drink tinto on the job or mango juice. Occasionally I will have a beer in the evening or on a day off, like yesterday for example."

Jardine thought about saying something but wanted to get down to business. "So, Paco, who are these Israelis you mentioned?' Jardine asked in a hushed tone.

"Not all Israelis per se, just one guy. Uri Yakov, a former Israeli soldier who owns Casa Jacobo. He runs it as a sex-hotel for amor-filled packaged tours to young just-out-of-the-service soldiers, fresh from their two-year mandatory service. His head of security is Nelson Valencia, former paramilitary leader. Not a man you'd want to meet in a dark callejón. If we go to La Brisa tonight, we'll see him for sure."

"La Brisa?"

"The bar up on the hill there." Paco motioned behind him. "It's the club everyone ends up at in Taganga."

"I thought it was La Vista?"

"It was. It's changed hands now. Yakov owns it."

Jardine nodded. "Sounds like it's a date then. Any chance this Yakov character has links to Mossad?" asked Jardine, fishing for new story ideas.

Paco lit a cigarette, took a drag and shook his head vigorously as he exhaled. "Not a chance. He's just a man looking to make money from the exploitation of our women. Pure and simple. Besides, if he were Mossad, they would need to declare it to us."

"Not sure Mossad likes to play by anyone's rules. He runs the business all by himself? I mean, with this Valencia guy as the muscle, of course." The words flew out of Jardine naturally, like he'd taken over the persona of a character in an espionage thriller.

Vanessa, the waitress, passed by their table again. Paco leant forward and touched her arm lightly. "Oye, Vanessa. What do you know about Madam Lagos? The tone of his voice had lost its playfulness from speaking her earlier. "We know she is occasionally around these parts."

Vanessa bit her lower lip. "Yes, she is, but... I don't want problems. She..." Vanessa looked left and then right and leaned in closer to the both of them. "Her name is Heidy Lagos. She's the madam for a popular brothel in Cartagena." She looked at Jardine as if filling him in on the context. "She's often around here, scouting new talent coming in from Santa Marta." She leaned back and smiled as if having a normal conversation with two customers.

Jardine reached for his phone to type out some notes.

"No!" said Vanessa in a frustrated whisper. "Wait till I leave, por favor. I've seen her in town many times. Once she was with Almirante Osorio."

"Almirante, as in a navy man?" asked Jardine.

"Yes, there are often naval ships docked in Santa Marta, they come to Taganga to party and rest."

"And how do you know he's an Almirante?" asked Paco.

"He told me. It's how he asks for food. He always says, 'una cerveza para el almirante'. He likes to talk about himself in the third person. Like he's a character in a telenovela. They also say…" her voice trailed off. "I shouldn't be telling you this… she turned to walk back to the kitchen.

Paco touched her arm lightly. "Please, Vanessa. You would be helping your country."

She crossed her arms, pouted and her eyebrows dipped in the middle, it seemed steam was gushing out of her ears. After a few seconds, she spoke: "They say Admiral Osorio is a sex fiend who tattoos the names of his sexual conquests on his body."

The two men leaned back with eyebrows raised, like elderly women who had just heard shocking yet juicy gossip. Vanessa sped off, carrying an arm full of dishes back to the kitchen.

Jardine mentally added the names to his list knowing full well they could be used as potential sources — no, characters — in his story. His mind ticked away with possible narratives that could weave the characters together as he felt the grey matter of his neural passageways unfolding and connecting.

The madam could be providing the terrorists with women...
surely they'd needed some stimulation before they blow
themselves up and reach paradise...? It would be plausible.
Brady had mentioned something similar. So, there would be a
kernel of truth to wrap it around. Paco had mentioned that
Yakov wasn't Mossad. Well, I'm the writer here and I have
creative licence. So, Yakov will become an undercover
Mossad agent monitoring the group. The Admiral? Now that
would be trickier. What would it take for him to be involved?
Perhaps he was caught in the brothel and then blackmailed to
work with fundamental Islamist terrorists? Compromise was
always a willing motivator for any man, especially a deco-
rated naval officer with, presumably, a family. Or perhaps that
was all too much. Sometimes the truth in Colombia is so
outlandish, that fiction is more believable.

Vanessa returned and whispered to Paco and Jardine.
"Oye chicos. You won't believe this, but there she is. Getting
out of the 4X4, across the road."

Paco and Jardine turned their heads slowly towards the
road. Underneath the shade of the mango trees lining the
street was a shiny black SUV with tinted windows. A tall
curvaceous woman stepped out, most of her face hidden
behind a large pair of Gucci sunglasses. She wore tight white
pants and a pale pink top with a short white jacket. Crossing
the street, she entered a small corner store, placed her hands
on the counter then pointed to something high on the shelf.
At the same time, she placed a medium sized sand-coloured
envelope on the counter. A group of older men sitting at the
table followed her movements into the store as if she were the
blue fluorescent light of a bug zapper, and they the hapless
flying beetles drawn in.

"She's the madam of a brothel?" asked Jardine incredulously. He always assumed they were older and more
matronly looking.

"Not what you were thinking?" replied Paco. "I had the

same reaction."

"I wouldn't say I'm an expert in brothel-owning madams, but I can't say I've ever seen one quite like her," said Jardine, turning now to Paco with eyebrows raised.

"She's an ex-Miss Cartagena, you know? Just missed out on being Miss Colombia 2005, in fact. Some say she never got over it," added Vanessa.

Two younger men sitting at a table outside the store stood up from their chairs and headed towards the entrance of the store. One entered and moved up alongside Madam Lagos. He gave the appearance of ordering the bill for their table. The other man waited outside, one leg bent casually leaning against the wall with one hand behind his back, while the other smoked a cigarette.

"They've got *sicario* written all over them," said Paco, glancing sideways towards Jardine. "If there's one type of Colombian I can identify it's the famous sicarios of Medellín." Both the men wore tight ripped jeans with small leather jackets and converse trainers. Their hair would not have been out of place on the album cover of an 80s metal band. This look was known throughout Colombia as the *sicario* look, the infamous hitman of Medellín who had worked for Pablo Escobar and his band of merry men.

Jardine took a swig on his beer and noticed the man in the store was leaving. Then his eyes moved to Madam Lagos, still waiting for the storekeeper but the envelope on the counter had gone. Madam Lagos was now on the phone. The man leaning against the wall pushed off with his leaning leg and followed behind his partner exiting the store. They both looked left and right in the trying-to-be-subtle-but-not-really way that suspicious looking characters often do, and sped off on a motorcycle.

Paco turned to Jardine. "A day in the life of a madam. Come, I have a place I want to show you. I think it will be of interest."

23

CASA JACOBO

THE TWO MEN CLIMBED INTO THE JEEP AND DROVE UPHILL AWAY from the beach along the dusty back streets of Taganga. After a few twists and turns, the usual gringo crowd thinned out and after passing two blocks of pastel coloured concrete huts with tin roofs, they arrived at a large concrete structure painted white with faux-Greek columns and a terracotta roof. A white concrete wall surrounded the building with broken glass and rolls of razor wire spread along the top to discourage any unwelcome visitors.

"Looks like they want to keep people out," said Jardine looking casually across the road from inside the jeep, his elbow resting on the open window.

"The opposite my friend. They want people to come in! But only if you pay the price." Paco continued to tell Jardine the story of Casa Jacobo. It had started as a hostel for everyday backpackers, travelling on the gringo trail in South America. It had become popular as a hangout for ex-Israeli soldiers after finishing their compulsory multi-year service and wanting a place to relax in the sun, smoke marijuana, snort coke, and bed as many women as they could. Taganga was a party town with laxed rules and so it was an ideal place for any such establishment to thrive. Eventually, the owner, Uri Yakov, realised he could cut out the dealers and pimps and began to charge an all-inclusive fee. After all, this was the Caribbean and all-inclusive resorts are not uncommon. Although unlike other all-inclusive resorts, this one included the additions of all-you-can-fuck and all-you-can-snort; a paradise of piña coladas, putas and pure cocaine. It was sex, drugs and reggaetón. In the late 2000s, business boomed and Yakov started to develop a small empire, buying up smaller cafes and bars in town, coffee plantations, shipping in women from different parts of Colombia and hiring ex-paramilitaries to run his security. Somewhere along the line, he became acquainted with Heidy Lagos, a former beauty queen and pre-pago, read: escort. And together, they became a small cartel controlling all illicit activities in Taganga and up the coast to Tayrona national park.

"He's really taken packaged holidays to the next level," said Jardine. "And it seems he knows his demographic."

Paco performed a U-turn at the end of the street and sped off down the hill again. They turned left onto another street, which went uphill again and then left into another street parallel to the compound. They were now a block away from the compound, but at a higher elevation. Paco pulled the jeep over next to a small corner store and ordered two glass bottles of coke, before he pulled out a pair of binoculars from the glovebox. From here, they could see slightly into the compound and could clearly see the street outside with a large green automatic garage door, which was the main entrance to the building. Jardine lifted the binoculars and observed the compound.

"Paco, surely this is too obvious…" said Jardine.

"Tranquilo. People around here don't ask questions or speak about what they've seen. *Sapos* don't last long in Colombia." Sapo — meaning toad — was the word for a snitch.

Jardine's instincts were telling him it wasn't a good idea to be out in daylight watching a cartel's compound, but then he didn't really give a fuck about what happened as long as it provided information for his reports.

"Is this the kind of information the British Intelligence is interested in?" Paco asked.

"Yes, very much so. Britain wants to do all it can to stop the spread of drug trafficking and exploitation of women in the world." Jardine took a sip of his coke before continuing. He realised he sounded like a cross between a dodgy used-car salesman and a Whitehall mandarin. Or perhaps the gap wasn't so big these days? "And it's the Yakov's and Madam Lagos' of the world we're interested in. Do you think Yakov will make an appearance?" Jardine asked, lowering the binoculars.

"Unlikely. He is rarely seen in public during the day. But, today's Saturday and like I said, it's likely he'll be at La Brisa later." As they talked, a black SUV with tinted windows sped along the street below and pulled up at the compound's military-green roller door. It stopped, and the driver beeped the horn twice in quick succession. Jardine noticed the Barranquilla number plates.

"Someone special? Lagos?" Asked Jardine.

"New clients more like it. They also offer an airport pick-up service," replied Paco.

Jardine, sensing something was about to happen, passed the binoculars to Paco and took out his long-lensed camera instead — a useful tool which fit his birdwatching purpose and also came in handy for non-avian related surveillance work. The SUV waited, idling in the empty street. As the roller door rose, two men with AK47s moved forward, almost into the street, and leant against the walls either side of the entrance, aiming straight out, as if they were expecting some action.

"More sicarios," said Paco. "One of our most famous exports, thanks to Señor Escobar Gaviria."

Jardine began to snap photos. A third man appeared in a khaki green shirt and cowboy boots and reached behind his back with one arm and placed something in the waistband of his jeans. Most likely a handgun. He motioned for the SUV to enter the compound. The SUV entered and stopped.

"That, mi amigo, is Nelson Valencia," said Paco, still looking through the binoculars. "Former paramilitary and now head of security for Yakov. It is also thought that he has links to the Oficina de Chiribito."

Jardine nodded and continued looking through the long lens of his camera while snapping photos of Valencia and the mysterious SUV. Valencia was short and stocky, like a small moustached barrel. He had a scar on his left cheek. He plodded towards the approaching vehicle as the passenger window lowered. Smiling and nodding, he reached into the vehicle giving the impression of shaking someone's hand. A document was produced. He analysed it for ten seconds before tapping the SUV's roof twice. It lurched forward into the compound as the roller doors began to close. The passenger door of the SUV opened just as the roller doors made its final descent. Jardine lowered the camera with a frustrated sigh. "Fuck," he said in an aggressive tone and then realised there was a young boy sitting on a stoop outside his passenger window. The boy smiled and giggled at him and then repeated his frustrated outburst. "Fuck!" Quietly at first, before repeating it again and then in quick succession, speeding it up and incorporating it into the tune of a famous salsa song. "Fuck, fuck, fuck, fuck, fuck-fuck." The boy continued his obscene, yet catchy tune as Paco turned towards Jardine.

"Valencia trained with the 'you-know-who' at the School of the Americas."

Jardine nodded, pretending to pay attention, but he

suddenly remembered Professor Villalobos's lectures and was sure he could incorporate 'School of the Americas' into a useful meme for the professor's class.

Paco continued. "He was part of Urrea's amnesty early in the 2000s, but like many others, he returned to a world of crime. What else would you do if you're trained to be a professional killer and it pays well?"

Jardine raised the camera again, but nothing was happening. The boy continued his expletive song but had moved inside the corner store. "What does he do for the Oficina de Chiribito? Surely not paperwork?"

"Security, contract killings, extortion. Whatever is needed. The Cartel leaders like to outsource their violence these days and keep a low profile. The days of Escobar — private zoos, jewel encrusted pistol handles, and gold-plated shitters are gone. Today's narcos live in a middle-class apartment, send their kids to private schools, drive a Prius and wear suits — Arturo Calle not Armani."

Jardine had read and written reports about many paramilitary leaders, and even interviewed low ranking members who had since left their former murderous occupations. He was always struck by the dark, uncanny charisma that many of them possessed. An indescribable feeling that on some level you could sit down and enjoy a beer with them, like them even, despite their numerous assassinations and drive-by killings.

"Yakov. Are you sure he'll be at La Brisa tonight?" Jardine asked.

"Let's hope so. It's one of his best hunting grounds, for clients that is. He's in charge of recruiting clients and Lagos the entertainment." Paco sighed, shaking his head. "Sometimes I don't even understand my own country. It's like one giant contradiction. Warm yet violent, caring but selfish, disorganised yet full of organised bureaucracy."

"I'll agree with on the bureaucracy side. If I even commit a crime in Britain, they'll need to contact the Colombian authorities for my fingerprints and all my other sensitive information. It's like you need to give your fingerprint just to buy a bag of crisps."

"Fingerprints are like signatures here," added Paco. "You can tell how much citizens of a country trust one another by the level of bureaucracy. And let's say that in Colombia, we have enough red tape to wrap around the world several times."

Paco started the jeep and they drove back along the mountain-hugging road leading out of Taganga. A minute out of town, on the outskirts of Taganga, they stopped at a hotel of small cliff-hugging bungalows overlooking the bay. They checked into two bungalows next to each other. Jardine thought about the day so far. He now had photo evidence, at least of Valencia and if he could snag a few snaps of Madam Lagos tonight, he would be able to put through a new report with photographic intelligence product. That ought to get the trail humming, he thought. Ambrose and London would have to believe him then. Although it would only buy him so much time, he would need something more concrete in the future. It's likely the response he would receive from London would be: interesting, if true, which basically meant find some more bloody intelligence product. In the meantime, however, he would need to get started before he left for the evening. He was dreading it, but it had to be done. He felt the resistance that many writers feel when they sit down to write a story, the nervous pang of failure and the all too common mantra: what if no-one likes my story?

24

INTELLIGENCE FALSO: PARTE 2

WHILE SHOWERING AND DRESSING, JARDINE WENT OVER WHAT HE had written in his head. Essentially, it was a nice simple story — a basic thesis or hypothesis. Two characters were involved in a much larger plot to establish a fundamental Islamist terrorist training camp in Colombia. It was the opposite of how he usually approached an intelligence report. It was more like writing a novel. He knew where he wanted to end up, now all he had to do was compile necessary information to meet the needs of his narrative. Fill in the characters with the necessary motives to reveal their agenda. It required an intricate weaving of fact and fiction to make it believable, wrapping the lies, like Garzón had suggested, in a kernel of truth. It was advantageous that in Colombia, the truth was usually stranger than fiction. Therefore, his lies, in some ways, would seem more credible than reporting the truth. It all seemed easy enough. However, inside of him, his stomach still churned out acid, which gave him the feeling he was committing a grave error, an error which continued to form a small seed in his throat. He supposed, or hoped at least, that the seed would eventually outgrow his throat and be forced out. Or he'd have to continuously swallow it for the rest of his life, because it was not that storytelling wasn't in his nature, it was that the past ten years of his life had pushed it out of him. He had become a calculating, human truth verifier, speaking with multiple sources and pinpointing the collaborative morsels of verity that rose to the surface. It was this part of him that needed to be killed off in order to set his story free, the inner ego dragging him to self-doubt to cease and desist. Just like the shaman had mentioned: part of you must die to change.

Besides, he was in the land of magical realism; the land where stories and journalism could be bound and sold as truth. After football and beauty pageants, it was practically the national pastime, although in reality with fewer yellow butterflies and raining flowers. It was an art that all the major Colombian TV channels were adept at. CRN and ParaCol leading the way on television. In print, El Heraldo Bogotáno and El Diario Colombiano. But the most voracious were the online media organisations. They were the true artistic tale-tellers. They spun more half-truths than a pathological bipolar spider.

Fully dressed now, he heard his phone beep with a WhatsApp message from Paco.

Meet same bar on the beach from this morning in an hour.

— FRANCISCO LEON

An hour? He still had enough time for another twenty minutes of writing. He picked up the remote and turned on the television. The Colombian news channel CRN was running with a photo of Presidente Soto from his university days. El Presidente had long, unruly hair and the beginnings of a scraggly beard. He was photographed next to Fidel Castro. The headline read:

'Presidente Soto, un comunista infiltrado'

The headline was a notion that Jardine recognised was false but wrapped in a kernel of truth. Jardine had read about the photo. In fact, he had even reported on it. Soto had met Castro, but so had other young presidential candidates, including the former right-wing president Urrea. Nevertheless, it was most likely having its necessary effect on the narrative of the peace talks. It confirmed biases and supported other half-truths. For example, that the former mayor of Bogotá and current presidential candidate was still an active member of left-wing guerrilla group M19 - a subtle form of mixing the truth with something false. It led him to think on which established truths were his lies resting? It was true that Heidy Lagos was running a brothel. It was also true that Yakov was helping her, most likely using his military experience and knowledge, and also providing a steady stream of ex-Israeli soldiers as customers. All facts. They had appeared in the Colombian media, had been mentioned briefly in some international news stories and were confirmed by worthy sources. It was also true that Lagos had connections with the brothel in Cartagena, which supplied women to the US President's secret service agents — the story Brady had told him. Maybe Lagos could also have such a connection? It had been reported in media around the world that there was a potential link between the women involved with the secret service agents and a mysterious sheik out of Qatar. What if Lagos was in fact working for the sheik who was after information from US officials while working clandestinely for an international terrorist organisation?

He poured himself another glass of dark rum and took a sip.

But how to explain the connection with Yakov? It would be unlikely the Qatari sheik would work willingly with an Israeli, unless... Jardine returned to his laptop and tapped furiously as the story flowed out of him like he had channelled Hemingway's advice to writers: "All you do is sit down at a typewriter and bleed." Or was that quote itself misattributed to the great writer? No time to fact check. At this stage, losing blood was the least of his worries.

After twenty minutes, Jardine stood up and slid his laptop back into a slim hard case. He placed it under the mattress. As he sauntered down the hill towards the beach, the reality of what he was doing once again flowed through him. The high energy adrenaline he had felt writing the report was slowly dissipating and he felt in two minds. Now I know how Veronica must feel when she's all fire and fury one day and sweet and cuddly the next. It was a strange kind of cognitive dissonance that he felt; a type of bipolarity between the two versions of himself. But, at least he felt alive.

25

LA BRISA

AS HE APPROACHED THE BEACH HE COULDN'T SEE PACO, SO HE sat on a wooden deck chair in a small restaurant immediately down the hill from La Brisa. A waitress strode over to him with long brown legs and light brown eyes. She giggled as if the sight of a foreigner still amused her. Despite there being a reasonable number of tourists, Colombia still hadn't become victim to the cynical and exhausted cycle of mass tourism that plagued other countries in the Caribbean. The waitress went to hand him the menu, but Jardine already knew what he wanted. "Una mojarra frita con patacones y papas francesas, un jugo de lulo con hielo y una águila bien fría, por favor." *Fried fish with patacon and french fries, a lulo juice and very cold beer, please.*

The waitress, calm as a meditating yogi, smiled and nodded her approval as she wrote down the order. "You speak Spanish very well," she said. "I knew you weren't going to be one of the other gringos that come here and only know una cerveza por favor."

"You mean, I don't blend in?" asked Jardine, a look of feigned shock on his face.

Her eyes looked up from the notepad. "Your accent says

Bogotá, but I'm afraid your face says gringuito," she said teasingly with a smile. "But I can tell you're different, you know. Usually we get a lot of people coming here only to drink, do drugs and well, visit certain establishments. Although it's worse in Cartagena. Have you been there?"

Jardine decided to avoid the question about Cartagena, he was more interested in human observations. "How could you tell I was different?"

"I don't know. I guess after years of observing people all day you become accustomed to that sort of thing." She turned with a smile and a wink and returned to the kitchen.

Jardine ate his meal and gazed curiously at the mix of people walking along the promenade. He mulled over his objectives for tonight. He would need more photos or a short video, something that would liven up the story and give him more credibility. It would show he's on the ground, capturing the real thing, not the usual dross he would report on stuck behind a desk in Bogotá.

A little white later, Paco arrived, and they both drank mango juice — at Paco's insistence — before strolling up the hill to La Brisa. Swirls of purple and orange drifted across the sky as they sat on a wicker cane sofa angled slightly towards the entrance and the sunset view over Taganga, the bay and the hills surrounding it. A riff raff of backpackers, locals, out-of-town Colombians and local business owners began to trickle in. Jardine ordered a bottle of Ron Viejo de Caldas, which sat in a bucket of ice with a glass full of freshly cut lime next to it. It was always good to be able to offer a glass of rum, one never knew when it might come in handy as truth serum. They had forgotten to deliver the soda and so Paco stood up and jogged to the bar. A man passed by Jardine, not recognising him. After a few moments, Jardine stood up, walked over to him and tapped him on the shoulder.

"Hi," said Jardine. The journalist nearly spat his rum back into the glass. Jardine went on with one eyebrow raised.

"What a pleasant surprise! I thought you were headed for San Agustin to cover the demobilisation process?"

"Err, yes, I was there for a week. Got everything I needed and well, you always hear Colombia has beautiful beaches." The journalist shuffled awkwardly on his feet. Jardine realised he never did speak to him when they met at El Villano in Bogotá.

Paco pulled up alongside them. "Who's your friend, Papi?" Paco's mode had changed, and it seemed all it took was the weekend to arrive before he slipped into a more relaxed vibe. He had somehow obtained a Hawaiian lei around his neck in the last thirty seconds.

"A journalist friend — VizFeed, right?"

"That right, we're activists as well as journalists at VizFeed."

"A journalist? Vea pues! Speaking of journalism. I'm getting some good intel from those girls over there," Paco said in English, pointing towards a wicker cane sofa further out on the terrace. "They gave me this flower necklace. Will report back soon. Oh and I know what you're thinking, *hermano*. I said I don't drink on the job, well," Paco glanced down at his watch. "It's now past 6 o'clock and besides, it's a Friday night!" And with that he swivelled and scampered back to the girls on the sofa.

"Need a top up?" Jardine asked the journalist, motioning to the bottle of rum. "Take a seat. How was your trip to Cauca?"

"Actually, I'm sitting with someone. You're welcome to join us?" the journalist offered.

Jardine glanced across at Paco. He was sitting on the edge of a sofa, his hands dancing in the air telling an animated story. Two blonde girls — Swedish, Jardine guessed — were sitting watching, their bright blue eyes wide open with a mix of amazement and amusement. "Sure. Let me bring the rum." Jardine picked up the silver bucket and walked with the journalist to his table. Jardine placed the drinks on the table and sat down next to the journalist. "And your friend?"

"He must be in the bathroom," replied the journalist. "Said he had a case of the sniffles. Poor guy! He kept inhaling abruptly through his nostrils and sniffling like he had pneumonia. Said he was on cold and flu medication. His glasses were glassy, and he kept fidgeting in his seat like he couldn't get comfortable."

"Twitchy?" asked Jardine.

"Yes! Couldn't keep still."

Jardine nodded and made the appropriate sounds, although he could think of another reason for the man's 'sickness'.

"He couldn't stop fidgeting and he has this peculiar grinding motion with his jaw. Like he's chewing a non-existent piece of gum." The journalist shook his head with worry. "So anyway, I haven't introduced myself. I'm Louis Munro," he said, pushing his glasses up the bridge of his nose. His previously neatly parted hair was now slightly ruffled.

"Jardine, nice to put a name to the face." Jardine put the man at about twenty-five, intelligent but naive, and with an emotionless face that made it hard to know what he was thinking.

"So, what do you do?" Munro asked as he lifted a glass of rum to his lips.

"Third Secretary at the British Embassy." Jardine had met the journalist in Bogotá and so couldn't fly with his bird-watching cover. He didn't know what Garzón and the others had told him.

Munro's eyebrows raised and a curious smile spread across his face. "Sounds fascinating. What kind of work does your position entail?"

"Jack-of-all-trades, really. Education programmes, business opportunities, political reports, whatever is needed to keep her Majesty's Government content."

Munro, who before seemed disinterested, awkward even at Jardine's presence, was now piqued. "So, what can you tell me about the peace process in Colombia?" The young journalist's demeanour had changed, like he was a projecting a more professional alter ego.

"What do you want to know? There's not much that you probably don't already know, I'm afraid. Most of what we get is from local media reports and the odd interview with the delegates. Didn't you find anything on your Cauca trip? People on the ground there would have a better indication than most."

"Ha! It turned out my interpreter didn't really speak English and so I only got dribs and drabs of information down there." The words 'dribs and drabs' grated on Jardine's ears in an American accent. Munro continued. "I wish I'd paid more attention in Spanish class in high school. Also, I realised I don't know if the guy was actually telling me the truth or just making the stuff up. I mean what he was telling me didn't match with what I already knew. He told me the FARC were involved in drug trafficking and well, maybe they dabbled in that, but their real cause was to bring about a fairer and more just Colombia. Their representation of women and their positions within the organisation are really very encouraging."

"You mean it didn't fit your narrative?" offered Jardine cheekily.

The journalist screwed up his face. "I was searching for the truth."

"How do you know what he was telling you wasn't the truth?"

"I hadn't heard it before. It didn't seem to make sense."

"Didn't make sense to you? Or in general?"

"To me. I have tight deadlines and need to churn something out pronto. And besides, I know what angle our readers will want. We all have to adapt to our audience, don't we?"

"I see," said Jardine, taking a sip of rum. "I agree with you on one thing. It definitely helps to know the lingo."

"You're telling me," Munro sighed. "I might end up leaving here without a story. Maybe I'll have to piece together some type of listicle instead: 'Top ten undiscovered bars in Colombia'? 'Five things no-one tells you about a country scarred by conflict'? That could work, right? Whatever keeps the editors happy."

"How about, 'This former country of conflict holds a nasty surprise'?" Jardine offered.

"I like that. That nasty surprise thing will really hook people in." The journalist scribbled onto his notepad. "People really can't resist clicking on something like that."

"I might have a story for you," said Jardine.

"Thanks, but I fly out tomorrow. I don't have time to investigate any further. Besides, this local journalist, my friend, he said he'd help me out."

"I mean if you don't want it I can always pass it on to a stringer from The Post or the Times, there are one or two of those in Bogotá…"

"No! Not the fucking Post or the Times! They're old-school neo-con propaganda!" His voice took on a seething rasp it hadn't previously had. The journalist's eyes widened as if realising something. He took a deep breath and said calmly, "I'll gladly hear your story."

Munro pulled out a moleskin notepad and tilted his head downwards while he scribbled notes. Before Jardine could begin, the journalist interrupted. "Wait, you don't know any neo-conservative capitalist, Trump-like figures, do you? Anyone who owns land, or lots of money or who has made homophobic or racist comments recently and is becoming popular? Maybe I could write a feature piece about that and then compare it to the US situation? Really, whatever you can give me, I need clicks!"

"Well there's plenty of those, although perhaps if you wait until the election next year—"

Munro interrupted again. "Or is there a politician who generally makes uneducated comments against the down-trodden?" Jardine opened his mouth, then shut it again and nodded.

"Well, not exactly one guy, more like a group. But try former president Urrea. He'll be right up your alley," Jardine replied. Munro continued scribbling in his notepad. After a few moments, without a reply, he stopped scribbling and raised his head. He saw Jardine looking over towards the edge of the terrace overlooking the sea. A voluptuous woman, he guessed in her forties, stood next to a large muscular man. They didn't seem like a couple, but clearly knew each other. Jardine recognised the woman from earlier in the day and the man seemed to fit his mental image of the paramilitary leader he had viewed through his camera lens earlier in the day.

Jardine turned to the journalist. "What about if I gave you a lead on a prostitution ring? Also, what if that prostitution ring had a connection to a potential espionage sting on the US president's secret service while stationed in Cartagena."

"The current president?"

"No, the previous one."

"Oh…" said Munro unable to hide his disappointment.

"What if it had potential links to a rich sheik out of Qatar?"

Munro's eyes lit up like he was a cartoon character opening a chest of gold. Realising the unprofessional look on his face, he cleared his face of emotion and sat back in his chair, adopted a serious air and took a gulp of rum, as if contemplating this new information. After a few seconds, he placed the glass of rum on the table and leaned forward.

"Oh, do tell!"

26

LA BRISA TRAE MENTIRAS

"So, you're saying she provides prostitutes to half of Colombia's Congress?" Munro shook his head in disbelief.

"Exactly. And a lot of navy and military men as well."

"Hmmm, it would make for a great story, but I'm afraid I need more juice." Munro leaned in now, as if the closer he got, the more information he could absorb.

The narrative was flowing, and Jardine felt confident. At least the narrative he was spilling now was the truth. "Well, that's her over there." Jardine motioned indiscreetly to the edge of the terrace with his eyes and head. "She provided prostitutes to the DEA and the former US president's secret service agents while they were here for the Sixth Summit of the Americas," said Jardine his eyebrows raised.

"That *is* a juicy story," said Munro nodding and smiling with a wink.

Jardine began to recount the story — half true, half fictional tale based on a true story. Just like a movie announcement: *these details will be dramatised for fictional purposes* as he recounted the saga of the US secret service agents in Cartagena in 2012. As Brady had told him, he mentioned that the men decided to pay a visit to a well-

known brothel in Cartagena. This he described as not necessarily a sin for a secret service agent alone in a foreign country, especially in an environment where carnal lust competed
with tropical humidity for air space. But it was most definitely a governmental sin. And in terms of security protocols,
it was as bad as a medieval blasphemy. Then he mentioned
the rumour of the connected sheik out of Qatar who may or
may not have been involved in funding international
terrorism networks. Next he added that it was not only the
secret service men, but the DEA were involved too. Jardine
then made the joke that all the US Government needed was
the CIA to visit Señora Lagos's establishment and the lucky
lady might have been able to apply for a lucrative government tender providing entertainment services to all US
government employees in Colombia.

As he finished his story, a slightly balding chubby man
wearing a leopard print shirt and rose-tinted round glasses
made eye contact with Jardine, and without being invited
approached the two men.

"Here you are! Thought you might have fallen down the
toilet," Munro said. "This is my friend. Feeling better?'

"Very much better. I went to the pharmacy for cold meds."

Jardine could think of a different type of 'meds' he was
acquiring.

"How are you? I'm Jaco." The man with the leopard print
shirt extended his hand and let out a sniffle. "First time in
Colombia?" Jaco asked Jardine. "I'm a regular around these
parts, been here three years. Although based primarily in
Medellín." Jardine recognised the accent as North American,
but with a hint of something else, a Slavic inflection?

The man poured himself a drink from the rum bottle and
then sloshed his hand in the ice bucket searching for a large
ice cube. After a few seconds of trying, he motioned for a
waiter. "Er, disculpe otra bebida por favor, oh, y bien frio."
The man spoke Spanish with a strong American accent. The

man turned to Jardine, in English now, "Did you want something as well? I can order for you if you like?"

"I'm fine with the rum," said Jardine in Spanish to the waiter. The waiter nodded and turned towards the bar.

"Jardine here is the Third Secretary at the Embassy," said Munro.

"In Bogotá? I'm based in Medellín myself. My partner and I have a business based there."

"What type of business are you in?" Jardine asked.

"Online business."

Jardine nodded to show he was listening.

The man's voice suddenly changed from casual to infomercial, without being invited. "We help maximise business-to-business sales funnel leads for small-to-medium niche online corporate coaching enterprises."

"Sounds complicated," said Jardine with a hint of irony in his voice.

The man didn't seem to notice and continued. "It's the way of the future. Got to have your niche and it's all about your persona. Your online brand is EVERYTHING these days. I'm part of a like-minded network. We motivate and coach each other to be the best person we can be."

"Good to have support, I guess. How do you two know each other?" Jardine asked.

"I posted in an expat Facebook group that I needed a fixer in Colombia and Jaco here responded," said Munro smiling. "Plus, he's got a background in journalism and so knows how we work."

Jaco nodded proudly.

"If you'll excuse me, I'm going to have a quick chat to someone." Munro stood up and walk towards the man and the woman on the balcony.

"Careful. Journalists don't usually have a great life expectancy in Colombia," said Jardine as Munro strode off.

Munro crossed the terrace and casually began to speak

with the woman Jardine had recognised earlier — Heidy Lagos.

Jardine continued to speak with Jaco for the next half an hour, listening patiently and nodding his understanding at the right times, all the while carefully watching Munro speaking with Madam Lagos. Jaco talked about how his network of people would support each other by commenting on and liking each other's social media posts to provide an illusion of interaction and interest in their videos, articles and posts. "You see, nowadays, it's all about authority. It doesn't matter if you know much about a topic. Everyone can be an expert, all you need is time and an audience. First, you need to pick a niche, then you simply read some books about it, you know, get an understanding. Then you paraphrase that and start to post videos and articles online. Anything that shows you know something about your chosen niche. That's when you need to be developing your online products. They could be courses, eBooks, factsheets, or motivational videos. Everyone is doing video."

Even British Intelligence, thought Jardine.

Jaco continued. "Now the only problem is that all of this can get lost in the noise of the online world. So that's when my network comes in with their comments and likes. It instantly looks like others are interested in your material. It helps with the tech company's algorithms. If you can crack those, it's a snowball effect. The more people like it and interact with it, the more it will be pushed to the top."

Jardine had not really been paying much attention, but on hearing this last part, his ears pricked up. "But the people who interact with it, they're not genuine, are they? Bots, I imagine?"

"Oh, of course not! They're genuine, real people. They want me to succeed, they're my network. I'm genuine as well. I want to help people, it's just hard to get traction, so we help each other out. It's not like I'm saying anything negative or wrong... occasionally you need to stretch the truth a bit."

"How so?" Jardine asked.

"For example, if I explain that I'm a middle-class, university-educated man from Chicago—"

"You're from Chicago?"

"For example... anyway, it doesn't exactly inspire people the way Connor McGregor inspires people, does it? You know, someone that's overcome difficulty and risen to the top of their game."

Jardine wasn't sure he understood the connection but responded anyway. "No, it doesn't. What if you've never done anything noteworthy in your life?"

"It doesn't matter! In that case, all you have to do is invent a little bit of a challenge you've had in your life. Something like you were addicted to drugs, but you overcame it. Or, you were three hundred pounds, but now you're two hundred. Something that inspires a willingness to change in people."

Jardine was intrigued. "How is this connected to your business?"

"That's your personal brand. It gives you street-cred, well, online-cred, I guess. People want a story, they don't want a product or service thrown at them. They're more likely to listen that way. And you know us humans, we love a good redemption story."

"That's true," commented Jardine. *What would my redemption story pan out like*? he thought. He was tiring of the man and so excused himself, going to the bathroom. To get there, he took a steep staircase descending behind the sofa where Jaco sat. He stepped down slowly, guiding his hand on the rail and entered the bathroom, contemplating Jaco's story. Two men, animated in conversation, followed him in. Jardine deducted one was Israeli and the other American. The American was telling the other a story of catching a huge marlin on a fishing charter the day before. However, it had split the line as it propelled out of the water. The classic 'one that got away' story, Jardine thought. Seems like we're all used to telling stories. Finishing his business, he began to ascend the staircase when he heard Jaco talking to Munro. He'd obviously returned from his chat with Madam Lagos. Jardine stopped halfway up the staircase to eavesdrop on their conversation.

"Are you still in touch with that online media company in Macedonia?" Munro asked. "The one that that dabbles in…" Munro paused, searching for the right words.

"The one that dabbles in online news services?" Jaco offered. Jardine couldn't see his face, but he imagined Jaco leaning in with a sinister smile spread across his face, like the Grinch that stole Christmas.

"Yes, that's it. You told me about it on the flight here. How does it work?" Munro asked.

Jardine glanced up and saw Jaco sip his rum. "They can write an article about whatever topic you need — a smear campaign against an enemy, a promotion piece for a product or blog post, they can even start a grassroots social media stunt for you. They've been doing quite a few of those. Identity politics is big these days, it drives a lot of traffic online. Not that long ago, they set up pro-white supremacy Facebook group and organised a march through a town somewhere in the US. Then they organised an anti-racism Facebook group and mentioned the white supremacy march. The two groups met, converged and mob mentality took care of the rest. Pure tribal warfare." Jaco let out a slow, deliberate laugh.

"Oh no, I don't want anything that drastic," Munro said, sounding genuinely concerned. "Something milder. A subtle article here and there. Can they do that?" asked Munro.

"Yes, I believe they can. What's it for?" Jaco asked.

"I might need them to dig me out of a hole. I may need some creative minds to come up with something more clickable. A subtle string of articles, professionally written, all truthful, nothing false or misleading. Spread out over a few weeks. As long as it gets clicks."

"Can be done, *my friend*. They can even play into whatever demographic you would like to see."

Jardine always thought it wise to be wary of people you don't know very well referring to you as friend.

"Great, I'll send you the details tomorrow morning. Where's our new friend?" Jaco looked down the stairs and made eye contact with Jardine. Jardine's blood froze cold, like he'd submerged into an ice-bath. But he remained calm and collected and continued climbing the stairs with confidence, like he had been in motion the whole time.

"How was your chat with the woman over there? Jardine asked Munro as he sat down.

"Oh, very productive. I think I have a few angles I can work on. How's this for a title: 'It's a Caribbean paradise, but it comes with a dark underbelly'. That's my headline. Well, that is, as long as the sub approves it." Munro looked pleased with himself and poured his fourth glass of rum.

"I was just giving him journalistic advice, what angles he should take and whatnot," offered Jaco.

"I like it. It intrigues the reader, piques their curiosity with an allure of forbidden knowledge. That will target a more sophisticated audience."

"Yes, that's what I was going for," said Munro proudly.

The three men continued drinking and were joined by a man with a Cuban accent who seemed to be well acquainted with Jaco. He was jovial at first, but Jardine heard Jaco mutter something to him in what sounded like Russian. The Cuban man's eyes fixed on Jardine before letting out a sly smile. Jardine couldn't put his finger on it, but something about the three of them rubbed him up the wrong way. There was something sinister about Jaco, like he was hiding something dark. Not dangerous, but definitely not to be trusted. After another ten minutes, Jardine made his excuses and left.

"Well gentlemen, it was nice to chat, but I had better rescue my friend over there." He motioned to Paco still talking with the two Swedish girls. The men shook hands and Jardine departed. Jardine wandered over to Paco and they continued to drink the night away, the rum flowed like wine at the last supper. Later both he and Paco would argue that the drinking was all part of the necessary cover, a need to blend in with the partying backpacker crowd. If he went home early, it would be too suspicious, he reasoned. And besides, Paco had introduced him to some very interesting people. All potential characters to be used in his story. There was Don Ernesto, a sugar baron from Sincelejo; the Ortega brothers, cattle ranchers from Valledupar; and Doña Margarita, a hotelier from Cartagena, scouting out new places on the nascent Colombian tourist trail. All could play a part in his quickly progressing tale, Jardine thought. Despite the fermented sugary rum coursing through his blood stream, it was at times like this in a drunken haze that he would think of Veronica. What was she doing now? Was she in bed, her nose buried in a book? Or at a work dinner schmoozing with the partners of the firm? I have to stay in Colombia, he thought. At least until Vero and I can work out a plan together.

The night progressed and at two a.m., a bartender aggressively rang a giant rusty bell hanging over the bar to signify last drinks. In an effort to begin to sober up, Jardine stumbled to the bar and ordered a glass of water with lime. He leaned on the driftwood bar, swaying like a three-legged dog when he heard the voice of a woman in his ear.

"Hola chico," said the voice in a costeño accent.

"Hola," Jardine replied elongating the 'a' on the end. He swivelled his head slowly like a clown at a fairground. "Eres tú!" he slurred. *It's you!*

"Si, soy yo," came the reply with a giggle as Madam Lagos motioned to the bartender for two more drinks. *Yes, it's me.*

"I mean, I saw you before speaking with that other man," Jardine motioned sloppily to Munro sitting on the sofa.

"I thought he was interested in some of the services that I offer, but I don't think he was interested. Also, he seemed like a journalist. I *hate* journalists."

"Oh really?"

"Unless of course they wish to talk about my past as a beauty queen that is. What about you?" Lagos scanned his body like a sculptor examining the final masterpiece for defects.

"Me? I'm not a journalist," Jardine replied.

Madam Lagos smiled and then launched into the usual barrage of questions she would demand of potential clients. How long in Colombia? What do you do? It was part of a process known in Colombia as 'según marrano'— *according to the piggybank* — sizing up a potential customer to see how much they might be willing to spend.

"Quiet night for me. I'm going diving tomorrow. With those two guys." He pointed to the Israeli and the American he'd heard earlier in the evening." It was a hastily made-up story, but it seemed to work.

Lagos nodded. "Ah, the tall one was my customer a week ago in Cartagena. Of course, I'm sure he's been telling everyone I run a fishing charter." So, the fishing story he overheard from the American in the bathroom was a lie, Jardine thought. Very deceptive. Two drinks arrived and she handed one to Jardine. "So, are you interested?"

"Interested in what?" Jardine feigned ignorance.

"Interested in my services?" She moved her eyes over her shoulder suggestively towards two women sitting at a small table. "A companion for the night? I have a large selection."

"Afraid not, I've got a special someone at home. I'm loyal, like a dog." Jardine instantly regretted his choice of words. Dog in Spanish – *perro* – meant he liked to sleep around.

Lagos giggled again. "If you need me or my services, I'll

be on the terrace until they kicked us out. And here's my number." She handed him a business card with the initials HL.

"Gracias, muy bonita la tarjeta," Jardine replied with a slur. *Thanks, very beautiful card.*

As Lagos left, Paco pulled up alongside him. "I'm escorting these ladies back to their hostel. You okay to get home?"

"Sure. I'm going to have a chat with that tall American over there and then home. Meet you tomorrow for lunch?"

"Sure, man. Chao!" Paco gave the thumbs-up sign. His linen shirt was now unbuttoned and the lei, previously around his neck, was now wrapped around his head. His transformation from straight-and-narrow military man to seductive Latino lover had unfolded within the space of an evening.

Jardine steadied himself and pushed off the bar towards the tall American with the story of the fish that got away.

27

ROJAS

JARDINE SAT UP IN BED SLOWLY HEARING A HEAVY RINGING IN HIS ears. Maybe the Cuban man from last night followed me home and blasted me with an invisible sonic boom ray, he thought. Or it might have just been the rum and its rough cousin – aguardiente. Colombians always tried to convince him that the firewater they drank didn't give you a hangover. After the eighth shot it didn't seem to matter too much.

He pulled the soft cotton bed sheet back in a swift motion and stumbled a few steps across the polished bamboo floorboards to the oak writing desk. He opened the plantation shutters above the desk to reveal the Caribbean Sea, laid out before him like a Mongolian steppe of glistening blue. A small flotilla of fishing boats bobbed away in the bay. The beach itself looked quiet, with only a few people walking along the promenade. He sat down, scratched the back of his head, yawned and checked his phone. He had a message from Professor Villalobos. It read:

CALL ME! Something has happened

— PROFESSOR V.

It's unlike the professor to be so direct. His messages usually contain more formalities than a P.G. Wodehouse character. He was about to call the professor when he saw another message from an unknown number with the prefix (888) – a US number.

Yo man, here are those photos. You wouldn't shut your pie hole about 'em. Nice to meet you, bro! Enjoy the rest of your trip! Peace out.

— +1 (888) 777 5792

Photos? He flicked over to his Photos app. To Jardine's relief, he saw the photos were not of him, but of Madam Lagos in a bikini on a yacht off the coast of Cartagena. He must have convinced her client – the tall American – to send them. He saved them in an encrypted password protected folder and called Professor Villalobos. It rang only once before the professor answered. "Señor Jardine! Thank you for responding. Are we safe to talk?"

"Quite safe, Professor."

"One of my colleagues has been murdered! Professor Rojas!"

Jardine gulped, his throat began to throb. The professor continued. "The police are saying it's a normal robbery. But, they don't take his watch. It was a Rolex, carajo! I mean, he was a guerrilla sympathiser and a Marxist, but even he needed to know the time, no? The watch was bought during a trip he made to Europe to a Socialist conference – bought in Switzerland. It would have been worth a few years of minimum wages in Colombia. No tiene sentido! *It doesn't make sense.*"

"Could it be politically motivated? Seems like many on the left will be under threat now that the FARC have laid down their rifles."

"That is my thesis. It is most definitely the work of the Paras or the BACRIMS. Terrible, just terrible…" The professor's voice trailed off.

"My condolences, Professor," Jardine said, trying to add as much sympathy in his voice as he could. The rum and aguardiente still seeped through his cerebral matter making his thoughts sluggish. The only sound, coming from somewhere in the dark reaches of his mind, was a voice asking, *what the fuck is going on here*? He glanced at his computer screen and saw a number of flashing icons shouting for attention from the Service's encrypted messaging system. He returned his attention to the professor. "Look Professor, it might be best if you lay low for a while. You know, stay at home if you can? Or at least change up your routine. Just like you always told me you did during Escobar's reign."

"No, Jardine. You don't understand. I fear they will somehow come for me. Requisaron mi oficina, papeles por todos lados. Hay que esconderme por un rato. ¿Reino unido seria una opción para ir?" *They searched my office, paper everywhere. I need to hide somewhere for a while. Is the UK an option for me?*

Villalobos's office had been searched? *There's no way we can offer him a safe haven in the UK*, thought Jardine. *He's not a valuable enough source. Sure, he gives us some good intelligence about the peace process and keep us abreast of the political situation, but, he's no Gordievsky.* "Professor, stay calm. Is there somewhere else you can stay until this blows over? This type of thing usually calms down. It's seems like they were only after Rojas anyway. Otherwise, you'd be…" Jardine didn't finish his sentence.

"I'd be what…? Ay dios mío!" The professor began to sob.

Jardine felt like crying too. It seemed his new-found confidence and charisma had been eliminated in his post-alcohol depressive state. The realisation of the situation slowly swept over him. His make-believe story was already having an effect on other people, the love of his life might be lost, an innocent man had been killed, and now, he'd made an elderly professor cry like a baby! He glanced out the window to the hills leading down to the bay. Something in Jardine stirred... it wasn't plant-based or external, it was coming from within him this time. A surge of energy and confidence swept over him. "Professor!" he said with authority. "Is there somewhere you can stay?"

The professor blew his nose. "Si, I have a sister in Tampa. I can stay with her. It's almost the end of the semester anyway. Mendez can take over while I'm gone."

"Good. Stay with your sister and this will blow over. I'll follow it up and assess the problem." Jardine felt a small sense of relief, like when you pass a person you vaguely know in the street and pretend not to notice them, and to your relief, they do the same. "I need to hang up, Professor. It's probably a good idea we aren't in contact anymore. Good luck." The line went dead.

Jardine exhaled heavily and looked out over the bay in front of him. He thought of Veronica and her wavy chestnut hair and deep brown eyes, her quick smile of perfect white teeth, and her soft caresses in the morning. In a decisive action, he opened his laptop and called Bogotá through encrypted video calling software. After a few seconds, a video screen appeared.

"Hello, old boy!" Ambrose was his own chirpy self. "Got a few rums in last night, did you? Lunch on the beach I see, followed by what I can imagine was a quick dip, and then drinks and dinner at La Vista."

"It's called La Brisa now."

"Oh. I tell you what, you took the bloody long way home. Seems you couldn't walk in a straight line!"

"How the fuck did you... Oh, we have those new tracking chips in our phones." *Can't scratch your ass without getting followed these days*, Jardine thought.

"Quite a view you've got there. It's pissing down here in the big bad Bog."

"How d'you bloody know that? You can't see the view with the tracking chips. It doesn't cover video."

"The latest spyware we are using. It's called Instagram, man. You posted last night, err, well, this morning actually."

Jardine discreetly typed in his passcode on his phone lying on the desk and tapped the Instagram icon. He saw the latest post he had made – a moonlit shot of Taganga bay with the hashtag #mooooooooooon. *Fuck*, he thought, *don't remember doing that*...

"Anyway, Jardine. There's been a development. It seems they've gone and offed a professor at Los Andes or was it La Nacional? Anyway, the usual rigmarole – two men on a motorbike, dark visors, bloke on the back with a pistol, close range, two shots, and just like Nancy Sinatra said, they shot him down."

"So I heard. Seems he was my sub-source from the report," said Jardine, slumping back in his chair. He always slumped when telling a lie, he wasn't used to being able to stand tall and straight and lie, not yet anyway.

"Bloody hell! I hadn't gotten that far yet. How did you—?"

"I just spoke with Flaming Flamingo," Jardine interrupted.

"Why, that makes perfect sense!" said Ambrose, a hint of excitement in his voice. "The bloke seemed a little bit Bolshie, wore a beret and everything. El Espectador is going with: 'Unión Patriótica: Temporada Dos' and El Tiempo with: 'Profesor Marxista Asesinado En Robo.' Funny the two sides they give. One say it's a standard robbery the other a targeted political assassination. Either way, it's standard Tuesday sort of stuff here in Colombia. I was thinking just this morning, at least it wasn't a human rights activist. We've had e-bloody-nough of those this year!"

Realising Jardine would have a chance to potentially

enhance his narrative, he said, "It seems that's just a..." – he searched for the right word – "a smoke screen. What they want us to see. Fake news if you will, Ambrose. But you and I, Ambrose, being in the intelligence business, we know that it's not always as it seems."

"Yes, indeed, very true, very true. I remember they used to always think..." Ambrose trailed off into one of his old stories. Jardine had heard it before and knew when to apply appropriate utterances and comments and add sounds of feigned interest. Finally, Ambrose came to the end. "...and that's the same as this bloody case! At least, that's how it seems to me. Nevertheless, you'd better add this to your latest report."

"Already on to that. I have some new information to add. Things are moving on up here. This DNI bloke really has helped me get to ground quickly. Who said they were all mañana, mañana on the coast?"

"Bloody hell, that's quick! You've always been a good one for liquid amber diplomacy. Feed them liquor till they tell you. Make sure you're triple checking everything you hear."

"I'll send it through to you first to check. I know you like to print it out and read a physical copy."

"Yes, never have got used to this reading on a screen business in the digital age. Let's see if I can send it to the right printer this time," said Ambrose with a chuckle. "They've re-mapped them, and it seems that I accidentally sent the last report to the bloody office common room! Went in there and luckily that new intern, Jose, was there. He told me nothing had come out. Imagine my relief, when I heard that. What with the new security protocols we have and everything."

"Yes, it would have been a shambles if Jose had seen it. I'm sure he's been vetted, but you never know."

"Yes, my thoughts exactly."

"I'll have the latest report through to you by the end of

today." *Not sure anyone in London reads them anyway*, thought Jardine. *Too busy trying to stop BP's oil fields becoming a caliphate.*

"Alright, old boy. I'll leave it to you. Speak soon"

Jardine hung up and opened the report from the previous day. He knew Ambrose had been speaking to Radcliffe. He always slipped 'old boy' into his lexicon after speaking to him, like he was channelling Radcliffe's spirit into his speech. For the next hour, Jardine sat at the desk and added the information about Yakov and Madam Lagos, along with the photographs he had received from the tall American, delicately weaving them into his narrative. After an hour, he sent though the report and switched on the television and scrolled through the usual 24-hour news channels: CCN, CNN en español, BBC World, Fox, Sky News, France 5, Al Jazeera and finally RTVE. Most had run the same story, and Jardine wondered if they all had the same source. He knew from the current state of journalism it wasn't a matter of who was the most correct, but who was the first? There was always time later to apologise. Besides, people were like fish these days, their memories only last as long as the length of a Tweet or a Boomerang video on Instagram. And if it wasn't liked, shared, commented on or retweeted, it failed to gain any traction and thus was lost in the obscurity of the incalculable number of bytes floating through cyberspace. It appeared all that was needed to make something popular these days was to overlay it with a puppy dog snout and ears or make someone vomit rainbows. Catching himself ranting in his head like a cranky baby boomer, Jardine's refocused back to the report he'd just sent. He wondered how it would be received. The old boys at Vauxhall Cross in London were not ADHD millennials with trigger thumbs hovering over a round smartphone button. They were probably reasonably good at decimating fact from fiction and calling the bullshitters where they stand. Although there was always WMD.

That was something that left doubt in even the most hardened intelligence agency advocate. Hopefully his lies wouldn't be that destructive, but hopefully the decision makers would be just as gullible.

LONDON MEETS LAGOS

AT TEN O'CLOCK IN THE MORNING IN A MEETING ROOM ON THE
fourth floor of a four-tiered beige building on the Thames,
hosting bottle green bomb-proof windows, a man wearing a
tailored McKenzie & Dartmouth suit, handwoven white shirt
and a tie in the colours of his private members only club held
up a report and began to read. "Now, moving on to issues in
South America." The ageing man continued on to mention
the run-of-the-mill issues of the day in Latin America: the
wave of left-wing populism dwindling across the continent,
Venezuela going through an economic crisis despite owning
the largest oil reserves in the world, Brazil turning to the
more authoritarian right and the re-emergence of Argentina
as an economic powerhouse. As he read, a younger assistant
clicked through drab PowerPoint slides revealing a series of
bland pie charts and bar graphs, concise bullet points and
rather dull stock photography. If it were possible to enter the
minds of the members of the committee sitting in the wood-
panelled conference room, it would come to light that it
wasn't only the uninspiring presentation or the topic that
didn't engage the room; everyone there knew that South

America had little to do with the fate of the world at that time.

"Now to the individual country reports," the man continued. He trailed alphabetically through Argentina, Brazil and Chile in much the same fashion as before. Updates on recent elections, opportunities and threats to British business interests and a host of other important issues.

"Move it along will you, Cavy," came the cry from a balding man in military uniform.

Lord Cavendish sighed and adjusted his Travellers Club tie and motioned to the assistant to continue to the next slide. As the slide changed, an intriguing image was displayed across the screen. Lord Cavendish glanced up nonchalantly and then, doing a double take, shuffled uncomfortably in his seat, coughing and spluttering as if a small crisp had tickled the back of his throat. "And... and now on to an interesting development in Colombia." His voice sharpened from the mundane and monotone to a more enthusiastic tone. The screen revealed the picture of a woman in her forties in a bikini on a yacht outside of Cartagena. Next to the picture of the woman was a picture of a muscular man wearing aviator sunglasses exiting what looked to be some sort of compound with faux Greek columns. The other men around the table sat up in their chairs and adjusted their glasses as if being awoken abruptly from an afternoon nap. Appropriate murmurs of approval and the odd comment such as 'how interesting' could be heard floating around the room. Lord Cavendish continued reading with an amusing smirk on his face. "The lady in the... well, normally I would called it a bikini, but it seems to have more in common with dental floss than swimwear."

The men in the room erupted in a communal chortle. "Hor hor hor, good one, Cavy," came the cry from a red-faced man in a beige suit, who slapped his knees and sputtered out a raspy laugh.

Lord Cavendish, Chairperson of the Joint Intelligence Committee (JIC) smiled smugly and nodded his approval before continuing. "Heidy Lagos is her name and it appears she is the owner of a network of brothels in Colombia that have been visited by a number of men of Middle Eastern origins who seem to have recently moved to the Colombian coast. She's quite the looker, as you can see. Former Miss Plantain 2002, we have been informed. An incredibly charming woman, it has been reported that she has been pursued by the relevant authorities in Colombia but has the uncanny ability to sweet talk her way out of any charges. It is also noted that she was quite a hit with the US President's secret service men a few years back before the Summit of the Americas."

"Typical Yanks, no discipline," came a cry from somewhere around the table.

Lord Cavendish continued. "Her known associate, not pictured here, is Uri Yakov, an alleged Israeli mercenary who assists Madam Lagos with security and provides a steady flow of clients in the form of young Israeli men, fresh out of their mandatory three years military service. However, it is being put to us by our man in Bogotá, that Yakov is actually a *Katsa*; an undercover Mossad Agent, monitoring Madam Lagos's Muslim clientele. It is thought that these customers have connections to either a Hezbollah faction, an ISIS affiliate or an Al-Qaeda cell. At the very least, some kind of fundamental Jihadi or Islamist group operating in Colombia. The man pictured is Nelson Valencia, a former paramilitary leader turned head of security."

"Absolutely diabolical!" chimed Sir Arthur Radcliffe, looking around the table incredulously, his eyes open wide and his bushy grey eyebrows raised like two small squirrels reaching up for a nut.

"I'm afraid the saga doesn't end there," Lord Cavendish continued. "It is believed these groups may be in cahoots with Colombian criminal gangs, remnants of the cartels, to traffic cocaine, which may or may not be utilised to potentially fund secret training camps in northern Colombia. In addition to this, our man has also reported that he reckons the recent assassination of a left-wing professor is the result of the victim's knowledge of these activities and connection to possible renegade Palestinian splinter groups operating in the area."

"I thought you said it was ISIS related?" asked the only woman sitting at the table.

"I heard Al Qaeda mentioned," interjected another.

"All of the above," added Lord Cavendish sheepishly, looking at the other side of the report to see if any footnotes had been left out. "It's all still up in the air, as it were."

"Never seen anything quite like it in all my time as Head of Operations," said Sir Arthur Radcliffe, shaking his head seriously before continuing, "Why it all makes perfect sense! The Yanks have gone cold on Latin America for the last ten years. That's why the whole continent went Bolshie. Look at the mess in Venezuela. Inflation to 1,300,000% and they're in bed with the Russians, Iranians and the Cubans. The new Axis of bloody evil — how do you say that in Spanish?"

"Axiso de evilo, I believe, sir," said a young assistant taking the meeting's minutes, nodding seriously and not understanding the rhetorical question.

A bespectacled man in his forties wearing a Hugo Boss suit leaned forward and raised his hand. "Why hasn't there been any chatter on the networks? Nothing picked up online at GCHQ through the usual sweep?" After speaking he leaned back in his chair and looked left to right around the table smugly.

"Well, there wouldn't be, would there, Cooper?" came the reply from an older man sitting across from him. "We're all so bloody consumed with technology these days. You think the terrorists don't know? They've gone underground, gone back to the old ways. The days before someone knew if you'd bought a kit kat at the local shop. These terrorists don't want us to know what adult material they've googled or to whom they've swiped left or right to on the latest dating apps. They've gone off the grid!"

"We must still go through the standard checks and balances. My superiors at Downing Street will want to see something more substantial," said Thomas Cooper.

Thomas Cooper was Whitehall's representative on the JIC and had been brought in at the recommendation of treasury to ensure MI6 was being fiscally responsible. His off-the rack Hugo Boss looked the part in briefings, but his lack of membership at a private London club meant he held a certain disdain for anyone else that did. This chip on his shoulder started as a small crumb, but had since grown to the size of a large tortilla chip, weighing heavily on his left shoulder, causing him to sit lopsided.

Attention turned back to the screen as Lord Cavendish continued the presentation. "Let's crack on. Thomas, perhaps if we provide some more background, it will provide more incentives for Whitehall? According to our sources, it is thought that this Mossad chap is, like I said, there to keep an eye on the growing influence of Hezbollah, or Al Qaeda, or ISIS or renegade Palestinian splinter groups in Latin America."

"And for the ladies and rum, too, I imagine," said another man with a slight wink to the table, met with a sliver of laughter from the committee.

Cavendish, trying to regain order in the room began to read directly from the report. "Heidy Lagos, alias: Madam Lagos, is a former 'pre-pago', known in English as a pre-paid.

"Prepaid? Like a phone plan, is she? Are you sure our man's not making this up?" interjected Cooper again, his eyes wide with disbelief.

"No, it appears it is similar to a call girl. I forget the

modern word," said Cavendish shaking his head while looking down at the table, as if trying to jog his memory.

"An escort?" offered Cooper, before shrinking back in his seat, realising he had answered too quickly.

"Yes, that's it. But with this system you, prepay her. That way all the business is out of the way and it gives the appearance that she wants to be with you because you're a dashing, charming sort of chap. Protects a man's ego I've been told on my trips to Colombia."

The group chortled again before Cavendish continued. "Now, no official intelligence channels from the Colombians will confirm Madam Lagos's connections, of course. She's supplied half the Congress with these 'prepaids'. In fact, I believe her establishment in Cartagena, El Oriente, is the club you visited, Secretary General Bellington, when you visited Cartagena with the Prince of Wales a few years back, was it not? Why, I even remember approving the expenses for it."

The Secretary General's face turned bright red as he mumbled and then managed to speak. "Yes… yes, that was it. El Oriente. Quite a good establishment. I was taken there by the Colombians, of course. Or was it the British Council that booked it for us? We were there for a literary festival you see. Anyway, I went along. Didn't want to seem impolite. You know how it is, when in Rome and all that. Although I didn't partake in any pre-purchasing or whatever it is you just mentioned. I handed in my receipts, everything above board, I assure you. Anyway, that's enough. We all know that it is highly likely this woman's intelligence is solid. Ladies of the night always make great spies — take Mata Hari for example!" The Secretary General's hands were open in front of him as if ending a magic trick.

A low cheer swept around the room. "Hear, hear!" "Quite right!" came the replies from around the table.

"Gentlemen, and lady, it seems time has gotten the best of us and I'm afraid we must press on. I'm getting the feeling that this is an important issue to the table. Do we approve then, to allocate a special dispensary budget to continue with this matter? All those in favour, say 'Aye'.

An overwhelming shout of 'aye' was heard around the table, except from the representative from Whitehall, Thomas Cooper, who muttered under his breath, "Bloody madness."

"We'll need more intelligence product, of course, photographic and visual intelligence, that sort of thing," said Sir Arthur Radcliffe. "I've mentioned that to Ambrose myself."

"Yes, you're quite right, Radcliffe. Knew you were the right man for Operations," said Cavendish with a stern head nod.

"Wait, we're not going to discuss this further? Surely there are more pressing issues that deserve treasury funds? We haven't gone into detail on developments in Venezuela yet... What's our position on the new interim president of the National Assembly? Or the Tri-border area in Paraguay..." interrupted Cooper.

"In time, Thomas, in time," replied Lord Cavendish using Cooper's first name. "We must be patient with these matters. We'll get to the Tri-border region when we get to Paraguay and Venezuela will come at the end. We must be very thorough in our analysis here and of course we need to go about this methodically and in alphabetical order. I know this may be a little out of your depth, but please bear with us." Cavendish had lost his chummy old boy tone and had turned on his condescending superior manner.

Thomas Cooper rolled his eyes for a moment, and then tried to smile through gritted teeth. "I'll make the necessary arrangements with the Treasury."

"Now, let's move on to matters in Ecuador..." Cavendish continued.

"Unbelievable..." muttered Thomas under his breath, crossing his arms and slumping back in his chair.

29

URIBIA

Having sent his second report, Jardine met with Paco for lunch at a small cafe in Taganga. After a recap of the events from the previous night, Jardine suggested they move on to the next step of their trip. "Paco, I need to get to Maicao."

"Maicao? What about your cover?"

"My cover?"

"The birdwatching."

"I'm sure there are birds in Maicao."

"I was thinking we go to Cabo de la Vela. They have flamingos there. It would suit your cover better."

"Flamingos?" Jardine thought of Professor Rojas, the sub-source for 'Flaming Flamingo.' Lifting his coffee cup without drinking, he stared at the wall above Paco's head. "OK, it will help me to plan my next move anyway."

After lunch, the two men climbed into Paco's jeep and set off north along the coastal road towards Riohacha and the Guajira peninsula. Having left Santa Marta and after passing Tayrona national park, the road became wedged between lush jungle on the right and the aqua marine Caribbean stretched out like blue tinted glass on the left. Small dark patches blemished the ocean, showing the sporadic colonies of coral. The road twisted slightly as they barrelled along, the wind blowing into the jeep cooling them from the hot Caribbean sun. As they drove, small trees with bright green leaves could be seen intermittently on the hills to the right. "You know what those trees are?" asked Paco.

"Coca leaf," replied Jardine.

"How did you...?"

"I've seen it near the Lost City, up there in the Sierra Nevada back when I was a simple backpacker *de verdad.*"

Paco smiled and tapped on the steering wheel. "You know it's the Kogi's who invented *the idea* of cocaína, although not in the form we know it today," he said casually. "They crushed seashells with coca leaves and mashed it all up to make a paste which they place on their gums. It allows them to talk for hours and hours, working out the mysteries of the universe, talking about the meaning of life. Talking and talking until the sun comes up."

"I know bankers and lawyers like that in London," said Jardine, looking sideways with a smirk. "I think they use the same technique."

Paco shook his head. "One of our infamous exports. It's a shame the leaf is not known for its traditional, medicinal properties."

"Hard to avoid I suppose when the stuff grows naturally. Especially in fertile ground like this." Jardine motioned with his hand to the mountains to their right.

Paco looked at him through the corner of his eye as he lit a cigarette. "As long as humans enjoy and partake in national stereotypes. As long as the English are known for tea, the Scots for whisky, the French for wine, the Argentinians for meat, then Colombia will, unfortunately, be known for cocaine."

Jardine nodded knowingly and spoke "Hopefully as time goes on, Colombia will be known more for its natural beauty, for its coffee, its emeralds, its flowers, and for..." Jardine glanced sideways at Paco. "...for its wonderful people."

Paco exhaled a puff of smoke. "Ojalá, my friend. Ojalá." *Hopefully.*

They continued in silence as Jardine reclined his seat and tried to sleep.

Passing Palomino and Dibulla, Paco spoke waking Jardine from his slumber. "La Guajira. No more lush green. Just desert, small bushes and flamingos until the northern most tip of the South American continent. The perfect place for the first stop on a birdwatching tour," said Paco.

Jardine stirred and looked out at the roadside. Small shrubs and an arid landscape had replaced the mountains. A horn sounded and there was a loud screeching of tyres from behind them. Jardine looked right to see a large black SUV overtaking them at breakneck speed.

"The fuck is that?" asked Jardine in a panic.

The SUV with tinted windows pulled up alongside them and hovered momentarily. Jardine held his breath and slumped in his seat. Before anything could happen, the SUV sped off ahead of them and swerved back into the correct lane. "Malditos barranquilleros!" said Paco while shaking his head. "They think they own the whole coast."

At the very top of the South American continent sits the La Guajira peninsula. A bleak, arid desert landscape where only the omnipresent wind made the heat remotely bearable. The constant whistling gale gave it an eerie, uneasy feel, like one feels on top of an isolated mountain. It was this remote outpost of the Spanish empire that former Governor Soto de Herrera declared in 1718, was, "Sin dios, sin ley y sin rey". *Without god, without law and without king.* The indigenous Wayuu who inhabited much of the peninsula never allowed

Europeans to fully take control of their land. They quickly learnt to beat the Spanish at their own game, using horses and firearms to fight back and level the playing field between themselves and *las conquistadores*. Constant visits from English and Dutch pirates, along with sharing a border with Venezuela — in which the Wayuu were allowed to traverse freely — led to a flourishing trade in contraband of all sorts, from plasma televisions, one cent litres of Venezuelan petrol, fake football tops and any number of illicit materials flowed relatively freely across the border.

Passing Riohacha, Jardine and Paco continued along a straight road for another hour. The landscape became swelteringly bleak, the only glimpse of vegetation an occasional cactus or scraggy short shrubs rising from the parched land. Occasionally a family of Wayuu walked along the side of the road, their bodies and faces covered by colourful flowing fabrics wrapped over them like capes. Eventually, arriving at the town of Uribia, they stopped to buy supplies. The town teamed with people. Wayuu men and woman sat on dirty plastic chairs under shelters made from branches, their colourful mochila satchel bags lining the street in front of them. Groups of men stood next to blue plastic drums used to fill two-litre fizzy drink bottles with cheap Venezuelan petroleum, its light brown-pink colour glistening under the belting sun. Sacks of rice and beans were loaded precariously onto the roofs of trucks and jeeps as the drivers hustled to fill their vehicles with passengers for the trip across the dunes to Cabo de la Vela. The blazing sun caused everyone to move in slow motion, exerting minimal effort to retain energy. Jardine and Paco entered a small bakery doubling as a corner store and sat down at a table and chairs. Paco fired off a list for lunch followed by two tintos, straight black coffee.

"Now you're even further away from *la nevera* now," said Paco as he sipped on his coffee. "Many people here consider

Bogotános as foreigners in their land. I guess they even think I'm a foreigner."

"Similar vibe in Maicao? Jardine asked, taking a sip of coffee.

"There it is a complex mix: Arabes, Colombianos, Venezolanos, Wayuu. It's very tolerant, but it's a smuggler's border town. A lot like a port, but a land port. Lots of mercancía crosses between here and Venezuela. Many of the big businesses are controlled by Arabes. As for the Wayuu, the border doesn't exist to them. They cross it when they want, their culture is on both sides of Colombia and Venezuela. They don't see borders like we do."

An elderly Wayuu woman approached them, her hand outstretched with a traditional Wayuu bag in the colourful Kanaasü patterns. It provided a stark contrast to her face which was completely black with face paint.

"Mochila? Hecho a mano, hijo," she said.

"You'd better buy one. You're on holiday remember?" laughed Paco. "A good place to hold your binoculars for bird-watching. That's exactly the thing a tourist would buy."

"But I already have a mochila at home in Bogotá!"

"Buy another. It will be good for your cover, man. Trust me."

Jardine reached into his pocket and gave her two 100.000 pesos notes. The lady smiled and handed over two brightly coloured mochilas with tassels. The woman took the two notes, examined them and placed them in the bag at her side.

"Wayuushe'? Bueno para el desierto," she continued, holding out a large cotton blanket-like cloth. It was large enough to cover someone from head to toe. It was a soft candy-red colour with intricate weave patterns in orange, brown and yellow around the border. Along the edges were gold tassels.

"I think this is more your style, Paco," said Jardine with a smirk.

"Maybe I should buy one for my wife? Oh, and my mother in-law of course. Need to keep on her good side, she already thinks I visit the putas when I'm away." Paco negotiated with the elderly Wayuu lady and placed the two large wayuushe' blankets on his lap. He picked up one of the mochilas and held it in his hands. "You know, these bags are made by the Wayuu women, they believe spiders taught them to weave and so each mochila and wayuushe' is unique."

The anecdote caused Jardine to think of the different strands of fine sticky-cotton string in which a spider weaves its web — much like the small intricate string of lies he had spun, which at that moment seemed to be running in straight lies. Hopefully he could keep them that way and not get them tangled up. Because the only thing that a tangled web is good for is trapping hapless flies.

Jardine and Paco finished their drinks and with their newly bought mochilas and wayuushe cloths, began the bumpy ride across the sand dunes to Cabo de la Vela. At first, they drove along a straight paved road, the asphalt ahead of them glistering and wobbling like jelly. After forty-five minutes, they turned off the asphalt on to a sandy track surrounded by tall thick cacti and low-level shrubs. Occasionally they passed several small thatched-roof shacks surrounded by tree branch fences sticking up like caiman teeth. The sandy track eventually petered out and they traversed a pancake-like desert, flat with vivid blue skies stretching out in front of them like an upside-down ocean. Jardine took out his phone, partly out of habit and partly because he wanted to see if he had a signal. Opening a news app on his phone he scrolled through the headlines until one article from a particular online media company caught his fancy:

'Meet the Madam who serviced the Secret Service'

He clicked the link and began to read. The article was well written and witty, weaving in a clear disdain for the ineptness of the current president. He checked Twitter; the article was trending. A trickle of other articles linked mysterious Middle Eastern visitors, also seen at the Madam's establishment after the Secret Service had been there. All was circumstantial, but the copy delivered enough taste to sweeten the palate and gave the allure of a more insidious threat than was immediately apparent. In the world of intelligence, it was known as 'playback' — the placing of modified stories into the media world where they would be multiplied, picked up and distributed. It turned it from an urban myth into a slightly more believable one. Only this time it wasn't playback from British Intelligence, but from a hapless journalist who couldn't find a serious story and had resorted to sensationalism.

Having arrived at the sleepy fishing village of Cabo de la Vela, Jardine and Paco found a small guesthouse on the lone road in the town and left their luggage. The town consisted of nothing more than a sandy beach track acting as the main street and small huts of concrete abodes with thatched roofs. On the other side of the road, each building provided a rancho, a small hut on the beach with hammocks for guests. Having settled in, and with beer in hand, Jardine crossed the sandy track and lay in a brightly coloured *chinchorro* hammock under one of the open walled thatched roof shacks. A slight breeze provided a gentle meditative sway as he glanced out towards the flamingo-pink sky in front of him. Wisps of smoky apricot sun teased the horizon, eventually blending with the pinks. He reached down beside the hammock and picked up his frosty beer and took a sip. Icy cold drops of condensation and damp sand fell down from the bottle on his bare chest, but he didn't brush them off. Looking at the setting sun, he began to reflect on the past few days. He'd been able to establish two more sources: Lagos and Yakov. Valencia even provided an interesting and menacing supporting role. The ball was in motion, although he still didn't know how London would receive the report. Professor Rojas was dead. Somewhere inside him, he felt responsible. But this was Colombia and people were assassinated every day for a whole number of reasons. Professor Rojas surely had people who wanted him dead and buried. He placed the beer back into the sand beside the hammock. Rojas had been a member of M19 back in the eighties... Hadn't he been responsible for his own death? If his life were taken, for whatever reason, wouldn't it be a type of redemption? Not in the vengeful, vindictive sense, but a general redemption for the world, a natural balance of sorts. How many did M19 kill in storming the palace of justice? Eye for an eye is still the rule of law in many places. It comes as natural to humans as eating, breathing and fucking. And nowhere was it truer than in Colombia. He looked down beside the hammock and saw the vibrantly chromatic mochila bag. Inside he had stuffed the equally colourful wayuushe' cloak, a gift from Paco. He took it out and examined the intricately woven patterns, thinking that Paco was right about the parallels it drew with a spider's web. *How does such a bleak environment motivate people to create such vivid colours and patterns*? he thought? The desolate, barren, desert landscape and the basic corrugated iron roofed huts were anything but complicated and colourful. Some would even say they looked hopeless and primitive. Yet the clothes, the hammocks, the bags, they involved intricate patterns with vibrant colours incorporating every hue of the rainbow. They had life. In that moment, two flamingos flew down and landed in the water in front of him. They roamed the shallows hunting small fish and crabs, oblivious to the human in the hammock. *Even the bloody flamingos are bright pink!* he thought. Maybe that's just the world — full of contradictions. Like Colombia itself, its past is full of death and destruction. Fifty years of internal civil conflict following a virtual civil war during *la violenca* years, yet the people are full of energy, generosity, laughter and non-stop dancing joy. If such positivity and beauty can come from such a place, then would it be possible for a blossoming, loving, caring relationship flourish from a violent trail of death based on lies? Jardine admired the swirls of rose pink and orange hues over the calm shimmering ocean as the sun set. The wind whipped softly through the rancho cooling the air. As well as the wind, Jardine heard a soft hum coming from the ocean. He sat up in the hammock and saw two kite surfers skimming the waters, their long blonde hair waving in the wind. A small drone followed them overhead, emitting a soft buzz, like the distant hum of a beehive. The flamingos didn't move as the kite surfers passed and disappeared from sight. Jardine continued watching the flamingos wading through the water looking for shrimp and crabs to devour. It was darker now as only a small edge of the sun could be seen on the horizon. Slowly a small blue flame appeared on the wing of one of the long-legged birds, growing and growing until eventually the bird burst into flames, engulfing the lanky avian species in a bright blue ball of fire. The flamingo didn't seem to notice and continued his waddle through the water. Despite his reasoning, it appeared the fate of Professor Rojas still weighed heavily somewhere in his subconscious. Or perhaps the ayahuasca visions hadn't quite left him.

30

AMBROSE TO HQ

THE PHONE IN AMBROSE'S OFFICE RANG AND HE ANSWERED IT within two rings. "Ambrose here."

"Ambrose, old boy! How is everything in the Andean tropics?"

"A few political assassinations, the odd cocaine bust and now they're telling us there are Venezuelan spies flooding the streets."

"Venezuelan spies? Whatever will they think of next?" said Radcliffe. "Now, I'm calling about those first two reports from Officer #397664. They were enough to arouse interest. The second report in particular was of great interest. It was given a four-star rating and was thrown around at the JIC meeting on Tuesday afternoon. The Treasury representative was sceptical, of course. Always are, the penny pinchers, trying to cover their tails and look like they're holding us ogres to account. So, they've said they want more."

"I believe Officer #397664 is following up a few of the leads as we speak. I'm sure it will bear fruit soon enough."

"When I say more, we want more visuals. I guess what I'm trying to say, Ambrose, is that what we really need is video intelligence product. It's the only way to convince the powers that be that there's really something going on."

"I see," said Ambrose, casually swivelling in his chair.

"Video will really get the ball rolling. If we can get footage of terrorists on the ground in Colombia, our people in Bogotá will have all the resources they need. We'll extend your chap's position to long term. He'll be vital, of course. In addition, if I may add an extra request."

"Of course, Radcliffe."

"Any extra additional video intelligence product, in particular, of that Madam Lagos woman will be looked on as favourable. Seems like a diabolical character, she really got the attention of the JIC. I think they're seriously looking to stop this exploitation of women business in its tracks."

"I'll pass the message on to my officer. Although, you know that's a big ask, sir. Colombia is not exactly a safe place to be photographing, filming and asking questions. As well as the Amazon jungle, there's a pretty dangerous concrete jungle out here as well."

"Yes, indeed. I remember from my time in Nicaragua in the 1980s. Very unpredictable region. But we need them all the same, at any risk. You know what it's like these days. We have to justify every penny spent. Every angle will be scrutinised. It's all about data, images and video footage to verify. You know what bloody happened the last time we took action upon intelligence without verification."

"This is hardly in the same league as WMD, sir."

"Yes, quite right. Nonetheless, the times are changing. We still have some of the old guard here, but we have to be more accountable…" the old man stopped in mid-sentence, "more careful these days. We can only rely on so much anonymous HUMINT. We need eyes on, as it were."

"Understood, sir. I'll speak with officer #397664 and make it clear he is to acquire additional, irrefutable video footage of fundamental Islamist terrorist activity. He's young, mid-thirties, so I'm sure he'll be up with all this new technology. Should be no problem for him to smuggle a bit of video out for us."

"What's he like, this chap?"

"He's a committed member of the team. Found himself a girl down here. He was due to be transferred to Yemen in a few weeks, before all this new intelligence product came about."

"Ah, to be young and on assignment. I remember it well. Had a girl in Prague, never was sure if she was a honey trap or not. Still good to adapt to the local culture, get to know the lay of the land and the lay of a bed. As long as it doesn't cost you in the end. By the way, what money is he receiving for his agents?"

"Not much. Only enough to keep them dangling."

"What about this girl of his? He was due to be transferred to Yemen?" The second question was blurted out as if Radcliffe had come to a certain realisation all of a sudden.

"You think she might be a honey pot?

"Yes, that was my line of thinking."

"She's been vetted. A very accomplished lawyer, in fact. Very intelligent girl."

"Right, well, that clears that up then. Nevertheless, treasury were sceptical. They always are the tightwads! How credible is this potential threat?"

"There was Hezbollah activity in the early 2000s. I don't see why it can't be true now. And just this morning there was talk in the international media about a potential Islamist threat using 'working ladies' in Cartagena to seduce the US President's secret service agents. It seems there's something afoot on the coast."

"Yes, quite. I read that too." Radcliffe paused on the line as if pondering what to say next. "Crazy world we're living in. Don't know what to believe anymore. It might almost be time for you and me to call it a day, Ambrose."

"You're quite right, Radcliffe. Too long in this spying game for us old dogs."

"Very well then. Got a bloody meeting with the Asia desk. Keep up the good work. Hasta luego, as they say down there, Ambrose."

"Hasta luego, Radcliffe."

31

CABO DE LA VELA

.

HAVING SHOWERED AND CHANGED, JARDINE AND PACO WALKED one block to a small bar, Juancos. They hovered outside while Paco finished his cigarette, looking up at the bright starlit sky. Jardine looked up at the restaurant's name. "Sounds like 'wankers'," he said not to anyone in particular. Several Wayuu women strolled passed them, continuing down the main street selling their colourful mochila bags, cloths and jewellery.

"The zone rosa of Cabo de la Vela," said Paco with a smirk, before taking a drag of his cigarette and then stamping it out on the sand.

They entered the empty thatched-roof shack. The floor was sandy and there were solid driftwood tables and navy plastic chairs crammed together in the small space. A bamboo bar stood in the corner and a mural of a lobster was painted on the back wall. A lone man leaned on the bar, seemingly asleep holding his head in his hands. Paco went to the bar and ordered two small Polar beers and brought them over to Jardine, sitting at a small table near the back wall. The barman walked over to a small jukebox in the corner, tapped at a few buttons and the machine burst to life with the sound of upbeat accordion and drums.

"I love this song," said Paco. "A classic vallenato number about a man who loves a girl but loses her."

"Aren't all vallenato songs about that?"

"Sí, but this one has a particular type of story behind it. You see, the singer was never particularly good at anything, not even vallenato. He couldn't hold a job, he wasn't good at school, he could barely play soccer. Then, one day, he decided to leave his hometown of Valledupar. Just took off." Paco took a sip of beer.

"I'm guessing it doesn't end there?"

Paco placed his beer on the table and continued. "No, my friend. So, the man disappeared, no-one knew where he went. He had a girlfriend at the time. Many said, well joked really, that he was off visiting his other girlfriends around the coast. Anyway, a year later, he returned with an old accordion, it had the colours of the Colombian flag painted on the bellows. So, he returns and not only is he a *diablo* on the accordion, but *dios mío* can he sing and banter with the best of vallenato singers. He wins La Pilonera Mayor Award at the vallenato festival in Valledupar and goes down as one of the best vallenato singers of Colombia."

"And the girl?" asked Jardine.

"I'm afraid that is not a happy ending. She got tired of waiting and had already married another man when he returned."

"Oh..." Jardine's voice trailed off.

"So, having lost the love of his life, he turned to drink and women and non-stop rumba and partying. He died alone, but with a tremendous skill, many prizes to his name and he'd managed to amass quite a few pesos. Many say — mostly old women, you know how superstitious they can be — that he'd made a pact with the devil to give him silky smooth fingers on the accordion and the particular timbre of voice and wit to be able to sing vallenato."

Jardine was silent, contemplative. Taking a sip of beer he thought to himself, *I hope I haven't done a deal with the devil.* As best he could remember, no-one he had come across had horns.

Paco finished his story just as two lanky men with long flowing sand-coloured hair walked into the bar. They both ordered beer and took a seat at a table beside Jardine and Paco. The hut was so small that they were within arm's reach. Jardine, looking sideways, recognised them as the kite-surfers. "I saw you two out there today. Impressive stuff," he said.

"Thanks man, it was a beautiful afternoon. There are not many places in the world like this. Completely undiscovered with easy access to the beach."

"The footage must be incredible, especially with that sunset in the background," said Jardine.

"Do you want to see it?" asked one of the men. "We do all the production of our videos ourselves. It has saved us thousands of euros. Really opens up our budget to travel to more far-off places, places where other kite-surfers don't venture. Like here in Colombia. Many won't come because of the perceived dangers, but we've been everywhere." The Dutch man rattled off all the places they'd travelled as the other pulled out a computer tablet from his small backpack. The four men huddled around the screen as the jukebox now belted out a slow salsa tune. It was dark inside the hut with only small fairy lights strung across the ceiling to light the hut. The video opened with a panning shot of the ocean as the drone rose up in the air. The sun shone across the smooth horizontal sea. As it reached a certain altitude, it swung around to reveal Cabo de le Vela below and in the distance, sand dunes as far as the eye could see. After a minute or so it moved in closer to the ocean to reveal one of the kite-surfers cutting across the sea like a water-running lizard from National Geographic. It swung around behind the man and followed behind for a moment before zooming out and then moving back in to focus on the second kite-surfer who was coming up behind.

"It's so clear," said Paco.

"HD with 1500-bit resolution all housed in a drone the diameter of a large pizza," replied one of the Dutchmen with a goofy grin.

"Incredible! It used to take a small Cessna fitted with thousands of dollars worth of camera gear to get this type of footage…" Paco stopped, realising he was giving away too much information.

One of the Dutchmen looked at him. "Cessna? Haven't heard of that brand of drone… Must be an older version. Are you a film maker too?"

"Ah, pues, not exactly. I own a farm and we need to take aerial footage of my family's property," said Paco, before sharing a relieved glance at Jardine.

"Oh right. Well, you should get yourself one of these. Easy to manoeuvre, efficient and you won't get a clearer image."

"What's it called?" asked Jardine.

"DZX Phantomas Pro drone with FLIB 4 camera."

"FLIB?" asked Paco. "I've heard of FLIR, but what's FLIB?"

"Infra-blue. It's ten times better than infra red."

Paco nodded, impressed.

Jardine had been looking at the footage with mild fascination — anything to take his mind of the task at hand and what lay ahead, for which he didn't have a clear plan. He secretly wished his life was like the two Dutchmen, without a care and travelling the world. It reminded him of his time spent backpacking. He had travelled with nothing more than a backpack and his own ingenuity, before the days of iPhone and Google Maps to calculate every inch of the terrain before you arrive, not to mention the plethora of blogs, guides and websites detailing all the destinations. Then, it was a leap into the unknown. Now, it was very different. Yes, he got to travel the world, but it was never with the freedom these guys had. There was always a reason for his going to places — talk to a source, check the situation on the ground, liaise with military or the police or a dissident. It was never exactly where or what he wanted to do.

The men continued watching the footage and ordered another round of drinks, followed by lobster, followed by more and more rounds of drinks. The small shack filled up with a few more intrepid travellers — foreign and Colombian — and some locals who congregated near the jukebox. The small hut had become crowded and sweaty bodies began to sway with the music with impromptu dance moves between the tables. Jardine decided to step out for some fresh air. He picked up his beer and weaved his way through the crowd to the door and exited the small shack. The darkness outside hit him. The only light a soft glow from two overhanging street-lamps dangling from a cable over the sandy road and the distant stars above. He could hear the waves lapping at the shore with a soft whoosh. Taking a sip of his beer, he looked up at the sky again. The stars shone with a fierce intensity like finely cut diamonds. His thoughts returned to those of earlier in the day whilst sitting in the hammock. It takes a desert to bring out the beauty in the sky. It's no wonder desert-dwellers know so much about the sky. The Bedouin, Australian Aboriginals, the ancient Egyptians. When there's nothing on land for us, nothing on the horizon, we look to the sky, he thought. The sky is where he looked for hope. Hope in the sky, just like the drones earlier this afternoon. A drone of hope. Suddenly, he had a realisation. The two intelligence reports he'd sent would only keep Ambrose and London on the line for so long. He needed something concrete, some-thing factual to really consolidate his story. The most convincing stories are the ones told to us by someone who saw it first-hand. Or, via video footage. No-one could argue with that. It even fit with the new direction the service was taking: the fourth generation of espionage. The chief had announced a month ago that the technological age posed an "existential challenge" to the traditional ways of operating and it was time for the organisation to "master covert action in the data age." What better data than video footage of a real life Hezbollah/ISIS/Al-Qaeda/Radical Palestinian splinter group training camp in the mountains of northern Colombia?!

He drained his drink, re-entered the hut and, after buying a round of drinks, strode over to the two Dutchmen sitting at a table in the corner. "Thought you two looked thirsty," said Jardine, placing the glistening ice-cold bottles down onto the wooden table with a thud.

"Ja! We're always thirsty," replied one of the Dutchmen. "Especially when the beer is so cheap! Do you know how much a beer is in Holland?" He shook his head and reached out for a bottle.

"I wanted to pick your brains about a few things, the drones to be more specific. My friend…" Jardine motioned to Paco who was frantically moving his hands in pursuit of telling a story to three American girls sitting at the bar. He turned back to the two Dutchmen. "He wants to purchase a few drones for his farm. Where did you guys get yours?"

"Well, electronics are not cheap in Colombia we have found. Did you see that girl caught with cocaine hidden in headphones and said she had bought them as presents? Ha! All electronics we have seen are even more expensive than Europe. It is not a good place to buy electronics, but…" the Dutchman took a sip of his beer before continuing. "There is a place down the road called Maicao. A friend in Bogotá told us about it. There, everything is cheap. That's where we bought our drone." The Dutchman sat back in his seat, pleased with himself for his advice.

"You know you can follow us on Instagram. I believe we tagged the place where we bought it."

"We have 250,000 followers," chimed in the other Dutchman.

"Is that a lot?" asked Jardine.

"It's enough for us to fund our travels and not have a nine-to-five."

"It's more like eight-to-seven in Colombia," added Paco, sliding up alongside Jardine.

Jardine took out his phone and added the Dutchmen's Instagram account and turned to Paco. "Paco, tomorrow we need to get to Maicao. I have a plan."

AN OLD FRIEND

THE NEXT MORNING AT NINE A.M., WHILE PACO WAS STILL sleeping, Jardine decided to check in with Ambrose. He dialled the six digit number which would route him through to the Embassy in Bogotá. The phone rang for longer than usual before Jane answered in a fluster. "Jesus, Jardine you won't believe what's happened here, it's been quite a morning!" Her voice held a sense of sarcasm, he didn't know if for humour purposes or as a coping mechanism. "There's been an attack near the Embassy."

"Cyber?"

"Bomb. Two casualties."

"Shit! What happened?" Jardine asked.

"They're calling it a 'targeted bomb assassination attempt.' Six blocks from the Embassy".

"Attempt?"

"You remember the ex-defence minister Loaiza? Two men on a motorbike planted a small explosive device on his windscreen at the traffic lights on Avenida Caracas with Calle—"

"Who are they saying is responsible?" Jardine interrupted.

"Some are saying it's a random attack by ELN for not

being invited to the peace talks," said Jane. "Others are saying there was a particular target in mind."

Jardine gulped. He thought about the information he had written in his reports. Mierda, not again.

"Who did it kill?" Jardine managed to croak out.

"Killed his driver and one of his bodyguards. Should have seen the footage. It's all over the telly. The remaining bodyguards managed to drag him out and get him into another vehicle."

"Jesus…" Jardine muttered. Although he felt relieved it was no-one from his reports.

Jane continued. "Fortunately, no British subjects were killed. Will mean less paperwork to fill out."

Jardine produced a number of well-placed laments through expulsions of air and human humming noises designed to show he cared. However, deep down he was relieved — just another attempted political assassination. *The bloke probably had it coming,* he thought.

"However, unfortunately…" Jane's voice began to tremble now. "In a separate incident, our beloved Don Carlos has passed away."

Jardine's body stiffened like concrete.

"They're saying it's a heart attack," she continued, her voice calming now, but still held a certain timbre that revealed she was shaken.

"What…what…" Jardine couldn't finish his sentence.

"On his morning break he walked down to buy a mango juice from the lady on the corner, as he always did. A few moments later, he was passed out on the pavement. An ambulance was called, of course, and he was rushed to hospital. They're sending a team out from London to investigate and take care of the funeral arrangements. FCO protocol when this sort of thing happens, even if he was a locally engaged employee."

Jardine didn't know what to think. This was too much of a coincidence. Professor Rojas, and now Don Carlos. Gone. Both after they were sources in his reports. Although after a few moments, he felt an ironic relief that it was only a heart attack and not something more sinister. That can't have been his fault? He didn't want to show his nervousness and so put on his formal telephone voice. "Horrible news. I just can't… can't fathom what's happened… Jane, could you patch me through to Ambrose?"

"Of course." Jane sniffed and let out a small sob. "One moment, and you take care up there, Jardine. Be careful!"

Jardine didn't know what else to say, he'd never dealt with death before, not like this. It had always been a footnote in a document, an anecdote from an informant, a quote on a page, a list of numbers in a table. Sure, there had been Rojas. But left-wing professors are killed all the time in Colombia. One became desensitised to it after a while. Plus, he'd never even met the guy. This had a more personal ring to it. He'd never dealt with such a personal life-ending fiasco. Especially, when deep down, he was beginning to suspect that these deaths may have been the result of love — his love for Veronica.

Ambrose cut onto the line with a small click. "That you, Jardine?"

"Here."

"Jane has obviously filled you in on what's happened. I've got a bit to sort out, as you can imagine. So, let's keep this brief. The Joint Intelligence Committee has seen your two initial intelligence reports. They seemed content with the photographic evidence you provided for the second report. Very content, in fact. They want more photographic and video intelligence product of Heidy Lagos, if you can."

"What about Yakov? Valencia?"

"They didn't mention them, strangely." Ambrose's voice

sounded genuinely surprised. "Lagos aroused interest because there's a big push for the protection of vulnerable women around the world and high priority on the international trafficking networks that facilitate these sorts of enterprises. Some on the JIC have put forward their willingness to come out themselves to Colombia and investigate. Maybe conduct their own undercover operation. So, any extra photographic or video intelligence product you can rustle up on Lagos will be well received."

"They're currently my sources. So, we will need to hold off on any undercover operations until I find out more about her clients." The last thing he needed was a real operations team snooping around after him.

"Yes, quite right. The JIC said themselves, the main interest is your mention of a potential fundamental Islamist terrorist threat. We've said it before, we need to meet the terrorists on their wicket and bowl the buggers out. I'll be talking with London again next week. They want video and photographic intelligence product. It needs to be one hundred percent verifiable. Clear primary source intelligence, direct from you. We can't trust any more third parties."

"Understood. Sounds like something the Ambassador would say."

"The Ambassador reads all your report and he is — as always — not entirely trustful of us. The Foreign Office still highly critical of the service you know."

"I'll have something by next week, Ambrose. In fact, got a lead I'm in the process of following up." Jardine tried to sound convincing and confident. "Still in the planning stages at the moment."

"Tops. We'll talk next week."

With a click the call ended. He thought of Don Carlos. He cared deeply for the man. On assignment, you were always drawn closer to people you work with. He'd been like a father figure to him. Although, no time to think about that now. The old Jardine would've moped around and let the emotion of the situation take control of his actions. But now, he knew what he had to do. He strode to Paco's room, banging on the door. "Vámanos, Paco! We have work to do."

33

MAICAO

THE FRONTIER TOWN OF MAICAO HAD LONG BEEN AN EPICENTRE
for contraband. The mere mention of the name in Colombia
conjured up images of cheap plasma screens, mobile phones,
economical booze, pirated DVDs and virtually-free petrol. It
was this robust and thriving commercial scene that attracted
Arab immigrants, settling in Maicao in the 1940s. It was
nothing new in Colombia. Arabs fleeing persecution from the
Ottoman Empire had established themselves along the coast
since the nineteenth century. However, it was the scattering of
minarets and the morning call to prayer from the Omar Ibn
Al-Khattab mosque that gave Maicao an air of a far-flung
outpost somewhere in the Middle East rather than a remote
peninsula in Latin America.

Jardine and Paco sped along the straight asphalt road
hugging the railroad to the Cerrejón coal mine until they
reached Maicao. They rolled into town just before sunset and
checked in to a small pension-style hotel in the centre.

The next day, Jardine woke to the wailing call to prayer
blasting in from all four corners of the room. He heard a
knock on his door and rose from his bed, instinctively posi-

tioning himself beside the door, not directly in front of it. "Quién es?"

"It's me," said a voice in Spanish. "Nice alarm clock, right? I'm going for breakfast, care to join?" asked Paco.

"I'll be down in five. Don't think I'll be getting back to sleep with this racket. Reminds me of church bells, lots of bloody noise!"

For a country with three prongs of the Andes protruding across its landscape and a lack of adequate infrastructure, Colombia is a notoriously difficult country to traverse. It is also famously expensive to transport goods across the country. It is four times more expensive to send a container from Bogotá to the port of Buenaventura, than it costs from Buenaventura to China. These high costs and difficulty has meant that if there's a cheaper way to import products, someone will find it. And so therefore the idea of the *contrabandista* — the smuggler — is famous throughout Colombia. No more is this apparent than in Maicao, which claims to host the cheapest electronics in the country. New plasma? Easy. Latest iPhone or iPad? As cheap as the factory in China. GPS for your car? Drive right up. Satellite phone? We'll throw in a GPS device for free. Not only electronics but any other number of legal and illegal goods can be found within its central marketplace.

The two men drove to Calle 13 in the centre and parked in outside a white store front with the name Importadora Electro-Paisa written in black letters. Two men sat out the front playing dominos. They entered the store, rummaging through the boxes of drones on display. "What about this one?" asked Paco, holding up a box with a futuristic looking picture of a slim jet-black drone. He passed it to Jardine.

"Made in China. Dutch guys said avoid the knock-offs. We need the South Korean model, the DZX Phantomas Pro drone."

"Ah yes, the image was pure perfection," said Paco.

It was in this moment that a sudden thought jolted into Jardine's mind. *Perhaps I don't want a perfectly clear image? That means it would be clear that whatever we find to film, a guerrilla training camp perhaps, would obviously not be a fundamental Islamist terrorist training camp. A bit of fuzz and grainy footage would be more ambiguous.* "We'll need something inconspicuous and small," said Jardine, hoping there was a small drone that had a crappy image. "And, like you said, with a clear camera, but not too clear…"

"Why not so clear?" asked Paco. "If we're birdwatchers, wouldn't we want a clear image?"

"I'm not sure birdwatchers even use drones... Wouldn't that be cheating? Besides, I mean… I need to be able to control the image, if you know what I mean…" Jardine's voice trailed off into a mumble.

"I have no idea what idea you mean, you crazy gringo… But, let's keep looking." Paco rummaged enthusiastically through a pile of boxes left in a messy heap on the floor. Merchandise was constantly arriving and heading out the door, barely giving enough time for it to be stacked and stored properly. As they sifted through the boxes, the two men looked up at three jet black SUVs, with tinted windows, rumbling through the dusty streets outside of the store.

"Marimbero?" Jardine asked the shop owner, using the name for the local marijuana growers.

"No sé, nunca los he visto por aquí. The Marimberos usually drive pick-ups and wear cowboy boots and hats. Those guys look more like la oficina de…." the store owner cut his sentence short, lowered his head and moved to the back of the store, obviously realising he'd already said too much in a town where you don't want a reputation as being nosey or *un sapo. A snitch.* As he moved to the back of the shop, the owner held up a package to Jardine and Paco. "This, mis amigos, is the best drone in Latin America. Just last week I had a Venezuelan customer who bought one. He said he had a project, a parade in Caracas to film. Was inquiring about how much weight it could carry. It must have been some sort of parade, he said it would go off with a bang! But anyway, I explained to them that it was deadly silent and could get close to whatever it is filming without being intrusive. Their eyes lit up at the deadly part. Maybe it would suit you, no?"

Jardine received the box and studied the specifications. After a moment, he looked back at the name and picture, it read: DZX Phantomas Pro. The same model the Dutchmen had mentioned. Jardine tapped the side of the box. "We'll take it! But do you also have anything smaller? Cheaper with a lesser quality image?"

The shop owner looked over his shoulder and then returned his gaze to Jardine, shaking his head. Jardine looked past the man, into a small bodega behind the counter where a beaded curtain was held to one side by a small hook. Inside he glimpsed a pile of mustard yellow boxes with bright red 'new' stickers.

"What are those?" asked Jardine.

"Those..." the man turned around and unhooked the curtain of beads. It swung down and rattled like the shake of a maraca, covering the entrance. "...are not for sale."

"I can still see them you know. The curtain is see-through," said Jardine.

The man looked behind him and shook his head as if it was not the first time he'd forgot that the beaded curtain didn't block the view. "It's a new product from China. But, I have a client already who has purchased all of them. They're cheap anyway, you wouldn't want them."

Paco stepped forward. "Do you pay your taxes, Señor?"

"Of course, I do. Claro que si."

"Because it would be a shame if DIAN were to find any inconsistencies in your paperwork." Paco placed a fake official badge on the counter. The man's eyes grew wide as if he'd seen a giant tarantula climbing up his leg.

"We are happy to pay the going price," offered Jardine.

The man was still looking down at the badge before tilting his head up towards them and nodded. The two men both grinned and Jardine pulled out his wallet.

With the drones bought, Jardine snapped a few photos around Maicao, mainly of the mosques and areas where people congregated. After an hour, they decided to drive a few hours down the road. The jeep rattled along from Maicao to Valledupar as the landscape beside the road became lush once again with verdant cattle-grazing pastures, and the Sierra Nevada de Santa Marta could be seen rising on the right, while the Serranía de Perijá mountain range rose on the left. Jardine reached into the back of the jeep and took a box out from under the wayyusshe' blankets, the colourful cloths they had purchased that covered their recent acquisitions. He examined the small box. "The Silent Wasp Personal Reconnaissance Aerial Drone for all your clandestine vision needs," Jardine read aloud. "A new product from RLIF Systems, designed to fit in the palm of your hand and scout locations with stealth and ease." Jardine frowned and reached into the back again and pulled out the other drone they had bought, comparing the two drones side by side. "It says the Silent Wasp is completely silent, although the camera on the Phantomas is clearer."

"That's why it's a reconnaissance drone, deadly quiet," said Paco with a grin.

"I think it's best we use the Silent Wasp first to scout out any locations we want to investigate, and then the Phantomas once we find something and we need clearer footage."

"A good plan," reasoned Paco.

Jardine shook his head slightly, not wanting Paco to see. It was finally happening. He knew — at best — they would find a small guerrilla camp in the mountains, he just hoped that the Colombian military didn't already know about it. Otherwise, it would already be common knowledge back at the Embassy and thus his plan would be a disaster. Or maybe he could pay local villagers to dress up and play the part? Too much planning, he thought. And besides, Paco is with me, he'd no doubt report it to DNI.

They continued until they arrived at the city of Valledupar, the home of vallenato music — the accordion-fuelled folk music accompanied by bongo drums popular throughout Colombia, and especially ubiquitous on the coast. Paco had planned to visit various government offices to obtain permits to visit the Sierra Nevada. Much of the land required permits from the local indigenous groups to visit. Arriving at a small guesthouse to begin their preparations for the ascent to the Sierra Nevada, Jardine decided to check in again with Bogotá. He pulled out his phone and noticed he had two encrypted messages. Pressing his fingerprint on the small circle at the bottom of the phone, he entered the separate password to enter the encrypted messaging application. WhatsApp wasn't strong enough for matters of this nature.

> **Final results from Don Carlos death. Not heart attack. Traces of cyanide in mango juice. Foul play obviously suspected. To be investigated further by visiting FCO team. Continue on current objective.**
>
> — THIS IS AN ENCRYPTED MESSAGE.

The ironic relief he had felt earlier dissipated in a foul swoop that rushed through him. Don Carlos *was* killed because of his report. The cherry-sized lump now lodged in his throat throbbed again as he began to breathe faster. He swiped to the second message from GCHQ:

Please contact us at your earliest convenience

— THIS IS AN ENCRYPTED MESSAGE FROM GCHQ

He exited the encrypted messaging app and dialled GCHQ. It rang before clicking after twenty seconds.

"Dawkins?" Jardine asked. Alex Dawkins was a GCHQ analyst Jardine had dealt with before.

"Jardine. Good to hear your voice. We've traced the number you gave us."

"And?"

"It's been tracked to a fruit juice vendor in a small town — Taganga, I believe it's called."

Jardine managed a smile. His little trick with the burner phones had obviously been taken seriously in London and Cheltenham.

Dawkins continued. "It seems they were dumped in a bin next to the juice lady, who appears to have fished them out and used them herself. So, we've learned bugger all about any terrorist connection, but our SIGINT transcribers now know the trick to a good mango juice. It's all in the strain apparently. A double strain is preferred to just the one, you see. The linguists have also been able to add some colourful new Colombian words to the service's Spanish glossary. Seems the woman was not happy the phones had been used in illegal activities."

"Shit! The classic call and run technique," lamented Jardine, trying to sound authentic. At least the incident had shown he was on the ground getting his hands dirty. A trail of failed false clues was at least giving his intelligence product an air of authenticity. Intelligence work is never perfect and clean like they'd have you believe in the movies. "Sorry it wasn't more of a help…" Jardine added.

"Well that's just it," Dawkins interrupted. "We didn't think anything of it at first. Like you, we thought it was

merely a classic burn and dump. But, in light of the occurrences with the cyanide in the mango juice in Bogotá, we
think there might be something more to this."

"Surely there's no connection to—"

Dawkins didn't hear Jardine and continued. "We think
there might be some type of fruit juice vendor mafia operating on Colombian streets, working in cahoots with potential
fundamental Islamist terrorist groups and perhaps with La
Oficina de Chiribito."

"I haven't... It's not something I've come across..."
Jardine spluttered.

"Sorry, Jardine? You're breaking up there. Ah, that's better,
can hear you now."

Jardine coughed and then responded. "Now that you
mention it," he began. "I did notice the juice lady receiving
small packages from nefarious looking men on motorcycles.
And that's where I first laid eyes on Lagos. Additionally, in
the past there have been known connections between paramilitary groups and Colombian drinks manufacturers,
including a world famous cola brand. " At least that part was
true. It would help in wrapping his lies in a kernel of truth

"Excellent. We'll add that in the notes section of the tran-
scription and attach it to your second intelligence report."

Jardine gulped. "Thank you, Dawkins."

"A pleasure. You keep away from that juice down there.
Best stick to the rum. Oh, and sorry to hear about Don Carlos,
I know you two were close. Make sure you catch the bastards
responsible!"

He hung up the phone and a small tear appeared in
Jardine's eye. He took a minute to think of Don Carlos and all
the good times they'd shared. Maybe this was all a mistake?
Maybe he should have just gone to Yemen to avoid all this
death? He forced himself to smile having read that if you do
so, the muscle memory in your jaw triggers a happy feeling. It
didn't seem to work as all he could think of was the loss of his

friend. After a few moments of quiet reflection, he forced himself to switch his mind to the task at hand. The juice mafia comment from Dawkins? It was as if the more he tried to avoid the inevitable, the more he was thrust further into his own lies. Soon the lie would become so big, that even if it was exposed as a fraud, too many superiors would have already signed off on it. And then, nothing would stop it.

34

AVIAN OPERATION

PERMITS IN HAND AND DRIVING OUT OF VALLEDUPAR, JARDINE and Paco passed a number of giant statues: a giant accordion, a giant lady dancing while holding up a corner of her dress, two giant guitars, two giant roosters in battle in the middle of a roundabout and towards the mountains, a giant statue of Jesus. Heading towards Bosconia, they continued for an hour on a dead straight road lined with lush green pastures on either side, before turning onto a paved side road. Trees lined the narrow one lane road and bent over slightly, creating a natural green tunnel of foliage and branches. Gradually, the road began to twist and turn, hugging the hillside, passing lone shacks painted bright greens, yellows and blues as they ascended towards Puerto Bello. Entering the town, they crossed a narrow one lane bridge and proceeded beyond, heading higher up the mountain. Here, the road became rocky, bumpy, and at times, muddy. It gave the impression of sitting on a giant overloaded washing machine full of bricks. Paco lit a cigarette with one hand while juggling the wheel with the other. He took a drag and turned to Jardine. "Colombian massage — gratis," he exhaled and smiled cheekily. "I should probably mention this now. Once we arrive at Nabusimake, there are no more roads."

"So?"

"So, we must go by mula."

"Mule?"

'Exacto. Or maybe donkey or a macho, we'll see what's available. You don't mind?"

"If the road's anything like this, a donkey will be a bloody improvement!" said Jardine.

After another forty minutes past Puerto Bello, they arrived at a large clearing full of wandering sheep and black pigs surrounded by rolling emerald-green hills. On the far side of the clearing stood a small village of stone huts with thatched roofs encircled by a waist-high stone wall. A small wooden gazebo-type structure above a weathered gate signalled the entrance. Jardine and Paco drove the jeep towards it as two Arhuaco men, one a teenager and one an elderly man, came out to meet them.

"Bienvenidos!" said the younger Arhuaco man.

"Hola!" they both replied in unison.

Arriving at the entrance, the young man shook their hands as they descended from the jeep and led them towards the entrance to the village. "My name is Juan," said the young man. As they approached the entrance, Juan extended his hand. "This is my grandfather, he doesn't speak much Spanish and so I'm here to translate and accompany you on your journey. They phoned ahead from the permit office in Valledupar to let me know you were coming." Juan and his grandfather were both dressed in white tunics over white pants with black wellingtons. His grandfather watched patiently and smiled, a white, woven, helmet-like hat on his head.

"Thank you, Juan. It's been a long journey," said Jardine.

"Maybe you would like a tinto?" asked Juan, lifting one of the backpacks on to his shoulder, the top of the backpack came undone and drone box was revealed inside. "Wow! Is that a spaceship?"

The two men entered the small village through the gate and continued with Juan and his grandfather until they reached a small hut. They drank sweet black coffee as Juan explained the rules of the village. It was not opened to mass tourism or the odd roaming visitor. It was necessary for visitors to be invited or registered before they were allowed to enter. The Arhuacos and the Kogi peoples of the Sierra Nevada wanted to protect their way of life from outside influence. That meant 'little brother' — the way they referred to outsiders — needed to register with the indigenous council. If it had not been for Paco arranging for them to pass through the village, it would not have been possible for them to enter.

"We don't mind little brother coming and visiting us. As long as you respect our way of life and our environment," said Juan, refilling their coffee cups. "My grandfather is the Mamo for this village, he gives you permission to be here."

"Of course, Juan. We are here at your mercy and we thank you for letting us stay the night before our onward journey tomorrow," replied Jardine. "I believe you will be guiding us tomorrow into the mountains?"

"That is correct. I know all this land — all the valleys and peaks, jungles and rivers. I will be able to take you wherever you desire within the Sierra Nevada. I believe you are bird-watchers, no? We have many different types of birds." Juan continued mentioning the different types of parakeets, hummingbirds, finches and quetzals that roamed the mountains. Jardine was familiar with some of them from the little research he had done prior to his trip and took a mental note in case it would be of use. The two men passed the night with Juan, his grandfather and the other villagers, eating dinner around a small fire before retiring to a small tent Paco had brought. The next morning, Paco, Jardine and Juan set off further into the mountains. The night before, Juan had said they would need to be careful as there had been some action lately in the mountains.

"Guerrillas?" Paco had asked.

Juan shrugged.

"Paras?" asked Jardine.

Again, Juan shrugged.

"Malos," he replied finally. *Bad guys*.

The donkeys stood in a wooden-slatted pen behind the village. Juan distributed them to Jardine and Paco as they loaded their backpacks and the two drones — which they had chosen to hide in old coffee sacks — onto the back of the donkeys. They set out from the village, slogging up a muddy zig zag track surrounded by rainforest and jungle. Stopping for a quick lunch, they continued for another few hours through verdant hills with scatterings of pine and mountainous jungle terrain with deep valleys. Occasionally, they were required to lead the donkeys through icy, fast-flowing rivers whilst balancing their backpacks on their heads. At various points, a lone Arhuaco man appeared a few metres away from them, wearing the traditional white tunic with black wellington boots. The man watched them for a few seconds and then vanished into the misty undergrowth, striding stealthily through the jungle with apparent ease. During one of these occurrences, Jardine stopped at what he thought to be a short Arhuaco man in the distance. As he moved closer, he realised he was gazing at a familiar face. An elderly man was sat under a tree reading an enormous leather-bound book, dressed entirely in white. "Paco," he turned and tapped his friend on the shoulder. "Do you see that man there?"

Paco turned. "Which man?"

As Jardine twisted back to face the path, he realised the man had disappeared into the undergrowth.

The three men continued until five o'clock, arriving at a small clearing with a thatched-roof rancho — a shelter —

covering five hammocks with mosquito nets. There were remnants of a fire next to the shelter surrounded by smooth river stones. Twenty metres down a dirty path lay a slow moving part of a river. They placed their bags on the ground, strolling down to the river to wash while Juan's brother and grandfather — who had since caught up to them — prepared food for dinner. That night they ate beans with rice, fried plantain and chicken around the campfire whilst Juan told stories of the Sierra Nevada and helped to translate for his grandfather as he told tales of how the Arawak and Kogi people believe the earth was created. He also recounted the significance of the poporo, a gourd-like object used to mix crushed sea shells with coca leaves. The mixture, applied to the gums, would allow the elders and shamans special insights and the ability to remain awake for days on end, chatting and uncovering the mysteries of the universe.

Jardine's ears pricked up during one particular story, as Juan translated, "We believe that the birds are sacred because they are all-seeing creatures. They can see the whole picture and therefore a better picture of things. From their point of view, it is easier to tell what is wrong or right, for all of humanity and for one's self."

"That's what we're trying to do," said Jardine, chomping into a drumstick. "See things from the bird's point of view." Since the lies had begun, Jardine had perfected the art of commenting without lying, but without giving away his purpose either.

Juan nodded. "That's why you bought your spaceship. I suppose it is a mechanical bird. Or a drone, as I believe they're called." Paco and Jardine looked impressed. Juan continued. "I've seen them on YouTube. What, you don't think we have internet up here? It seems you picked the best model. They say the Phantomas has the best HD definition and easiest flight capabilities."

Jardine stopped eating and smiled. "It seems like I've underestimated your knowledge, mi amigo."

"Have you ever seen this land from above?" asked Paco.

"No," said Juan. "What is it exactly that you're looking for?"

"Birds, all types of birds," replied Jardine.

"You don't have birds in your country?"

"We do, but here they're very different, much more colourful and full of life."

"Juan, we have some information that there are some illegal armed groups operating in this area and we want to be sure that we're safe," Paco said. "Have you ever seen any camps?"

"I have seen them from a distance. We can usually track them down. Just last week we spotted a camp, not too far from here, near a river. I will take you near there tomorrow morning, but we won't disturb them."

"Will it be easy to avoid them?" asked Jardine. "I mean, they don't patrol or anything like that?"

"With your drones it will be much easier. It won't be as noisy as the military helicopters, they all scatter when they hear that. We can see their movements and avoid them. Anyway, they are mainly active at night and the early morning, before the military have had their *huevos pericos*."

"We move out at first light," said Jardine with authority. It seems the bull had returned, and he was ready to execute his operation with success.

Waking an hour before sunrise, the men ate breakfast and packed their bags before moving further into the Sierra Nevada. Juan's brother and grandfather headed back to the village and would meet them later down next to the river. Reaching the edge of a steep hill leading down to a deep valley, a space in the trees revealed a stunning view across valley. In the distance, the snow-capped peaks of *Simón Bolívar* and *Colón* hovered behind barren mountains, leading down to smaller hills and valleys of green spread out in front of them like an undulating emerald carpet.

"There's a camp over there." Juan pointed downwards, to the bottom of the hill and across the river below. "Malos," he added.

"Let's set up here," said Paco, unpacking the drone boxes. "I imagine we'll spot some condors flying through this valley."

"Like I said before, we should send the Silent Wasp first to scout out the territory and then the Phantomas for better quality imagery. With the Wasp, we'll be able to get right up their noses without detection," said Jardine in English — to avoid Juan understanding — as he helped Paco assemble the drones. After ten minutes, they had managed to assemble the small Silent Wasp Reconnaissance Drone and the three men huddled together, sitting on a large rock watching the small video screen on the controller. The Silent Wasp lifted up with a soft buzzing sound.

"Put it in silent mode!" said Paco in an agitated whisper.

"It's not a bloody mobile phone, you idiot... Oh, you're right, here's the silent switch." Jardine flicked a red switch on the remote control and the buzzing stopped. The mountains were silent now, only the faint sound of running water could be heard from the river below and the odd squawk from distant birds. The drone rose out over the valley passing the upper canopy. Jardine angled it to the west as it hovered over the treetops moving in fluid motion. The view on the screen showed a crimson sun rising through the clouds casting a soft blue mist across the valley. It fogged up the camera slightly as the Silent Wasp glided effortlessly across the treetops. Several condors flew by as Jardine angled the camera lens towards them before descending into the valley and crossing the river.

It continued across the tops of the trees to the other side, passing a small clearing in the canopy where movement could be seen. Jardine stopped the drone momentarily and angled the camera to zoom in as it hovered a hundred metres above the clearing. The mist was slightly thicker closer to the treetops and the three men arched their heads closer to the remote-control screen.

"Kogi?" asked Jardine.

"Or Arawak. I can't really see with all that mist," said Paco.

"Even I can't tell, it's too misty," said Juan.

Several figures in white cloaks appeared below running across the clearing.

"It seems like either Kogi or Arawak," said Juan. "We have some other groups up in these mountains."

"Bugger," muttered Jardine, turning to Paco. "Thought we had something there. Stick out like ghosts in the night down there with the white tunics running through the jungle."

Juan laughed softly. "We call the men in military fatigues the ghosts of the day. You can hardly see them camouflaged in the jungle."

The drone rose high above the canopy again and followed the river looking for signs of movement. The footage showed the drone tracking the steep valley with a raging washing machine-like river at the bottom. Small hummingbirds zoomed across the river hovering over flowers along the banks. Jardine followed a few of them to give the impression he was interested. A toucan appeared flying in circles like it was drunk. Jardine watched it curiously as Juan moved in closer to see the screen more clearly. "There! I knew there was someone up here."

A lone man, wearing all black, waded through the river at a narrow point, a black rucksack balanced on his head. One hand was up holding it steady, the other grasping an AK47.

"What's he doing there?" asked Jardine. He lowered the

drone closer to the river. Another man also wearing black could be seen on the river bank with an AK47 slung over his shoulder, dangling behind him.

"Guerrilla o Para, Paco?" asked Jardine.

"Guerrilla," replied Juan sharply before Paco could answer.

Paco and Jardine looked at Juan with amusement. "I thought they were all 'malos'?" Paco asked.

"You think I can't tell the difference? As well as identifying different plants and wildlife, it's important we can differentiate between the human species as well."

Paco and Jardine smiled and moved the drone further towards the two men. The drone was now sixty metres above the two men and had not been detected. The Silent Wasp was living up to its name.

"Seems they haven't noticed it," said Paco. "Although the image is grainy, it's hard to make out their faces."

"Don't think it matters a great deal, it looks like their faces are covered in a black and red hood anyway," said Jardine in English.

Paco leant back. "They have all the hallmarks of the ELN. You see…"

Paco explained the history of the most active guerrilla group still operating in Colombia — El Ejército de Liberación Nacional. The National Liberation Army, Colombia's second revolutionary left—wing armed group, inspired by Marxism and liberation theory. The guerrillas usually wore military fatigues with their trademark black and red hoods and arm bands. However, at night they would often wear all black, taking off the red part to avoid being seen in the jungle. It appeared that the guerrillas were yet to change into their camouflage fatigues and were only just beginning their morning routine of a brisk exercise drill, followed by breakfast and ideological classes.

"There must be more of them close by," said Juan, his eyes

filled with excitement like a kid playing a video game. "People watching is much more exciting than birds!"

Jardine toggled the joystick and moved the drone away from the river over the trees until they saw movement coming from a small gap in the jungle canopy.

"Aha! There!" said Jardine.

A group of black-clad figures were star jumping under the treetops. The small clearing was covered by overhanging branches, meaning that only a small proportion was visible from the sky. The guerrillas, just beginning their morning training routines, moved from star jumps to jogging on the spot before undertaking various stretches and a small obstacle course, consisting of running and hopping through tyres lying on the ground. A smaller group to the side crawled with their rifles under barbed wire, wriggling along like human-sized worms. To the untrained eyed, it was not dissimilar to the stock terrorist training footage shown on the evening news at the mention of Al Qaeda, ISIS, Al Shabaab, Hezbollah or any other terrorist organisation.

"We have no reports of guerrillas operating in these mountains," said Paco. "This will need to be reported to Bogotá."

"This is what I suspected. My intelligence says that they're a recent grouping of dissident FARC guerrillas who have joined the ranks of the ELN, trying to fill the power vacuum left after the FARC's disarmament," said Jardine. "They have even recruited a large number of Venezuelans crossing the border into Colombia."

Paco nodded in agreement.

As the guerrillas conducted their training, three figures emerged from the thick undergrowth and moved out into the clearing. They stopped under a tall wax palm and leaned against it. They seemed relaxed, like they thought the wax palm was providing sufficient cover for them from above. Jardine zoomed in, keeping the drone still. A bespectacled man in military fatigue with a bushy black beard and thick, short wavy hair lit a cigar. He gave the impression of a young, black-bearded George Lucas.

"AC," whispered Paco.

"Don't think so, not out here, Paco. I thought you'd be used to the heat coming from the coast," replied Jardine.

"No, not that, *pendejo*. The man with the beard, ball of hair, and cigar," said Paco. "He's known as AC. We've been after him for decades!"

"Why do they call him AC?"

"It's his alias."

Jardine looked at Paco confused. Paco shrugged and added. "Maybe because he's from Bogotá? *La nevera* — the fridge in the mountain."

"Really?" asked Jardine.

"Or maybe it's just the initials of his real name?"

Jardine zoomed in further, taking several screen shots of the man known as AC smoking a cigar. His mind was already moving ahead. That photo would give him an extra advantage. There was something about the photo he knew London would like. But, what was it? The man fit the archetype for a guerrilla leader. But, from a distance and with the slightly grainy footage, AC's hair seemed unlike hair, more like a round hat. Not dissimilar to an Ayatollah's or a Shia cleric's turban. A bulbous cloth of fur sitting on his head. *That's it*, he thought. *There's my visual proof that Hezbollah are operating a terrorist training camp in Colombia!* The previous intelligence reports were vague enough to gerrymander a Hezbollah influence into the mix.

Paco stood up and moved over to the other drone box. "It's time for the Phantomas. We need clearer footage. I'll need video proof to send to Bogotá."

"I think we have enough with this, Paco. Besides, this is a joint operation, this will go through our channels as well," said Jardine.

"It needs to be clearer. I mean look at the photo. It's not very clear at all! For all intents and purposes, the man we know to be AC could just be a man wearing a round cloth around his head. We need more clarity!"

"Let's quit while we're ahead. Near enough is good enough, and besides, the Phantomas is louder, there's no guarantee it won't be heard."

"It's a risk we need to take."

Jardine rolled his eyes as Paco picked up the Phantomas's remote control and motioned for Jardine and Juan to come over. Jardine hit the 'return home' button on the Silent Wasp and set the controller down on his backpack. He stepped towards Paco and helped him ready the Phantomas. After a few moments, the Phantom rose in the air with a similar buzz to that of the Silent Wasp when it first launched.

"No silent switch this time," said Paco. "Let's hope they don't hear it."

"It is very loud, Paco. Perhaps we should call it a day," Jardine offered.

"The day is just beginning."

"It's just an expression. Let's have a coffee and think this through," Jardine coaxed, trying to persuade Paco to abandon his plan with the Phantomas drone. The video footage was much clearer, and it would undoubtedly be easy to see that the man was in fact the infamous, secretive ex-FARC guerrilla leader — AC — and not a potential Hezbollah commander training new recruits in the mountains of northern Colombia. Although in reality it appeared he had joined the ranks of ELN.

The Phantomas rose rapidly and traversed the same route as the Silent Wasp, crossing the river and arriving at the small gap in the treetops. It was still several hundred metres above and had so far avoided detection. The guerrillas were still training and now engaged in mock hand-to-hand combat jousts. Paco began to lower the drone as the guerrillas finished their training. They gave each other high-fives, hugged and patted each other on the back. While they enjoyed their post-training elation, it became apparent that a few of the guerrillas began to glance upwards. Paco continued lowering the drone and panning the camera from side to side looking for AC. The guerrillas began to run frantically now towards the cover of the trees as Paco continued panning the drone's camera, briefly capturing some of their faces revealing looks of horror as they ran like scattering ants.

The next action happened in a split second.

Paco panned the camera until he witnessed a lone guerrilla kneeling on one knee, head tilted, squinting with one eye while his other eye looked through the scope of a large tubular object resting on his shoulder.

Before Paco could react, he saw a puff of grey smoke followed by a flash of orange and white light as a rocket-propelled grenade obliterated the drone, sending a thunderous explosion echoing across the valley. A fireball lit up the sky. The smoke from the explosion blended with the morning mist as a cacophony of bird noises erupted, squawking through the jungle. The Phantomas's control screen turned immediately to a black and white fuzz.

"The fuck happened, Paco?" asked Jardine, his voice agitated, but still in a whisper.

"Guerrilla with an RPG! Shot the fucking thing!"

"Buenísimo!" exclaimed Juan, impressed with the explosion. He giggled to himself and shook his head. "It's not the first time I've seen them blow things up. But usually it's the other way around. A military helicopter blowing up a coca farm." Juan walked away a few metres and pulled out his cell phone. "I'm calling my uncle to see if he heard it down the hill. If he did, the military will be up here soon, and we'll be caught in the crossfire."

"That's if these narco-guerrillas don't get to us first. They're clearly onto us. We need to make tracks. Juancito, you know a way out of here?" asked Jardine. The words flew out of his mouth in a split second, surprising him with his decisiveness. Juan nodded and then held the phone up to his ear. Jardine began to pack things up as Paco stuffed the controller back into its case and then helped Jardine. Five minutes had passed, and they were packed and ready to go. "We need to get down the mountain. We'll need to get back to the jeep and then on to somewhere away from here. I think we've outstayed our welcome this time," said Paco.

They began to pack the bags back onto the donkeys. "There's no time for that," said Juan.

"We're not going to just leave these donkeys here? These are good donkeys," said Paco in disbelief.

"All animals are good. This is simply part of the cycle of life…" said Juan. "I can fetch them." Before Juan had finished speaking a shot swished past the three of them and hit a tree three metres away with a solid thwack. A sniper rifle.

"Fuck! They're here already!" said Jardine.

"Impossible! They weren't that close to us!"

They left the donkeys and ran for cover behind a nearby boulder. "We need to get to the other side of that clearing," said Juan, pointing out over their heads.

"Do you think they saw where we went?" Jardine asked. Paco held up a palm frond above the boulder to test the waters. A flurry of bullets tore it to shreds, this time from something more automatic than a sniper rifle. The three men looked at each other. Juan's eyes darted around the clearing. "Let's run around the rim of the clearing. It'll take a little longer, but at least we'll have some cover with the jungle."

Hunched over, the three men ran following the edge of the clearing. They seemed to be clear for the first half, but a string of machine gun bursts echoed out and the ground behind them puffed up with dust as if small moles were throwing up dirt in their wake. They arrived at a small path and managed to enter a rocky track that led downhill. They ran along the path until they saw a fallen ceiba tree. "Over here," said Jardine, crouching down behind the fallen tree. The three men were puffing and panting like a trio of asthmatic dogs as they stooped down behind the fallen ceiba. After a few minutes, they heard voices running down the track behind them.

"Did they see us?" Paco asked Juan.

Juan shrugged and picked up a small, smooth rock and studied it. The voices stopped. There was an ominous silence. Then, rapid machine fire rattled across the jungle floor thwacking against the thick trunk of the giant ceiba tree. Paco pulled out a Glock 9mm. "Standard issue from los gringos during Plan Colombia," he said as he clicked the safety off and raised his hand above the tree. He fired six shots indiscriminately towards the machine gunfire. When he stopped, another flurry of bullets was returned in quick succession. "Estamos jodidos," said Paco. *We're fucked.*

The woody pelting of bullets continued for another minute and then stopped momentarily.

"They're reloading," said Jardine.

"Down here." Juan was motioning beyond the track and further down the hill which led to a fast-flowing river. "It's our only chance."

The three men scrambled, slid and scurried down the hill through ferns and small bushes before crossing a clearing of waist-high grass, arriving at a small cliff with the river gushing below. "This will take us downriver to my village," said Juan.

"Take us how? There's no boat!" exclaimed Paco.

"Jump in and grab whatever you can to stay afloat," said Jardine, taking action. "There are tourists at Palomino that pay money for this type of experience. Besides, what other option do we have?"

The three men looked at each other. Then, with a calm face, Juan looked to the sky and jumped into the raging white wash below. Paco crossed himself and followed. Jardine was left on cliff by himself. He looked back and saw two black-cladded men with red and black hoods emerge from the jungle into the clearing. Had he seen a flash of white robes as well? He didn't have enough time to tell. He thought of the bull he had seen and ridden in Bogotá. Take it by the horns, he said to himself and jumped, dropping like a pin into the river below.

The glacial water momentarily took Jardine's breathe away as he surfaced gasping for air and manoeuvring his arms to stay afloat in the raging torrent. He caught a glance of Paco and Juan ahead of him, both had managed to find a short log to cling to as they barrelled down the river feet first. Jardine swivelled his body so that his feet faced downriver and managed to guide himself successfully through a section of rapids without drowning. Eventually, he found himself next to Paco, and with an outstretched hand, grabbed onto the log keeping him afloat. The river raged for another ten minutes as they battled dormant boulders and stray branches caught up in the raging, icy torrent. After another ten minutes, they arrived at a wide section of the river where it was calm and the current slowed. They could hear gushing water ahead of them and Juan yelled out to them, "Waterfall! Swim to the side!"

"Paddle, Paco!" yelled Jardine as the two men paddled furiously with their arms while kicking their legs to reach the riverbank. It was at this moment that Jardine noticed small glistening creatures jumping up out of the water around him.

"The fuck are these things…?" he asked.

"What are you talking about? said Paco.

"They look like shrimp."

"Shrimp? In a glacial river in the mountains?" asked Paco in disbelief.

The fist-sized shrimp leaped in and out of the river like small invertebrate dolphins following the wake of a boat. Paco and Jardine scrambled onto some rocks at the riverbank twenty metres before the waterfall. Juan was already there, sitting on a rock watching the two men with amusement. They lay on their backs, chests heaving as they looked up at the equatorial sun blazing down on them. Jardine sat up and looked back at the river. The shrimp-like creatures continued springing from the water like hyper-active lemmings, oblivious to the fall ahead. "Why aren't the shrimp swimming to avoid the waterfall?" Jardine asked.

"Did you get knocked on the head?" Paco asked, now also sitting up.

Jardine blinked and shook his head. Maybe the vision from the ayahuasca still hadn't worn off?

The three men, still breathing heavily, followed Juan over more giant, smooth, egg-like rocks leading from the side of the river until they reached a muddy path. They followed the path for two hours, finally arriving to a small dirt track.

"Mi tío!" Juan motioned one hundred metres down the rocky track.

"I thought there was no jeep access up here?" whispered Paco.

"That's what we tell españoles y gringos," Juan said with a grin. They jumped into the idling vehicle and drove back to Juan's village of Nabusímake.

35

THE TOUCAN

ARRIVING BACK AT NABUSÍMAKE, PACO AND JARDINE SPENT AN hour with Juan and his grandfather thanking them for their hospitality and for guiding them. "What will happen now?" asked Jardine.

"The military will come and maybe find the guerrillas." He tilted his head slightly. "Or maybe the guerrillas will simply go to ground and find a different spot to camp and evade them another day."

"But you and your village will be safe?" asked Paco.

"Claro que si! They don't bother us any more, the military makes sure we are safe. I'm sorry we couldn't see more birds."

"No problem, it turns out you were right. People are more interesting than birds," said Jardine, patting Juan on the back.

Paco and Jardine drove back to Puerto Bello and entered the bakery and ordered coffee. Paco turned his head and winked at a girl on the next table, as if he knew her. The girl smiled shyly and giggled.

"So, what's next?" he said with eyebrows raised like a curious puppy. Paco's transformation was complete. He had managed to completely shake off his rigid ex-military self. He seemed more relaxed and without a care in the world, as if being chased down a mountain by murderous narco-guer-rillas had not happened. At least, not to Paco. Jardine's chest still pulsated like he had a wind-up toy trapped in his thorax. Although he didn't feel scared, he felt alive.

"I need somewhere to rest a while," said Jardine, picking up his coffee cup but not drinking. "At least for a few days. Send this incident through to Bogotá, who will then send it through to London."

"Yes, I should report too…"

"No! I mean, if I report it to London and mention how valuable you were, then maybe it will get back to your supe-riors via London. That would look favourable on your behalf. If you report it direct to Bogotá, someone else will just take the glory."

Paco reached for his coffee cup, picked it up and studied it. "You're right," he said, taking a sip. "Rodriguez always steals my thunder."

Jardine noticed the woman at the next table glancing at them curiously. Over Paco's shoulder an elderly man who had been staring at them smiled, and gave Jardine the thumbs up sign. "Do you think the townspeople here speak to the guerrillas? I can't help but feel we're being watched. It's defi-nitely time to be somewhere I can blend in with the crowd again," said Jardine.

"I know just the place, my friend," said Paco, motioning a cheers with his coffee cup. "Oh, and in case we get into more trouble, take this."

———

After the mountainous roads of the Sierra Nevada, the road to Cartagena was flat and green. Earthy brown cattle lined endless lush fields with the misty Sierra Nevada slowly disappearing behind them. In the passenger seat, Jardine pulled out his phone to check the news. Scrolling for a few minutes he came across an article in El Tiempo:

'Fuga de gas en restaurante siriano'

Opening the article, he read of an explosion in a Syrian restaurant in El Parkway in Bogotá. There had been two casualties including a General from the Colombian army. "It can't be possible…" he said to himself. The cherry-sized lump previously lodged in his throat increased in size again. The adrenaline feeling of earlier had dissipated. Could it be the same restaurant? It wasn't like there were many Syrian restaurants in Bogotá, let alone in Teusaquillo.

He dialled Ambrose's number who answered with a tinge of frenzy in this voice. "Jardine, little busy here at the moment. I guess you've read the news?'

"The gas leak at the Syrian restaurant?"

"No, Colombia beat Peru 2-1! They'll be in the World Cup!"

"Oh…" He could hear blaring salsa music, bongo drums and people cheering in the background. He assumed they were downstairs at the British Council watching the game on the big plasma screen televisions in the cafe. Someone blew loudly on a vuvuzela.

"I saw an article about a 'gas leak' in a Syrian restaurant in Teusaquillo. Seems a bit suspicious and the General killed was one of my sources — Toucan Loco."

Jardine could hear Ambrose's distant voice, like he didn't have his mouth to the receiver. "I really shouldn't, I'm on the job, got some reports to… Oh bugger it! Solo un poquito, Natalia." Jardine could hear the distinct glug of an aguardiente bottle being poured.

"Did you say something, Jardine? Can't really talk as I'm downstairs at the British Council. The whole city's gone bonkers. Just had a shot of *guaro*!"

Jardine realised he had been living not under a rock, but on top of a rock — the Sierra Nevada — for the last few days.

"Gas leak in Syrian restaurant. Any news?" Jardine repeated.

The sound of partying subsided. "I've just ducked into a classroom. Gas leak? Yes, I did hear something about that. The newspapers are saying gas leak and we've heard small explosive device from the police. Looks like an extortion job. Apparently, the owner wasn't paying his way in the neighbourhood."

Jardine's blood went cold, like injecting gazpacho soup. An explosive device? It always amazed him how such events could go virtually unnoticed in Colombia. If it were in Britain, it would be front page fodder with a news crew following the event live. In Colombia, a small explosion was page four or five news, one of those small square box articles where they mention a local event to fill space. It also surprised him how blasé he'd become about such events.

Ambrose continued. "Apparently there had been a few attempts earlier in the week, which weren't successful. It was kept out of the news, for good reason, obviously.

"The General killed was Toucan Loco," Jardine said now.

"Toucan Loco? Why that's one of your sources! Not having much luck, are they?" said Ambrose. "What have you been up to anyway?"

"I'm headed for Cartagena to write up my next report and send it through."

"Going for the signing of the Peace Accords?"

"Signing of the peace accords?"

"It's taking place in Cartagena tomorrow."

Jardine really had been living under a rock. He'd forgotten all about it.

"We didn't get a guernsey, of course. Only the Ambassador. I'm off to San Andrés tomorrow anyway to meet with a source about BP's oil rights. They figured because my father's

Jamaican I'll be able to establish a rapport with them. Oh, and I almost forgot to mention. The Venezuelan station has mentioned recently that their foreign minister is being investigated by the Yanks for his nefarious connections. Seems his father — a Syrian national — was responsible for fundraising for a Hezbollah faction in Venezuela. Thought it might come in handy for you."

"Thank you, that might be useful. Enjoy San Andrés, Ambrose."

"OK, just one more shot y ya no más...!" Ambrose's voice trailed off as he hung up.

Jardine looked out the window of the jeep. His thoughts were scattered and his mind became cloudy once again, like the mist that washed down the Andes towards Bogotá each morning. He couldn't help but wonder how on earth had he allowed himself to become entangled in this falsifying affair? He began, somewhere in his sub-conscious, to mentally count the number of deaths. He didn't know if they were all his fault, or simply a typical week of strange, unexplained political assassinations and extortion retaliating bomb blasts that occurred in Bogotá from time to time. If the victims were journalists or human rights activists, he wouldn't have bat an eyelid. That nefarious thought caused a flicker of hope to flash through him... He also thought about what Ambrose had said and he realised that whatever report he sent through in the next few days would not be heavily scrutinised. Ambrose would be in San Andrés and the Ambassador would be at the peace dialogues signing in Cartagena. It would only be London that would really analyse the footage and the report. And so far, they seemed to be hoovering up his intelligence product like a dodgy vacuum salesman.

36

CARTAGENA

THE HOTEL CHARLESTON SANTA TERESA SITS ON THE EDGE OF the colonial city of Cartagena next to a stretch of fortified wall that separates it from a coastal road and the Caribbean Sea. Outside is a square surrounded by palm trees where horse-driven stagecoaches mingle, waiting to ferry tourists around the walled city's famous brightly coloured houses with bougainvillea drenched balconies. Pulling up to the entrance, Jardine checked in and unpacked, arranging his laptop and notepad on a desk overlooking the square while beginning to sift through the drone footage. He briefly read through his previous reports to maintain the previous narrative and make sure he wasn't omitting any crucial plot lines or characters. It was exhausting work. Not because it was difficult to write the report, but because his conscience wouldn't allow him to push the nagging thoughts that he was doing something wrong to the back of his mind... thoughts of death and his potential responsibility for it. Turning his attention back to the report, he decided to provide a summary for each video. He would suggest to his superiors to read the summary prior to watching the video. That would mean the reader was likely to confirm their own biases based on what they had read — the video would merely act as confirmation of these biases. It would tell them what they wanted to see, rather than act impartially. Everyone in the service had undergone anti-bias training, but like all corporate training, it was never put into practice. Jardine poured himself a frosty glass of dark rum and lime, lit a cigar and began to type. He did not usually smoke, but desperate times call for, well, cigars.

Intelligence Report 3

FOR SECRET INTELLIGENCE SERVICE EYES ONLY

LOCATION: SANTA MARTA, COLOMBIA

ANALYST: O.W.J./#397664 (Intelligence Analyst temporarily promoted to Intelligence Officer Status)

SOURCES: Primary in-field video intelligence product

REPORT TITLE: Video footage of Hezbollah terrorist training camp in the Sierra Nevada de Santa Marta, Colombia.

EXECUTIVE SUMMARY: Recent new video footage undertaken by Officer #397664 and a Colombian DNI liaison officer shows evidence of an Islamist terrorist training camp in the Sierra Nevada de Santa Marta. Due to the footage, it is thought to be a Hezbollah training camp funded by shadowy forces emanating from Venezuela. This has been verified by Caracas station who confirm that influential ministers in the government of that nation are involved with Hezbollah in Latin America.

This assessment includes one video in two parts, a summary of each is below. For maximum effect, it is highly advisable to read these summaries before watching the video footage.

He stopped to take a sip of rum and then started on the summary for the first video.

Video One — Initial terrorist training footage

Video one clearly shows a number of terrorists in black fatigues, reminiscent of recent footage from Lebanon, Syria and Northern Iraq. The black fatigues are a trademark of fundamental Islamist terrorists, as are the trademark 'running through tires' exercises visible in this footage.

Note: (1) This footage confirms previous intelligence product from the now deceased sub-source (#397664 — 003/01) of Agent (#397664-003), alias: Flaming Flamingo, a source who is now in a self-imposed exile in Florida due to the danger imposed on his life.

Jardine now took a puff of the cigar and sat back and thought for a few minutes.

Video two — Confirmation of Hezbollah factions active in Colombia

Video two indicates that the likely group involved in this training is Hezbollah. This is clearly visible as one of the leaders, seen smoking a cigar under a palm tree in the video, is wearing a black hat similar to that worn by Shiite mullahs of Lebanon and the Ayatollah of Iran.

Notes: (1) This intelligence has been confirmed through the service's Venezuelan station — confirmed by Officer #456935.

(2) This revelation was in turn confirmed by Heidy Lagos — a known supplier of prostitutes to members of a terrorist organisation.

(3) In addition, it is believed to be linked to the recent explosion — thought to be a targeted assassination — in a Syrian restaurant where Agent (#397664-006), alias: Toucan Loco was killed. Toucan Loco had alleged that the restaurant was, in fact, a front for an unspecified Islamist terrorist organisation with funding from Venezuela.

(4) Global mobile phone tracking by GCHQ has confirmed the potential threat of nefarious operators involved in a potential fruit juice mafia controlling large numbers of mango juice vendors throughout Colombia. This threat, while outlandish, has precedent. Local drinks manufacturer, Bonoposto, and a famous international cola brand have previously been tied to paramilitary groups. Additionally, the recent cyanide assassination of Don Carlos, head of security at the British Embassy in Bogotá, further confirms the targeted nature of such a criminal organisation. It is thought they also have links to the *Oficina de Chiribito*, who in turn have links to Hezbollah.

Additional Footnote: A short video clip of clearer terrorist training footage is attached to show the severity and high threat level of such a revelation. Unfortunately, this video intelligence product was cut short due to the presence of an anti-aircraft RPG grenade launcher which inhibited the acquisition of additional, clearer footage.

Jardine took a break. It was amazing how fast he could write a report when there was no fact checking or verification required. Or at least facts that he had made himself. He felt free, like he could really open himself up and unleash his creative side. Within an hour he had finished the report, which normally would have taken an entire workday. He clicked on the first drone video and watched it one more time to confirm that the footage corresponded with what he had written. He watched the drone rise and cross the river, flash by the Kogi camp, or was it an Arawak camp? He didn't bother to stop and verify. Now, passing more trees and the river, the drone finally arrived above the ELN camp. The vision showed men clad in black fatigues undergoing some type of training. It had all the hallmarks of an Al-Qaeda, ISIS or Hezbollah training video. The final digital zoom, which identified AC — one of the most wanted guerrilla leaders in Colombia — was sufficiently blurry to warrant the explanation of a Shiite mullah or ayatollah wearing a turban. It was uncanny how much AC looked the part. Even Jardine himself was beginning to believe it. The blurry vision of the Silent Wasp helped to distort any inconsistencies. He pondered this for a moment, returned to his report and included a final summary.

Final Summary: Due to the appearance of a Hezbollah training camp with support from the Bolivarian Republic of Venezuela, further surveillance and analysis is requested to verify and further investigate these claims. It is requested in the form of…

He finished the report with the suggestion that his position should be extended indefinitely, with an increase in pay-band due to his new operational expertise and experience. He leant back in his chair and took another sip of the molasses-y dark rum. Having finished the report, Jardine went downstairs and sat at one of the tables outside on the terrace. He pulled out the cigar he had lit earlier — a Montecristo imported from Cuba — and lit it again. As he sat there and watched the traffic moving outside the entrance to the hotel, he saw a convoy of black SUVs fly by. He had grown accustomed to this during his time in Colombia. It could be anyone from an important businessman to a politician to the British Ambassador. He leant back in his chair and took a long drag on his cigar. He finally felt he could relax. He had done everything he could and now it had to play the waiting game to see how his reports would be received. The small cherry-sized lump in his throat pulsated slightly. Somewhere in his stomach he knew it wasn't right, but he managed to squash the feeling with another sip of rum. He thought about calling Veronica to tell her he could stay in Colombia, but then thought the better of it. Patience is required before he could be sure of anything in the land of magical realism.

37

AN INVITATION

Veronica Velasco entered the room and sat on a plush leather chair opposite Alejandra Velazquez, the partner at her law firm. She smiled warmly and leant back in her chair in a relaxed posture. "Hola Veronica, everything well with you I imagine?" she said warmly.

"Si, señora Velazquez."

"You know I like to cut to the chase and so I wanted to ask you... How would you like to go to the signing of the peace accords in Cartagena? My cousin is in the *Miniserio de Relaciones Exteriores* and he has access."

"Me? I..."

"You're moving up in the ranks of the firm and I think it's important that you witness an important step in this country's history. Besides, you could take a few days after to relax with that gringo of yours. The one that seems to make you so happy." She winked and smiled. "I'm sure he would like a break from the cold Bogotá nights, no?"

Veronica felt a slight thud in her chest. I miss him, she thought. "Oh, si, that would be lovely. Thank you, Doña Aleja. It would be a wonderful opportunity and I'm sure Oliver would love it." She felt bad about lying but didn't want to bring up what had happened. She's right though, Ollie would love it.

"Well, I'll let Ana Maria work out the details with you and she can organise flights and the hotel."

"Muchas gracias, eso es una oportunidad muy especial." *Thank you very much, this really is a special opportunity.*

Back at her desk, Veronica opened her laptop and tapped her fingers softly on the desk. All these opportunities, advances in my career, more money, promotions, fancy car and a better apartment... they all mean nothing if I can't be with him, she thought. What's the point of all of that if I am unhappy and alone? She checked her email and saw the details of the hotel from Ana Maria. The Hotel Charleston Santa Teresa. What's the point of staying in a fancy hotel if you can't share it with anyone?

38

PEACE AND INTRIGUE

JARDINE HAD ARRANGED TO MEET PACO AT CAFE DEL MAR, AN open-air bar/restaurant on top of Cartagena's fortified wall with sweeping views of the ocean, the old city, and skyscrapers of Boca Grande. Jardine walked along the wide fortified wall and sat at a table, placing his mochila on the seat beside him with the strap wrapped around the chair leg — standard protection against thieves in Colombia — and ordered a mojito and grilled fish. He swivelled his wooden deck chair so that he could still gaze out towards the ocean, but angled slightly towards the entrance to observe anyone entering. A warm Caribbean breeze blew slowly through the open-air restaurant, ruffling the large Colombian flag perched on the wall beside him. It was in this moment that his mind began to drift back through the situation he had got himself into.

He felt surprisingly calm, as if all the action, death, lies and trail of assassinations had yet to enter his mind and slowly chew away at his subconscious. Or maybe it was the love he still felt for Veronica that calmed him, for that was the only authentic feeling of truth he had left. We all share the fiction of love and if enough people believe in something, it becomes a literal truth, doesn't it? *So, if love is truth, then my reasoning of lying for love must also be true. Isn't love what forms the basis of humanity? Therefore, I'm only doing my duty to humanity while loving my soulmate and doing whatever necessary to keep that love alive.* He was happy with his theory and while taking a sip of his minty mojito, he wrote it down in a dusty notebook in case he had to use it in the future, in a hearing of a Royal Commission into negligence in intelligence, for example. He couldn't exactly put it in an intelligence report, but it would be useful to convince someone that he was justified in his lies. Lies. Such an ugly, dirty word that makes you feel like you're committing murder. How bad was a lie for love?

Paco entered wearing a pair of dark jeans with a light-coloured denim shirt, camel-coloured suede boots and his colourful Wayuu mochila bag slung over his shoulder. He moved as he always did, with smooth panther-like strides, a tinge of swagger all while keeping an effortless charm and charisma — a delicate cross between rugged and sophisticated, but personable, humble and by no means arrogant. He gave a knowing nod to one of the waitresses. *He obviously knows her*, thought Jardine. Paco stopped to talk with her for a few minutes before waving to Jardine. "Cartagena, a perfect mix of love and cholera. Ying and yang, fire and water, air and earth. Women of the night and men with wallets," he said sitting down.

"What are you drinking?" asked Jardine.

"Your mojito looks particularly refreshing." He motioned to the waiter and ordered two mojitos. "I think this counts as off duty?"

Jardine took a sip of his mojito and nodded.

Paco continued. "So, I found out some information while you were finishing up your reports." Paco commented that he had spoke to some contacts in Cartagena and that there was a rumour that El Tigre Blanco was in town. But as often was the case, rumours were just that, a good story with little substance. "Even if he is in town, it would be with the Colombian authorities help. However, it's not even certain that he exists."

"El Tigre Blanco? Well, if he's wearing white tonight, he'll be hard to pick up. All the peace accord signing attendees at the Patio de Banderas Convention Centre are dressed in white linen," said Jardine.

"Ah, yes. We should probably head that way after dinner. At least to have a look, I mean."

Jardine nodded with a mouth full of fish.

"Then," Paco's eyes lit up, "after that, I'll take you to a clandestine salsa bar I know. Since going on this trip with you it's like my energy for life is back again. Before it was reports, reports, and reports. Uno se cansa de eso." *One gets tired of that.*

"Sounds like a plan. I've enjoyed my time with you too, Paco. A little adventure always does wonders for the soul. It will be a good end to our time together." Jardine raised his glass in a toast and clinked it with Paco's glass. Wanting to glean whatever extra information he could for his latest report, Jardine decided to change the subject. "So how is the DNI transition over from DAS? What are they working on at the moment? Obviously, you can't tell me everything, but what's going on behind the scenes?"

"All progressing well. We are currently digitising our report system. In fact, we are working on a new form of intelligence report inspired by SnapChat and all of that new app communication technology. It's an intelligence report which, once deciphered by the reader, automatically deletes itself."

Jardine raised his eyebrows, impressed. "Like a digital self-destruct mechanism. What if no-one reads it?"

"Then it will automatically self-delete after one hundred days."

"Not one hundred years?" asked Jardine.

Paco smiled. "That seems to be the agreed upon time-frame. Of course, this is only for top-secret intelligence." Paco took a sip of rum and coughed and sputtered. "I forgot to tell you!"

"What is it?"

"I received such a report from DNI in Bogotá this after-noon. I'm sorry, the conversation with the waitress distracted me."

"What happened, carajo?" Jardine asked.

"It seems someone has assassinated Señora Lagos. And Yakov is either missing or laying low for a while or may be dead, we just don't know for sure yet. It came with an accom-panied police report — one that doesn't self-delete."

"Read it out," Jardine motioned with his hand. "But, in English, we don't know who's listening."

Paco pulled a small tablet out from his mochila and began to read using the slightly archaic style still used in official Colombia documents, translated into English.

"On the thirteenth day of the—"

"Get to the important bits!" interrupted Jardine.

"Sorry…" Paco trailed his eyes over the page mumbling to himself before finding the important information.

"Señora Heidy Lagos succumbed to her wounds of multiple gunshots to the abdomen. Also at the scene, the blood of another individual was found, presumed to be a foreign national of Israeli origin who we believe is injured. It is also high likely that he is missing as he was not to be found at the scene of the crime."

"Well that would be obvious," commented Jardine sarcas-tically. He needed sarcasm to calm his mind and help process all the information that was currently swelling in his mind.

Paco stopped for a moment to clear his throat and then continued. "It is worthy to note that the head of Señora Lagos was intact, and no form of mutilation had occurred, which obviously rules out any paramilitary activity. Nor were there any signs of political or ideological slogans, which therefore discounts the guerrilla. It is out of the question that the Colombian military would undertake such a targeted assassination because the 'kill-a-crim-for-cash' incentives of the past have ceased to exist for the last two years. It is equally unlikely that this was the result of the BACRIMS as, according to the Government of the Republic of Colombia, they do not exist. Therefore, this leaves us to believe that this is the work of an international terrorism ring with the possibly of links to Venezuela, as they are socialist pigs and like to support this sort of thing."

"Does it really say socialist pigs?" asked Jardine.

Paco looked up from reading. "We always get sent the first draft, before it has been edited for the media."

Paco continued. "Furthermore, it is thought that the Foreign Minister of Venezuela, Señor Juan Antonio Tafur Kabachi is aiding this terrorist organisation with petroleum money from the recently nationalised state oil company of the Bolivarian Republic of Venezuela."

"Jesus…" said Jardine.

Paco scanned the paper. "There is no mention of a man named Jesus."

"No, I meant… nevermind." Jardine swatted his hand as if to signify 'don't worry about it'. That is quite a story, he thought to himself. Even he couldn't have written something like that. The Colombians seemed to be beating him at his new found career of falsifying official reports.

"They had it coming, you know," said Paco. "Sometimes death is the best justice in Colombia. It's unlikely they ever would have spent any time behind bars. And if they did, it would've been behind the bars under house arrest in a mansion with a jacuzzi and a plasma screen. Just like Escobar in *la cathedral*. They would probably even get a subscription to Netflix."

"You're right. That does make it seem more palatable. Justice is not often so swift in deciding the bad from the good." Jardine shook his head. "But surely there must be some honest authority in Colombia that would've brought them to justice?"

"There are many men of integrity, but more integrity just means more money in Colombia. And Madam Lagos had tonnes of that," said Paco, shaking his head.

The deaths of Uri and Vanessa, on a moral level, didn't hit Jardine. No one deserves to die, he thought. But if people do bad things and get bumped off, well that didn't grate as hard as an innocent person. He wasn't sure if there was a philosopher that had come up with a theory that would support him, but he liked to think there was. Maybe some type of moral philosophy that warranted, or indeed encouraged killing bad people. Like a vigilante paedophile killer he had seen on Netflix. Surely that was something to be applauded? In fact, many of the deaths had happened to people who had been involved with causing death in one way or another. But still, he began to feel a slight sense of guilt. He felt the most guilt about Don Carlos. He felt as guilty as cookie monster must feel at a diabetes convention. A nervous, shaking blue furry wreck. It seemed death was circling him like vultures to a carcass and the lump in his throat throbbed as his heart began to increase its tempo to a caleño-style salsa romp.

The two men continued their dinner as Paco ordered a serving of ceviche. It was a Tuesday night in the off-season and no cruise ships were docked, so the main thoroughfares of Cartagena were strangely empty and quiet. Most people in the vicinity were to be found towards the Convention Centre for the peace accord signing. After dinner, they crossed through the old city arriving to the well-known *torre de reloj*, the clock tower at the entrance to the walled city. Walking under the small archway, they came out to a small plaza outside the convention centre. People had congregated all around, the streets heaved with people dressed in white. They managed to push through the crowd, progressing forward to be able to see the president and a host of dignitaries sat on a stage outside in the open air. A woman stood on the stage announcing the end of Colombia's internal conflict. "Now, the moment the whole country has been waiting for: the official and definitive signing of the peace accords."

Jardine turned to Paco. "Is this it, Paco? Peace in Colombia?"

"God knows. The only thing I know for certain is that I know nothing."

"Sounds very philosophical."

"All the lies that have been told on both sides means that even if the accords are signed, that's only the beginning. The real work comes after. What follows will determine the real possibility of peace in Colombia."

The woman on the stage continued, explaining the document would be signed using a pen made from a bullet. A potent symbol to show the end of the conflict. She summed up her speech by saying, "Las balas escribieron nuestro pasado, la paz escribira nuestro futuro." *Bullets wrote our past, peace will write our future.* Simonchenski stepped forward to sign first, followed by President Soto. Then the two men faced each other and shook hands to a roaring crowd, cheering, applauding, and waving white handkerchiefs in the air. A chant of: "Si se pudo, si se pudo, si se pudo" emanated from the crowd. Followed by *Viva Colombia, Viva! Viva Colombia, Viva!* A wooden birdcage of doves was brought on stage and opened, releasing the flapping white-winged creatures up into the air. Military jets zoomed overhead letting off jet streams of red, yellow and blue – the colours of the Colombian flag. People raised their heads – and phones – to the sky, taking in the momentous occasion.

Jardine, overcome by emotion, turned to Paco. "Paco, there's something I have to tell you. I haven't been reporting on guerrilla movements, or the paramilitaries or the BACRIMS."

"What do you mean?" asked Paco, his brow furrowed.

"I've been inventing false intelligence about an Islamist terrorist organisation training in the Sierra Nevada. I have a girlfriend, and well, I wanted to stay in Colombia and…"

"Que?" Paco interrupted while looking confused. "You mean to tell me, you…" His voice trailed off as he looked over Jardine's shoulder, his eyes wide with excitement. "Hijo de dios… I think that's Valencia?"

Jardine swivelled around slowly to see Nelson Valencia's arms crossed, watching the doves fluttering up in the sky.

"What's he doing here?" Jardine asked. Another man stood next to him, it seemed to be a personal bodyguard. Valencia tilted his head as the man beside him whispered in Valencia's ear. Valencia laughed now as if the man had told him a joke and nodded as they both swivelled and headed away from the crowd towards the clock tower, the entrance to the walled city. "We need to follow them," said Paco.

They followed, walking casually behind Valencia and his goon, hanging back twenty metres as they proceeded back under the torre de reloj, through a small plaza, and down Carrera 7 towards the outer wall of the old city and the ocean. Valencia stopped to buy a single cigarette from a street vendor as Jardine and Paco stopped to inspect a man selling panama hats. Having lit his cigarette, Valencia slapped the man on the back and they continued passing the Tcherassi Hotel, an Argentine parrilla restaurant and the former house of Gabriel Garcia Marquez, before turning right onto Carrera 2. Paco and Jardine followed and began to walk faster once Valencia had turned the corner.

"Wait here," said Paco, jogging to the corner of Carrera 7 with Carrera 2, as Jardine waited outside Garcia Marquez's former abode. A large illustration of García Márquez was painted on a wall with the quote, "Ningún lugar en la vida es más triste que una cama vacía." *No place in the world is sadder than an empty bed. It's like they know my life in this moment,* thought Jardine. He stood there staring at the wall in silence as Paco's quiet footsteps pattering down the street filled the steamy night air.

39

A WITNESS OF PEACE

VERONICA WATCHED THE DOVES FLY UP INTO THE HUMID NIGHT air and the crowd erupted with applause. President Soto and Simonchenski waved enthusiastically to the crowd as everyone stood from their seats. Cheers of *Viva Colombia* followed by the reply: *Viva* erupted as the various spectators hugged, cried and smiled jubilantly as the sun slowly descended. Peace in Colombia. *At least for the time being,* she thought. The ELN were still active, BACRIMS continued to control certain areas of the country, and there was no guarantee that the demobilised guerrillas would all, indeed, demobilise. Added to all that, how safe would these former guerrillas be? And how long until they were sought out, found and then assassinated, just like the days of the *Unión Patriótica*, the former political party of the FARC during the 1980s.

The doves continued to flutter upwards as military jets barrelled the skies above. Most of the crowd raised their heads and phones to capture the moment. Veronica lowered her gaze and glanced around at the crowd. There were important people from all over the country and the world, with many Ambassadors and foreign dignitaries amongst them.

She was scanning the happy and jubilant faces when her eyes fell upon a familiar silhouette towards the back of the crowd. It can't be? She did a double-take and squinted, as if trying to verify what she was seeing. Ollie? She saw the profile of Oliver Jardine, his head to the side talking to a tall man in a light denim shirt. She picked up her handbag and moved briskly through the crowd towards him. *What is he doing here? Is this the plan he had? Or was that just an excuse for one last party in Cartagena?* She was perhaps one hundred metres from reaching them when she saw Jardine and the man were now looking into the crowd and subtly whispering to each other. Then they sprang to the side and headed briskly in the direction of the walled city. It seemed as if they were following someone. She tried to move closer but the further back she got the denser the crowd became as they gathered and surged forward to see the handshake and the continuation of the peace ceremony.

Reaching the edge of the crowd, she arrived at the clock tower sitting on the wall of the old city and spun around looking for a trace. Which way did they go?

40

THE STREETS OF CARTAGENA

THE EVENING WAS CALM AND STEAMY. HEAT STILL RADIATED OFF the asphalt beneath their feet and the surrounding walls as Paco came jogging back to Jardine. There was nobody in the streets except for a couple of mangy dogs running ahead, sniffing litter, and happily wagging their tails as they moved from bag to bag. It felt eerily quiet and gave one the feeling of a long lost colonial Spanish outpost forgotten in time. It seemed almost everyone had abandoned the walled city for the peace accords.

"Where did they go?" asked Jardine, as Paco came closer.

"They entered a wooden garage door up there on Carrera 2. I think it's a side entrance to the Hotel Santa Clara, they…"

The two men heard a low rumble, like the distant revving of engines accompanied by fast paced rhythmic beats. "Do you hear that?" asked Jardine.

"It sounds like techno music mixed with a strange melodic snake charmer tune over the top," said Paco as he looked over his shoulder back down towards Carrera 2. "For one thing, it's definitely not vallenato, salsa or reggaetón."

They peered ahead down the empty street. The dogs

continued their tail wagging rubbish expedition down the lone Carrera.

"I can't tell where it's coming from," said Jardine. The music echoed and bounced around like an erratic chant in an empty canyon. They glanced back towards Carrera 2, glancing at the stucco peeling off the fortified seawall at the end of the street. On the left, small wooden balconies floated above, overflowing with vivid fuchsia bougainvillea cascading down over the whitewashed walls. On the right, a copper colour wall with high barred windows ran the length of the street, a sole lantern illuminating it. The music grew louder and louder as they realised it was emanating from the street Valencia and Paco had just entered. Walking forward cautiously, they were now almost at the intersection, when three black SUVs flashed by in quick succession.

"The fuck was that?" said Jardine.

Their walking became a jog as they reached the end of the block, stopped and peered around the corner, staying out of sight. The three SUVs had stopped half way down Carrera 2, engines still idling. The music had stopped and four men with AK47s stood in the street — two on either side of the SUV's back passenger door and two on either side of a large wooden garage door. A lone couple walked by at head height atop the sea wall to their left. Apart from the couple, the street was empty and two old street-lamps at either end of the block formed an eerie glow. Squinting, Paco and Jardine witnessed two of the men with AK47s scanning the street as three men wearing white robes stepped out of the middle SUV, followed by two men wearing woven sombreros *vueltiaos*. The five men entered the garage while the four men with AK47s remained outside.

"That's the door Valencia entered?" whispered Jardine.

Paco nodded. "Looks like he's got some visitors."

"The white robed people, did they look like sheiks to

you?" Jardine whispered to Paco in English. The week speaking only in Spanish had taken its toll on his tired brain.

"They weren't that stylish. I mean they wore just basic white robes,"

"No, tonto! Sheiks, not chic! *Jeques*," said Jardine in Spanish, to emphasise the word.

"What would a group of sheiks be doing here? Are you sure it wasn't El Tigre Blanco? That could have been him in his white *traje de luces*. Like a young Vicente Fernandez, no?"

Jardine shook his head, unsure what he had just seen. "I don't know. All I saw were three men in a flash of white. But they looked Middle Eastern to me, not Mexican."

Jardine and Paco ducked down and tried to crane their necks further around the corner. Jardine shifted his weight between his feet, but in doing so accidentally kicked a crumpled beer can lying on the ground. A tinny rattle echoed down the empty street.

"Que hijueputa fue eso!" shouted one of the men. *What the fuck was that?!*

One of the men began to jog towards them as Paco and Jardine swivelled and strode away stealthily from the corner back towards the Garcia Marquez house.

"Fuck!" hissed Jardine. "They're coming this way, Paco!" They continued walking briskly while glancing at each other nervously.

"Que hacemos?" said Jardine. What do we do? Jardine suddenly wished he had a gun, like an intelligence analyst from a Tom Clancy novel.

"I have an idea," whispered Paco. He reached both hands down in to his mochila hanging at his side. "*Mira*!" Paco pulled out one of the multicoloured Wayuu cloths they had bought in Uribia. "Do you have yours?" he motioned to Jardine.

Jardine felt down his side into his mochila. *Thank Christ I didn't take it out*, he thought. "Yes! I have it."

"Quick, compadre! Throw it over you and walk slowly, bend your back, follow my lead," said Paco, hunching like a small elderly man.

Jardine whipped out the sarong-like cloth and whisked it over his head. It managed to cover him head to toe. Paco, already having taken out his cloth, was shuffling a few steps ahead of him.

The man with the AK47 arrived at the corner leaning his gun against the wall and peering around.

"Quién putas está allí?" *Who the fuck is there?* He yelled down the street, his voice echoing off the walls.

Jardine and Paco continued to shuffle their feet along the road covered by the coloured Wayuu cloths.

A second man with an AK47 appeared now and glanced down the street. "Que es?" he asked, looking at the first man.

The first man looked towards him with a furrowed brow. The edges of his mouth raised slowly into a smile. "Solo malditos Wayuus." *Just bloody Wayuus.* They lowered their guns, and both let out a nervous cackle before turning around and walking back to their post. Jardine and Paco continued shuffling as if they were a harmless pair of elderly Wayuu women out for an evening stroll. They had walked nearly half an entire block before they realised the men had left.

"I came here to get away from that sort of thing," said Jardine, pulling off the cloth. "I thought Cartagena would be safe. I was only supposed to file my report and await further instructions. Now it appears I'm the lead operative in a sting operation."

Paco smiled from under his cloth. "Many say we are the land of magical realism, but I tend to think we're a plentiful tierra of truth-is-stranger-than-fiction. Is this part of your false intelligence report?"

Jardine gave Paco a deadpan look. "What do you make of what we just saw?" asked Jardine.

"Did you see the number plates?"

"Barranquilla?"

"Exactly, the same SUV that was following us since Santa Marta," said Paco.

"Maybe Valencia has been on to us since Taganga?"

Jardine didn't want to believe it. He didn't want to think someone had been following him. The old him would have ignored it, pretended it wasn't there, dismissed it, oblivious to the unconscious damage it was doing. However, he was no longer the old him, he had changed, and he knew he had to take action.

"Paco, we need to get back there and stop whatever Valencia, or El Tigre Blanco, or whoever it is, are up to. Can you…" As Jardine spoke, small yellow items appeared to be falling from the sky, surrounding them like glowing yellow butterflies.

"Flowers?" asked Paco, holding his hand in the air to touch them. They hit his hand with a slight fiery-sting. After a few seconds, a pulsating chuff-chuff-chuff sound came from the sky above. A bright spotlight appeared overhead and shone on them for a few seconds before tracing along the street towards Carrera 2 and around the corner to the wooden door. They heard the men with AK47s begin to shout and the rhythmic rat-a-tat-tat of machine gunfire cracked through the silent night like an octopus on speed playing multi-ball cricket.

Glancing upwards, Jardine and Paco saw a Sikorsky UH-60 Black Hawk banking sideways before stopping and hovering at the end of the street. A man sitting behind a mounted M134 Mini-gun aimed at the street below, yelling in Spanish. On the other side of the chopper, four men in tactical gear rapidly descended on ropes, holding IWI Tavor TAR-21 assault rifles.

"Not flowers, sparks!" said Jardine with confidence. "Let's get back to that corner."

As the descending commandos hit the ground, they took

up position behind a delivery van parked in the street, whilst screaming, "Alto! Alto o les disparamos!" *Stop or we'll shoot!*

A voice over a loud speaker thundered across the night. "Que se rindan, están rodeados." *Surrender, you're surrounded.* The man in the helicopter manning a M134 Mini-gun swivelled from side to side, ready to fire at the drop of a sombrero. The men with AK47s not used to obeying instructions, wedged themselves between two of the SUVs, placing their weapons on the roof — one aiming towards the helicopter and the other toward the men on the ground. A few seconds later, four more men scurried out from inside the building and took up positions amongst the parked SUVs.

The orders were repeated over the loudspeaker. *"Que se rindan." Surrender.*

A large man with a handlebar moustache adjusted his sombrero and aimed his AK47 up at the Blackhawk, muttering, "Hijueputas de mierda," under his breath before letting off a heavy flurry of shots towards the helicopter. The spray thudded into the five-centimetre Kevlar plate on the bottom of the helicopter causing the man on the M134 Mini-gun to swing into action and return fire, spraying bullets down on the men like confetti on a newly-wed couple exiting a church. Valencia's men ducked and took cover behind the SUVs, unable to return fire.

From inside the garage, a man appeared with an RPG balanced on his shoulder. He began to steady himself and take aim at the Blackhawk, but the helicopter jerked upwards and banked out over the ocean away from the building, escaping the range of the RPG. The remaining commandos and Jardine and Paco were now alone near the corner.

With the helicopter gone, the group of men among the SUVs now focussed their attention to the commandos behind the delivery van and sprayed heavy fire liberally. From the corner, Jardine and Paco could see the men bunched together behind the van, still unable to return fire.

"Oye, les cubrimos mientras se dispersan," Paco yelled to them. *We'll cover you while you spread out.*

Paco pulled out two Beretta M9s from his mochila bag and passed one to Jardine.

"Know how to use it?" asked Paco.

"Why didn't you tell me you had those? What happened to the glock?"

"I left the Glock with Juan. Picked up these from a contact here in Cartagena. Know how to use it?" Paco repeated more urgently.

"Even an analyst can fire a pistol," replied Jardine.

Jardine and Paco tilted their bodies around the corner and let off a quick succession of shots towards the men amongst the SUVs. Valencia's men, taken by surprise ducked down and hid behind the SUVs, giving two of the commandos enough time to scoot across the narrow street into the side street with Jardine and Paco. The men leant their backs against the wall, their chests heaving up and down as they recovered their breath. Two commandos remained behind the van as Valencia's men stopped firing, allowing an eerie silence to fall over them as all groups considered what to do next.

"Vamos, parcero. We need to get out of here," said Paco. "This is getting too *caliente* for us."

"We can still help, I need to do something about Valencia. My conscience won't—". In that moment, another group of fatigue-clad men approached from beyond the Garcia Marquez house, jogging up the Carrera wearing tactical gear, night vision googles and carrying M4 Carbines.

"The Compañía Jungla Antinarcóticos," said Paco.

The group arrived and exchanged words with the two commandos. One of them looked towards Jardine and Paco nonchalantly, did a double take, and then spoke. "Leon, que hijueputas haces aquí?" *Leon, what the fuck are you doing here?* A man who appeared to be the leader of the group took a few steps towards Paco, his hand outstretched. Paco introduced the man to Jardine as 'El Capitan'.

"We've been on a small birdwatching adventure to La Guajira and the Sierra Nevada," said Paco.

"Birdwatching?" The Captain seemed confused.

"Nevermind. What's going on here?" asked Paco. "We saw Nelson Valencia enter ten minutes ago."

"Valencia? We have intelligence that there's a leader from a Islamist terrorist network meeting with members of the La Oficina de Chiribito."

"Fundamental Islamist terrorist network," corrected Jardine under his breath.

"ISIS?" offered Paco.

"Hezbollah," said Jardine confidently. He had to appear like he believed his lies at least, even if it was getting above his head.

Paco and the Captain looked at him, surprised.

"Both wrong," the Captain said confidently. "It's a leader of ISIS here to negotiate a deal with La Oficina. We believe they are..." The Captain continued. As Jardine listened, he felt a small apple-sized lump in his throat. If Colombia really were a land of magic realism, the apple would have engulfed his neck enough to perhaps stop his breathing. In some ways, in that moment, he would've preferred that.

"ISIS? Here in Colombia?" Paco asked the Captain.

The apple dislodged momentarily, and Jardine managed to blurt out a sentence. "It's not ISIS or Al-Qaeda or Hezbollah. It's *El Tigre Blanco* meeting with Valencia! The intelligence has been falsified! They're just stories, *cuentos,* fairy tales!"

Paco looked sideways at Jardine with disbelief and a look of what-the-fuck on his face.

"El Tigre Blanco? We have information he was arrested yesterday at an abandoned airstrip in Sinaloa, Mexico," replied the Captain.

"What?" said Jardine, looking puzzled.

"We must press on," said the Captain, not having changed his expression from his standard emotionless poker face during the entire exchange. The Commandos, joined by the Capitan's Jungla Company, began to prepare. Apart from the odd click of a gun and a few whispers, the streets were still deadly silent, as if all the men were respecting the various signs plastered around the old city that read: 'Please respect local residents when you leave this establishment and keep noise to a minimum.'

Paco and Jardine followed the Captain back to the corner. Jardine's initial shock at the carnage about to unfold in front of him suddenly felt like it was rushing out of every pore in his body. His shoulders lowered, his neck loosened, and his feet felt like feathers, able to lift him up into the sky. He walked towards the Captain. "Capitan, there has been a mistake. I'm the analyst responsible for—"

"Listo compañía!" interrupted the Captain in a whisper.

The helicopter had returned now, hovering five hundred metres out over the ocean, out of range of the RPG, but close enough to be of effect, if needed. The Jungla Company and the Commandos inched forward. Several of the men crossed themselves, a final prayer before moving in. If it were possible to see their facial expression under their dark green face paint, they might have looked worried. The men formed a line, each placing their left hand on the shoulder of the man in front and then moved forward in silent unison, an anti-ballistic shield out in front. The man with the RPG moved forward and aimed at the advancing group as they inched along the wall. Before he could pull the trigger, a small flash of light emitted from the helicopter as a bullet whistled through the air, penetrating the side of his head with a loud thud like a small rock into a watermelon. He fell slowly as the RPG clanged to the floor.

The Commandos continued forward as one of them threw a grenade, landing among the men between the SUVs. It blazed a bright light then exploded, killing two of Valencia's men instantly. They pushed on further and began to pick off the men one by one with tactical efficiency. Valencia's men did all they could with their return fire, spraying bullets towards the advancing Commandos. A man on the roof, aiming downwards, managed to shoot one of the Commandos in the neck before another flash from the sniper in the helicopter caused him to fall, his arm left dangling over the edge of the building's roof. The remaining commandos continued to advance, picking off the remaining men before reaching the large wooden door of the building, and disappeared inside.

41

THE CITY OF WALLS

THEY MUST HAVE ENTERED THE WALLED CITY, THOUGHT Veronica. She strode forward entering through the right arch under the clock tower and walked through the small plaza, arriving at the corner of Calle 34 and Carrera 7. Looking down Carrera 7, she saw red and blue flashing lights a few blocks down. *What's happening down there*? She advanced forward down the narrow street until she reached Parque Fernandez de Madrid. The humid air was moist against her skin and she pulled her hair up into a ponytail. Reaching the park, she noticed a large police and military presence; all streets heading north towards the Garcia Marquez house and Hotel Santa Clara were barricaded and maned by military personnel. The park was quiet except for a small group of people who had gathered to watch the commotion happening on the corner. She approached one of the men on the barricades, a young steely faced man in military fatigues.

"Que esta pasando aqui?" *What's happening here?*

"No se puede decir por medios de seguridad." *I can't tell you that, it's confidential.*

"Puedo pasar? Estoy hospedado en el Hotel Santa Clara."

She tried to lie to see if she could pass. *Can I get through? I'm staying at the Hotel Santa Clara.*

"No señorita. A nadie esta permitido en este momento." *No, young lady. No one is allowed through at the moment.*

She tried to look beyond the barricades but couldn't see to the end of the street. *Why do I have a feeling Ollie is caught up in all this mess*? She bit her lip nervously while tapping her foot impatiently. *I hope he's not caught up in this. Why would he anyway? He said so himself, he's always behind a desk, in the political section of the Embassy. Why would he be involved in a military operation*?

42

EL SHOWDOWN

"AYÚDENLE Y YO LLAMO A LOS MEDICOS," SHOUTED A Commando who hadn't entered the building. *Help him while I call a medic.*

Paco and Jardine ran forward to help the fallen Commando shot in the neck. As they reached him, he lay on his back, his breathing was raspy taking in short breaths. Paco loosened the man's shirt as Jardine removed his helmet and they both lifted the top half of his body and propped it up on the curb. They resisted the urge to ask him, "Are you okay?" or "Where does it hurt?" like a doting mother, knowing it wouldn't help. Instead Jardine managed to say in Spanish, "Help is coming." He ripped off a piece of the man's shirt and used it to apply pressure to the wound on his neck. A few seconds after he'd pressed down on the wound, the Commando spoke in English, "Thanks, old boy."

Jardine nodded and then twisted his head slightly in confusion, not expecting to hear a British accent.

"You're British?" Jardine asked. The Commando, still breathing heavily as crimson liquid flowed from the small wound, replied, "It's me, boyo." His words held a slight Welsh lilt.

Jardine looked closely, it wasn't easy with the khaki green and black face paint, but the well-manicured moustache hadn't changed. "Don Carlos?"

"Si, señor," replied Don Carlos, this time in Spanish.

"But... but... I thought you'd been poisoned by mango juice? Or was it papaya?" Jardine looked downwards to the left as if trying to recall an important fact. "And you speak English? Like a Welshman..."

"That's because I *am* a Welshman. Well, half-Welsh at least. Real name's, Jones. Carlos Jones. Dad was Welsh, and mum was a Paisa. The mango business was all a show to throw the buggers off the scent," replied Don Carlos.

Jardine's head whirled. He couldn't think of what to say or ask next.

Don Carlos coughed three times as small squirts of blood trickled down his chest. He looked Jardine in the eyes. "Don't worry, looks worse than it is, I imagine. Think the blood's going straight down the old oesophagus. Any word on the medic?"

"I'll check." Paco stood up and jogged over to the other Commando who was calling for a medic.

"What are you doing here though?" Jardine asked. "Who are the 'the buggers' you were trying to throw off the scent?"

"Valencia. He's always been a wanted man, but there was never any great impetus to track him down. You know how it is here. But it seems doing deals with an Islamist terrorist organisation was a step too far. So, they finally pulled in *las junglas* to track him down."

"Don Carlos, that bit about the Islamist terrorist organisation, it's not tr—"

"Medic can't get through," Paco interrupted, yelling from twenty metres away. "We can take the military jeep around the corner, get him to the Naval Military Hospital."

"Let's get him up," said Jardine. "Come on..." Jardine stopped to think of what to call the man.

"You can still call me Don Carlos, old boy. I've grown quite fond of it."

Jardine smiled. "Come on, time to save your neck, hombre." They lifted Don Carlos up and stood either side of him. He put his arms around their necks as they walked him around the corner to the jeep. They shuffled together, as if in a strange version of a three-legged race.

"There's also another reason we targeted Valencia," said Don Carlos.

"What's that?"

"It's why I signed up for the whole 'death-by-mango' incident. Paramilitaries were responsible for killing my uncle and his family. They owned a small shop in rural Antioquia. They were accused of collaborating with the guerrillas and the paras mowed them down. I was training in the British military at the time. It changed the whole course of my life."

Jardine shook his head without saying a word as he continued with Don Carlos and Paco to the jeep.

"Even if I die today because of this," he pointed to his neck, "I'll be content if we get Valencia."

Finally, they arrived at the jeep parked in the side street facing the seawall.

"Let me open the back tray so we can lay you down," said Jardine, as they leant Don Carlos on the jeep's bonnet facing the street. Jardine jogged round the back to unlatch the tray and rearrange a number of boxes.

"I'm guessing the keys are somewhere in the front," said Paco, jogging around to the driver's side of the jeep. "Mierda, they didn't leave much room." The jeep was parked close to the wall and Paco tried to squeeze himself into the driver's seat.

"Must've been Ramirez, always parks too bloody close to things," chuckled Don Carlos.

As Jardine rummaged through the back of the jeep and Paco squeezed into the driver's door, a side door to the building opened and a lone man with a scar on his left cheek exited, holding an AK47. The man's eyes fixated on Don Carlos leaning against the jeep. Don Carlos, staring back, locked eyes with the man. They were two competing lions that have just spotted each other.

"*Valencia, hijueputa de mierda,*" said Don Carlos as he reached down to the belt on his thigh for his SAS-issued Glock 19. But Valencia had already managed to raise his AK47 and with the brisk pull of the trigger, spurted a small flurry of shots. Don Carlos's Glock clattered to the ground as his body fell with a slap on the pavement, followed by the echoing footsteps of Valencia as he ran down street.

Jardine, having heard the shots, picked up the Beretta that he still had in his pocket from Paco and fired three shots in quick succession into Valencia as he ran. He fell to the ground with a thud, his AK47 scrapping the road by his side. Racing around to the side of the jeep, he saw Don Carlos slumped on the ground, barely breathing and coughing up even more blood. "Don Carlos, you're bleeding everywhere," said Jardine.

Don Carlos coughed and looked at Jardine. "Valencia?"

"Lying in a pool of his own blood."

"Good lad, it's a bloody shame we couldn't get to spend more time together, Ollie."

"It's only a shame if you die on us. We'll get you to the hospital. Paco!" Paco was still wrestling with the door.

Don Carlos shook his head weakly. "I'm done for, mate."

"This is all my fault," said Jardine shaking his head. "I never should've lied in those reports, I only wanted to stay in Colombia and be with Veronica. I never thought it would come to this…"

Don Carlos had his eyes closed and didn't appear to hear what Jardine had said. Jardine shook him softly. "Don Carlos, I'm sorry. I thought you were dead and now you're alive, it's…"

Don Carlos slowly opened his eyes. "This might sound like a contradictory thing to say, but in war there are a lot of lies and a lot of love. Life is full of contradictions. For Queen and country. And while I'm at it, for Comandante Bolivar, La Liberator."

Don Carlos slumped sideways his eyes frozen open with death.

43

R

In a suite at the Hotel Charleston Santa Teresa, Jardine sat in front of a laptop screen as R – the head of MI6 – sprang to life via video link. "You couldn't make this stuff up!"

Jardine looked upon the Chief's slightly upturned nose as he spoke from his office in London. He looked to his left at the British Ambassador, who was sat next to him with a serious expression on his face.

R continued. "I've read a few Garcia Marquez novels in my time, and of course, I love my spy literature, but this is something else entirely! In all my years, I've never heard of such a diabolical plan. Well, except from those sneaky Russians. But they're a whole different kettle of Siberian fish. Now the Russians, they..." R's voice trailed off as Jardine thought of Veronica. Her light caramel coloured eyes, her soft brown skin, her wavy hair that sprouted in every direction, her smile, her touch, he missed it all. I need to call her, he thought. But first, he needed to confirm what would happen with his future in Colombia.

"But anyway..." R – after his personal anecdote – had returned to the conversation at hand. "Who bloody knew, eh? It's just like Brecon Beacon Mountains all over again, we caught those cheeky buggers training up there! Who knows what this lot were concocting up there in the Sierra Nevada? Anyway, Jardine, is it?"

"Yes, sir."

"Yes, well, we'll need you in Colombia for a good while longer to sort this mess out. Seems like you have the guts for it after your discovery. How does another three years contract sound?"

"Excellent, sir."

"I'll get HR to write it up now and send it through."

"Thank you, Chief. As you know, I'm committed to combating terrorism at its source and if the source is here in Colombia, I'll need to be here."

"That's the spirit! You're not only a good analyst, but it seems you've done a bloody good job with those drones. I'm not very tech-savvy myself, but by god, did you bring in some class-A intelligence product with them."

After Don Carlos's death, Jardine had been picked up directly by the Ambassador's security team and whisked to the Ambassador's suite. Speaking to R via video link, and with the Ambassador breathing down his neck, he still didn't quite understand what had occurred and was attempting to squeeze out more information without giving away that he had absolutely no idea what they were talking about. "I had to think on my feet and drones seemed like the logical method for extracting the footage," said Jardine vaguely.

"The idea to quickly fly over that ISIS training camp – genius! After a little play with the footage, we were able to slow it down, verify then pinpoint those white robed buggers running around in the jungle."

"White robed?" asked Jardine, trying to land it somewhere ambiguous between a question and a statement. A hot flush swept through him like he'd downed a hot tea in one gulp. His mind raced back to the jungle when he had flown the drone over the treetops and flashed by a group of people in white robes; what he had assumed was a Kogi or Arawak camp.

"Yes, it was quite sneaky of them. Yemenis, Egyptians, a Tunisian, and a few Venezuelans. All funded by a mysterious Sheik out of Qatar. Ingenious plan! Why, they simply wore their usual dishdasha cloths and it blended in with the local Arhuaco and Kogi people. If you slow the footage down, you'll see the men running around with their AK47s, skipping through tyres, ducking and weaving under barbwires, stabbing the odd stuffed coffee sack with their bayonets. God knows what they were planning, the dastardly bastards! The poor Arawak and Kogi had no idea, of course. They would've never allowed that to happen in their territory.

"I can assure you it was nothing," said Jardine, now trying to sound confident. "It really was nothing more than a quick flyover before it was shot out of the sky. In fact, I'll need to put in a reimbursement claim for that. I still have the box and the receipts I think…"

"Don't worry about that. You'll be reimbursed."

There was still one thing Jardine wanted to ask. "A question, sir. If I may?"

"Yes, go on."

"What did you make of the Ayatollah looking man. The one with the hat and glasses?"

"Ayatollah looking man? Ah yes, we read it in your report, but thought you must have confused the guerrilla leader, AC, with a Shite mullah. It's very easy to do under the circumstances."

"It's pronounced Shi-ite, sir. Two syllables."

"Oh, yes, quite right."

"One more thing, sir. Something I can't get my head around." There was at least one aspect about which Jardine could show genuine ignorance. "Don Carlos, or Carlos Jones…."

"Ah yes, Carlos Jones, well he was one of ours…"

R went on to recount a brief history of Don Carlos – an undercover MI6 operative with the Colombian Military. He'd been a bright student of history when he decided to join the British Military. It was the death of his uncle, something that affected his mother a great deal, that motivated him to work his way up the ranks to become part of the SAS. Because of his fluent Spanish and ties in Colombia, he was chosen to train the Jungla Commandos as part of a small group of SAS members in a joint SAS/MI6 assignment. It was from there that he was selected for a top secret position, not even Ambrose knew. Only a select few in London were ever made aware.

R's voice returned. "Bloody good officer. He'll be sorely missed. There'll be a service for him in Bogotá, which you'll be attending, I'm sure."

"Of course," said Jardine.

"It will be a top-secret service. His wife, yourself and Ambrose. Everyone else already buried him after the mango incident."

Jardine nodded. "I wouldn't miss it for the world."

44

HOTEL SANTA TERESA

THE FOLLOWING DAY, PACO CAME TO THE HOTEL TO OFFER Jardine a ride to Bogotá on a Colombian Airforce plane. The Colombians wanted to return the favour for his work in tracking down Nelson Valencia and the Islamist terrorist group. He jumped at the chance, not wanting to spend a plane trip with the interrogation of the British Ambassador, who still seemed suspicious.

Paco strode casually towards Jardine who was lying on a sunbed, poolside on the roof terrace of the Santa Teresa hotel. The soft yellow dome of the San Pedro Claver church rose up behind the pool with the Miami-like skyline of Bocagrande in the distance slightly to the right.

"Were you pleased with my tourist guide services?" asked Paco approaching.

"Yes, I'll have to recommend you," Jardine replied without turning his head.

"But we didn't really see any birds." Paco advanced a few more steps, the sun shining brightly behind him.

Jardine turned his head now, looking upwards towards Paco. "My sources were enough, they were named after tropical birds."

"Tropical birds?" Paco looked confused. "For example?"

"Flaming flamingo."

Paco shook his head with a smile. "Next time you lead a secret mission, try using more aggressive sounding bird names águila, halcón, etc." *Eagle, falcon, hawk, etc.*

"We do that, too. I was trying to be a little more 'creative'. It can get very drab and dreary when you all you do is conduct interviews and write reports."

"I see. It seems your reports were very 'creative', or should I say, 'sexed up'?

Jardine looked downwards pondering. "It turns out it's easier to make stuff up rather than report the truth."

Paco nodded. "You know my former boss retired and started writing spy novels. He knew the security situation so well that he would often predict what would happen in his fictions before it actually happened. What is it that he used to say?" Paco stopped to sip the coffee in his hand. "Ah, that's it! 'I've been overtaken by events.' That's what he used to say. That's what's happened with you, Jardine."

"I didn't write a novel."

"No, but a falsified intelligence report is better than a novel. It's somewhere between a craft and work of art."

"A work of art no-one wants to buy."

"From the look of it, everyone bought it. Hook, line and sinker. You could write a novel. The first one could be about Colombia. It's hot on the radar these days. It seems everyone wants to know about cocaine kingpins. Don Pablo, Popeye, Cartel de Cali. You could write about that?"

"I think there's enough of that out there already," said Jardine winking at Paco.

Jardine looked over Paco's shoulder. The sun shone in his eyes and squinting, he could make out a silhouette of wavy hair. "Vero?" he asked.

Vero ran towards him screaming as she leapt forward to embrace him. "I'm sorry, I didn't mean what I said. I missed you. I saw you yesterday but couldn't get through to you as they'd blocked the street off. Then, I overheard a conversation about the operation just a few streets away and it involved the British and I...I... Oh, I love you so much." She burst into tears as she wrapped her arms around him.

"It's okay, I'm okay and we're okay." He kissed her forehead and hugged her tightly looking down into her glistening brown eyes. "I can stay here now. The Chief has approved it. I need to speak with Ambrose in the office, but I'm here for good. No Yemen, no Syria, no Iraq. Here in Colombia. They need me for a new reconnaissance team."

"*En serio*? Really?" she asked.

"Really," Jardine replied, placing his arm around her and leading her down the ramp into the hangar.

"I'm sorry," Veronica repeated. "I don't care if I have to go to Yemen, or Syria or Iraq or even the moon! I would go anywhere with you. Maybe we should just escape from all this? Wherever, I'm ready to be with you for the rest of my life. I didn't mean all those things I said, you're the most important thing in my life. What's the point in being promoted if I can't be with the man I love?" She burst into tears again and gripped him tightly, like a small koala to its mother.

"You're not going to introduce me?" a voice sounded from beside them.

They both turned. Jardine smiled. "Vero, there's someone I'd like you to meet." Jardine introduced them, and Paco stepped forward and greeted Vero. "I now see why this man wanted to become a novelist?"

"A novelist?" Veronica asked raising an eyebrow.

"Si, un cuentero," replied Paco. *A storyteller*. "His stories have a habit of coming true. Although in Colombia that's a tough job, the truth usually outdoes the fiction."

"Don't listen to this guy," Jardine said with a smile. "I'll tell you all about it on the ride home." Jardine patted Paco on the back. "Will we see you in Bogotá someday, Paco?"

"Only if you lend me a scarf. It's freezing in *la nevera!*"

45

AMBROSE'S DECISION

JARDINE KNOCKED TWICE ON THE OFFICE DOOR AND THEN LET himself in. Ambrose was sat in his chair looking out the window at the mountains. "Morning, Jardine. Heard what happened in Cartagena from the Ambassador. Who would've thought?" Ambrose swivelled on his chair to face him, stood up and outstretched his hand. "Congratulations! We might make an operative out of you yet."

"I wouldn't go that far. The DNI Agent, Paco Leon, did most of the heavy lifting. I simply went along for the ride."

"Very capable the Colombians," said Ambrose nodding. "But, just image it! ISIS training in the Sierra Nevada de Santa Marta. And they were in cahoots with Valencia. My money would've been on Hezbollah, like your report said. But ISIS? Not a chance! And right under the Colombian military's noses. Not to mention the Yanks — they had no bloody idea!" He shook his head in disbelief.

"I didn't believe it myself at first, to be honest," replied Jardine. "Thought it was something out of a novel — a fiction."

Ambrose nodded. "To be honest, I thought you were making the whole bloody thing up! Until I saw that footage, that is. I kept it quiet though, retirement is calling me and the last thing I need is an analyst telling porkies under my command. Imagine the frosty send-off I'd receive."

Jardine felt something bubble up inside his throat. The lump in his throat felt like an apple. "I did make it up…" he blurted. The apple-sized lump dislodged and as he gulped, it vanished.

"What?" Ambrose looked incredulous.

"But I was overtaken by events," Jardine replied quickly.

Ambrose furrowed his brow with a puzzled look as if slowly processing the information. After ten seconds he spoke. "Well, that was the most accurate, least factual account of a terrorist training camp we've ever encountered."

"I'll take that as a compliment, sir." Jardine nodded and smiled.

"So you bloody well should! We usually get it wrong when we make it up, but you got it right!" He shook his head in disbelief. "You mean to tell me that…" Ambrose went on to question Jardine about all the finer points of the operation, what was true and what was false, why he did it and what was his motivation. Jardine came to the end of his explanation. "So, I can assure you, Ambrose; nothing like this will happen again. In fact, if anything, I think the whole exercise has improved my skills in the intelligence world."

Ambrose nodded and considered what Jardine had just said. "Yes, I could see how that might be true. Still, I'll be putting in a recommendation for termination of your employment with British Intelligence."

"What? But…" Jardine's mouth was wide open with disbelief.

"Look," Ambrose interrupted. "I'm close to retirement. I did my time and went up the ranks and here I am. Do you see yourself as me in thirty years?"

"Can I lie just one last time?" asked Jardine.

"Well, after your porkies, you'd better start telling the truth," said Ambrose.

"Then, no. I can't see myself in your position. In fact, the thought terrifies me," said Jardine truthfully.

"Well then, count this as a blessing. Go see your woman and go and start a new bloody life with her! Of course, you have a right to appeal if you disagree with my decision. We've moved on since the Tomlinson days, but I think it's for the best if…"

Jardine scurried out of the office before Ambrose could finish.

46

A NEW ASSIGNMENT

JARDINE SAT DOWN AT HIS DESK AND TYPED FRANTICALLY TO finish the report. It had to be finished by the end of the day, his new boss was a different kettle of fish altogether to Ambrose. He continued typing, the deadline looming larger over his head, tap, tap, tap. The data was looking insufficient and so he thought about adding a few extra pieces of information to inflate the figures. But, something inside him stirred and he managed to stop himself. He no longer had to lie, no longer had to tell stories to distort reality to fit another agenda. He was free of that, an independent entity with a clear vision of who he was and why he was here. After years of not understanding himself and being at the mercy of others, he finally felt he fit in his skin and could just be himself. He no longer had to lie every day.

Tapping through the last line of the report, he heard a muffled scream coming from downstairs. He descended the stairs slowly and immediately felt tension. A cool air blew upwards filling his nostrils with a slightly salty scent. It reminded him of having a bloody nose. Still descending the stairs, the muffled voice became clearer…

"Did you finish? What's our status?" his new boss stood at the bottom of the stairs flanked by two burly men.

"Yes, here it is. Are you sure you're ready for it?" He looked at the two men. "What's happened?"

His boss stepped forward, kissed him on the cheek and slung her arm around his neck. "So? Tell me, what's our status?"

He looked down at the report. "Well, according to BestTravelAdvice.com," he glanced up now, looking into her eyes. "We are the most popular Boutique Hotel in Southern Spain."

Veronica's eyes lit up and the sides of her mouth rose, revealing a flash of white. "Yay! Fantastic news! I knew we could do it, mi amor." She wrapped her arms around him and looked up at him lovingly. Then, she took a step back. "Oh, I almost forgot. These two men are here to fix the leaky sink in Room 3. Could you show them where it is?"

ABOUT THE AUTHOR

Lachlan Page has lived in Colombia, South Korea, Europe, and Nicaragua. Before becoming a writer, he worked as: a volcano hiking guide, a red cross volunteer, a marketing analyst, a language teacher, a university lecturer, and an extra in a Russian mini-series. He currently resides in Sydney. *Magical Disinformation* is his debut novel.

Visit www.LachlanPageAuthor.com to sign up for news, updates, free content, and much more.

Coming soon... Oliver Jardine - Book #2

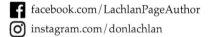

facebook.com/LachlanPageAuthor

instagram.com/donlachlan

ACKNOWLEDGMENTS

My thanks to the team at Jericho Writers who provided me with valuable advice and direction on the manuscript and for expertly editing early drafts. Likewise, shout out to the guys at Ebook Launch for a wonderful cover design and for working so diligently in coming up with perfect cover for the book.

To my parents. immense gratitude for always encouraging me to follow what I've wanted in life and providing a steady supply of book to read as a child. Your on-going support has always meant so much to me.

Thank you to Adina Stan for reading an early draft and providing valuable feedback.

The country of Colombia (and its people) provides the setting for this novel. It's a country of outstanding beauty and warm, friendly people. A land of snow-capped mountains, vast grasslands, misty rain forests and steamy jungle, rolling hills of coffee plantations, white sandy beaches, and coastlines on both the Atlantic and Pacific oceans. A land which, according to National Geographic, contains 10 percent of all animal species on this planet. I'd encourage anyone who reads this book to learn more about her and all that she has to offer. Oh, and it's ColOmbia not Columbia... #ColombiaNot-Columbia ;)

While living in Colombia, I came across a number of people who left a profound impression on me. I thank all of these people (too numerous to name!) for their friendship, company, and — at times — all round craziness. In particular, gracias a Pepito Perez y Juan Mata (not their real names) for their expert knowledge on security issues in Colombia and for confirming some of my research and notes.

Last, but not least, thank you to my lovely wife, Monica, for always being there for me and encouraging me to continue and press forward with publication of this novel, despite all of the setbacks and challenges that presented themselves along the way.